BURIED
LIES

ALSO AVAILABLE BY STEVEN TINGLE

Graveyard Fields

BURIED LIES

A NOVEL

Steven Tingle

CROOKED
LANE

NEW YORK

Copyright © 2024 by Steven Tingle

Published in the United States by Crooked Lane Books, an imprint of The Quick Brown Fox & Company LLC.

Crooked Lane Books and its logo are trademarks of The Quick Brown Fox & Company LLC.

Library of Congress Catalog-in-Publication data available upon request.

ISBN (hardcover): 978-1-64385-912-5
ISBN (ebook): 978-1-64385-913-2

Cover design by Jerry Todd

Printed in the United States.

www.crookedlanebooks.com

Crooked Lane Books
34 West 27th St., 10th Floor
New York, NY 10001

First Edition: October 2024

10 9 8 7 6 5 4 3 2 1

For Jess

1

Looking back, when Dale asked me if I wanted to see a dead body, I probably should have said no. But I was bored. I'd been sitting on the deck of my rented cabin for hours, drinking beer, eating chips and guacamole, and staring at Cold Mountain like it held the answers to life's deepest mysteries. So far the mountain had yet to reveal any of its secrets. But if I'm good at anything, it's waiting.

My name's Davis Reed. I'm forty-five years old, five feet ten inches tall, have short brown hair, and wear a constant five o'clock shadow courtesy of an expensive stubble groomer my sister gave me for my birthday two years ago. I live in a small cabin in a teeny tiny community called Cruso that sits on the western end of North Carolina. If you don't know the geography of North Carolina, the state's got three distinct regions: beaches in the east, mountains in the west, and something called the Piedmont in the middle. I've seen all three, and I'll take the mountains any day of the week.

I said Cruso was teeny as well as tiny, and I wasn't kidding. It would be a one-red-light town if it had a red light, but it doesn't. What it does have is a convenience store, a volunteer fire department, a golf course, and a Mexican restaurant that serves the best guacamole in Haywood County.

How I got to Cruso and ended up renting the cabin is sort of complicated. The short version is this: in the fall of last year, I moved here from Charleston, South Carolina, where I'd followed two depressing months as a traffic cop with two depressing decades as a private detective, the kind you hire to hide in the bushes and take photos of cheating spouses and chase down insurance frauds. One of those cheating spouses turned out to be my brother-in-law Greg, who at the time was a sergeant with the Charleston PD. I won't bore you with the details of my confrontation with Greg other than to say it ended with me getting shot in the leg and almost dying of blood loss on the floor of a storage unit in Mount Pleasant. When I was released from the hospital, I decided to get out of Charleston and recuperate in the quiet solitude of the mountains and try my hand at writing a book. That led me to Cruso and the cabin, but not a whole lot of solitude nor a whole lot of writing.

So there I was, sitting on the deck of the cabin, enjoying the unseasonably warm March weather, drinking a bottle of my home-brewed IPA, and having a staring contest with a six-thousand-foot-tall mountain when I heard a vehicle coming up the long gravel drive, followed by the squawk of a siren. My landlord, Dale Johnson, never arrives quietly, but he does arrive often. I guess if I lived with my dad, I'd get out of the house as much as possible too.

"How do you eat that shit?" Dale said when he squeezed himself into a deck chair next to mine. And I mean *squeezed* literally. Dale is a big guy. I don't know if it's politically correct to call anyone fat these days, but let's just say Dale is the kind of guy you don't want to see walking down the aisle of an airplane when the only empty seat is the one next to you. I'm surprised they make law enforcement uniforms in his size. Yeah, Dale is not only my landlord, he's also a deputy with the Haywood County Sheriff's Department. Actually, he's the head deputy, a fact that never ceases to amaze me.

In the five and a half months I've been renting the cabin, Dale and I have become fairly close. We're about the same age; we both love brewing and drinking good beer; and last November, just a month after I moved in, we survived a somewhat lively adventure involving three murders and some seriously nasty bad guys that culminated at a hiking area next to the Blue Ridge Parkway, called Graveyard Fields. Almost getting killed together seems to make people bond.

When Dale finally got comfortable, he let out a long sigh, then hoisted a sixty-four-ounce glass jug to his lips.

"That better not be my beer," I said, even though I knew it was.

Dale ignored me as he chugged. He wiped his lips with his shirt sleeve, then said, "You write anythin' today?"

"I was about to, but now you're here, messing up my flow."

"Bullshit. I don't know nothin' 'bout writin' books, but if I had to guess, I'd say if you've been workin' on one for five months and ain't written a damn word, then maybe writin' ain't your strong point."

I topped another chip with a glob of guacamole and shoved it close to Dale's face. He smacked it away, and the chip sailed over the deck railing like a dead bird. Dale doesn't eat anything from El Bacaratos, or El Bacteria, as he calls it.

"You should do one of them podcast things 'bout that bomber crash," Dale said. "All you gotta do is talk. How hard can that be? People don't read shit no more nohow."

"You know, it wouldn't hurt you to pick up a book."

"Why do I need a book? I got a TV."

Dale and I bickered back and forth for about an hour, when suddenly the sound of AC/DC's "Highway to Hell" filled the air—Dale's ringtone. It took him a good fifteen seconds to wiggle the phone out of his pocket and get it up to his ear. He didn't bother saying hello.

"Whatever it is, cowboy, I'm off the clock." Dale listened for a moment, then frowned. "Why? Who is it?" Then a beat later. "Dammit, Earl, just tell me." Silence for a few seconds, then. "Fine. I'll come see for myself."

Dale grunted, pushed his mass out of the deck chair, and let out a burp that sounded like a cruise ship leaving port. Then he asked me the question I should've said no to.

But I didn't.

2

"What's going on?" I asked, following Dale through the cabin and into the kitchen.

"Some dude got hit in the head with a golf ball, and it killed him," Dale said. "That's all Earl would tell me. Meet me at the golf course. And make it quick."

With that, Dale was out the door. I was about thirty seconds behind him when I heard his patrol car crank up, followed by the sound of gravel spraying across the drive. The golf course was only about five miles away, but I knew Dale would make it there in less than four minutes. No matter where he's headed, Dale drives like he's attempting to go back in time.

I limped down around to the gravel clearing and my Mercedes SUV, the most expensive thing I've ever bought. When our parents died in a car crash, my sister and I both inherited a hundred and ten thousand dollars. I was fairly sure her money was growing steadily in some sort of IRA. My cash had disappeared like your lap when you stand up.

When I got behind the wheel, I noticed something on the windshield. I turned on the wipers and watched a broken tortilla chip and a glob of guacamole smear across the glass.

I took it nice and easy down the winding gravel drive, then turned left onto Highway 276, a twisty two lane that snakes through Cruso to a small community called Bethel, and on to Waynesville, a tourist town full of real estate offices, restaurants, and stores that sell the kind of knickknacks certain people describe as charming.

I kept the Mercedes under forty as I drove past the fire department, community center, and small homes that dot the hills surrounding the highway. I always drive slow. I consider the speed limit to be just that: the limit. It doesn't mean you have to go that fast.

4

A few minutes later I crossed a small bridge that spans the east fork of the Pigeon River, then turned right onto Country Club Drive, where a small sign welcomed me to Springdale Golf Club. I'd driven past the course dozens of times since moving to Cruso, and although I knew the place was open to the public, I'd never once been tempted to explore it or drive through the community of homes that surround the course. I'm not really the country club type.

After a few hundred yards, I saw a sign that read "Golf Facilities," with an arrow pointing to the left. That led to a large parking lot where a few sedans and SUVs were parked among an ambulance, two small firetrucks, and five patrol cars.

I stepped out of my Mercedes and looked around for Dale. A second later I saw him barreling toward me in a golf cart. He skidded to a stop just inches from my feet.

"Did you have a flat or get lost? Or both?" Dale said.

"So where's the body?" I asked.

"Out on the golf course, dumbass. I radioed Earl. They're on the fifteenth hole. C'mon, let's go check it out."

I stared at the golf cart while Dale patted the passenger seat.

"Can I drive?" I asked.

"Fuck you. Now hop on."

* * *

Dale floored it and we passed several buildings I figured to be the pro shop, restaurant, and so on. A few well-dressed folks milled around, and each one eyed us suspiciously as we went by. At least Dale, in his uniform, looked official. I, in my ratty jeans and twenty-year-old LL Bean sweatshirt, looked more like a guy you'd see holding a cardboard sign at an intersection.

I hung on for dear life as we bounced over fairways; past bunkers, tees, greens; and through a dried-out drainage ditch. The course was hilly and teeming with tall pines and hardwoods, with no golfer in sight. The place seemed deserted.

"Do you know where you're going?" I yelled over the sound of the engine.

"Brother, I know this place like the back of my hand. I used to work here when I was in high school. I watered the greens at night. Let me tell ya, ya learn to get 'round a place when ya got to do it in the dark."

Suddenly Dale jerked the wheel and turned onto an asphalt golf cart path. We followed the path around a sharp curve, then past a teeing area where an etched wooden sign read "No. 15, Par 4." The hole was long and straight and steep. The fairway rose like a lush, manicured ramp to an elevated green far in the distance. I glanced to the left and saw another fairway running parallel to the one we were on, separated by a few tall trees. In the middle of that fairway, several deputies stood next to four golf carts. Dale noticed them too.

"Dammit, Earl," he mumbled. "That's sixteen, not fifteen."

Dale turned the wheel and flew toward the group at full speed, as if playing a game of chicken. Not one of the men budged. At the last second Dale slammed on the brakes and spun the cart counterclockwise, causing me to tumble out onto the grass.

While the men laughed, I brushed myself off. During my time in Cruso, I'd met several of the local deputies and was on good terms with most of them. There was Earl, with his bushy white mustache and large turquoise belt buckle, certainly not an official part of his uniform. Next to him was Mike, young, clean cut, all business, a nice guy from what I'd seen. Tommy was there too. I didn't care for Tommy, and I felt sure the feeling was mutual. That lively adventure I mentioned earlier, the one with the three dead bodies and nasty bad guys? For a short time, maybe a day or two, I had been a "person of interest" in that adventure. I think Tommy still considers me as such.

I pushed myself up and glanced behind the golf carts, where, in the middle of a large bunker, a gray tarp was stretched out over a motionless lump.

"How's it hangin', Davis?" Earl said. "You 'bout got that book finished?"

Before I could answer, Dale walked over and smacked Earl on the back of the head. "This is sixteen, cowboy, not fifteen." Dale then motioned toward the bunker. "So what's the story?"

"I'll let Phil tell it," Earl said.

Dale looked around. "Where is he?"

"Went to take a leak," Earl said, pointing across the bunker to where a thick line of trees bordered the right side of the fairway. Among the trees a large pond reflected the late afternoon sun. On the other side of the pond sat a one-story house with a small deck and tall windows covered in what looked to be thick blue curtains. As I stared, I thought I saw one of the curtains move.

Dale growled, then asked Earl if he'd seen the Vols "beat the shit" out of the Bulldogs. I zoned out and took in the scenery. The hole we were on looked like a tough one. From where we stood, the fairway sloped down for a hundred, maybe a hundred and fifty yards, then leveled out just short of a small creek that twisted its way in front of an oval-shaped green. In the other direction, up the fairway, I could make out an elevated teeing area, with two golf carts parked next to it.

I heard a loud cough and turned to see a man in khaki pants and a blue-and-white-striped dress shirt appear out of the trees near the pond, and recognized him as the county medical examiner. He walked in our direction while fighting with his zipper. As he approached, he extended his hand toward Dale.

"Keep your pissin' hand to yerself, Phil," Dale said. "Now tell me what happened."

Phil cleared his throat, then turned and spat onto the fairway. "Officially, I'd say it's blunt force trauma. The deceased was using a rangefinder to gauge the yardage when—boom!" Phil raised his left hand and abruptly slapped the side of his head. "A golf ball strikes him in the left temple. And that's all she wrote. Wrong place, wrong time. Freak accident."

Dale turned to Earl. "Who got here first?"

"First responders from Cruso," Earl said. "They were out here in less than twelve minutes after the call came in. Man was already dead when they got here."

Dale turned back to Phil. "I didn't think a golf ball could kill ya. Hell, when I played baseball in high school, I got beaned with a line drive right between the eyes. I just shook it off and kept playin'."

I wanted to say, *That explains a lot,* but I bit my lip.

"You were lucky," Phil said. "In some cases a blow to the head like that can cause a subdural hematoma, bleeding under the skull that could have killed you within hours or even minutes. Head injuries are strange business."

Dale rubbed a spot between his eyes, then stepped to the edge of the bunker. "So he was standin' in here when he got hit?"

"That's right," Earl said, pointing to an area near the tarp. "His golf ball's there. His playin' buddies confirmed it was his. There's another ball close to it, almost buried in the sand—looks like somebody stepped on it. That's the one that hit him. His rangefinder's there too."

"All right," Dale said. "So who hit the ball that killed this dude?"

Earl spread his arms. "Nobody knows. His playin' buddies were mindin' their own business when all of the sudden they look over and see the man layin' in the sand. Thought he'd had a heart attack."

"Did they hear anyone yell *Fore*?" I asked.

Phil and the rest of the group turned in my direction. Dale gave me a look I took to mean *"Shut the fuck up."* So I did.

Steven Tingle

Earl pointed toward the adjacent fairway, hole fifteen. "They said some-body was playin' alone over there. After they realized what had happened and called 911, two of 'em drove 'round in their golf carts, lookin', but never found nobody. We've searched and can't find nobody either. Keith and Boner are over on the other side of the course right now, lookin'."

"So nobody knows who hit the ball?" Dale asked.

"I told ya, his buddies thought he was havin' a heart attack," Earl said. "They didn't know he'd been hit with a ball 'til later. So whoever hit it had time to skedaddle."

Dale turned to Phil. "Could it a been a heart attack?"

"It's possible," Phil said. "But the deceased has got a whopper of a contu-sion near his left ear. He was obviously hit, and that's most likely what killed him."

Dale turned back to Earl. "So where's his buddies?"

Earl pointed up the fairway toward the tee. "I sent 'em up there to wait for you. One of 'em's freaked out pretty good. Guess he ain't used to dead bodies."

"Ain't no one should be used to dead bodies," Dale said. Everyone nod-ded, and I realized that occasionally Dale was capable of hitting the nail square on the head.

Earl then stepped into the bunker and grabbed a corner of the tarp. "You ready, big man?"

Dale responded by taking a tin of Copenhagen out of his shirt pocket and filling his mouth with tobacco. He nodded and Earl pulled the tarp away like a magician performing an illusion. The dead guy was face up. He looked to be in his early to mid-seventies. And he actually looked peaceful. The only thing out of the ordinary was a red knot the size of a cherry tomato near his left ear. I stepped over to Dale, whose eyes looked like they were about to pop out of his skull.

"Do you know him?" I asked.

Dale mumbled something incoherent.

"Who?" I asked.

"Prentiss Wells," Dale said, motioning for Earl to come near. Earl dropped the tarp and walked over to us.

"Has the shit already hit the fan?" Dale said.

Earl snickered through his bushy white mustache. "Not yet. But the fan's spinnin'. And the shit's on its way."

8

3

"Who's Prentiss Wells?" I asked.

Dale didn't speak. We were back in the golf cart, headed up the steep fairway toward the sixteenth tee, where three golfers stood next to their golf carts. All three were male, middle aged, and dressed for a day on the links. Despite their dead golfing partner, the three men were still wearing golf gloves, golf caps, and golf shoes, and one guy had a club in his hand.

"Hey, buddy," the golfer holding the club said to Dale as we walked toward them.

"Well, if it ain't Jimmy Fletcher," Dale said. "How you been, Double F?"

Jimmy extended his arm, and he and Dale began to shake hands, but Dale immediately jerked away.

"Take off that damn sticky glove," Dale said. "It's like grabbin' a glue trap."

Jimmy's face reddened as he slipped off the glove and stuck it into his back pocket.

"So whatcha been up to?" Dale asked.

"Same ol', same ol'," Jimmy said. "Still in Waynesville. Still selling loans."

"We need to catch up some time," Dale said. He glanced at the other two men. "So who's who?"

"I'm Rex Pinland," one of the men said. He wore a green argyle polo shirt and salmon-colored pants held up by a thick white belt, the kind of outfit that gave golf a bad name. "I work at Wells and Butler. That's Prentiss's firm."

The third man was a short guy with curly black hair peeking out from under a Titleist cap. His face was as white as a sheet. "What's your name?" Dale asked.

The man stayed silent and stared off into space. I wondered if he was in shock.

"Snap out of it, buddy," Dale said. "What's your name?"

Jimmy gently elbowed the guy, who suddenly emerged from his trance. He stammered for a few seconds, then finally muttered: "Freddy Sizemore."

"So what happened, Double F?" Dale said. "You hit a bad shot and whack Wells in the head?"

Jimmy grimaced. "It was awful, buddy. We were waiting for Prentiss to hit, and all of the sudden he falls down in the bunker. I thought he was having a heart attack."

"Did you see the ball hit him?"

"No. I was on my phone. My girlfriend wanted to know when I'd be finished playing."

Dale turned to Rex. "What 'bout you?"

"I was on my phone as well," Rex said. "I dropped Prentiss off by the bunker, then drove over to the rough to wait for him to hit. I was checking my voicemail."

To Freddy: "Did you see it?"

Freddy shook his head.

Dale pointed at Freddy's feet. "Why's your shoes all muddy?"

Jimmy answered. "While we were waiting for Prentiss to hit, Freddy went into the trees near the pond to take a piss. It's pretty muddy back in there."

"So nobody was lookin' at Wells when the ball hit him?" Dale asked.

"Buddy, you have to understand: Prentiss was as slow as a turtle," Jimmy said. "He'd stare through his rangefinder for ages before he'd hit. Whenever it was his turn, we'd all pull out our phones. But when I finally looked over at the bunker, Prentiss was face down in it. Freddy was running over to him, and I yelled for Rex."

"Okay," Dale said. "Then what?"

"What do you think?" Jimmy said. "We turned him over and tried to rouse him, but I think he was dead before we got to him. I couldn't find a pulse."

Dale turned and looked down the fairway. I turned as well. The view was magnificent. In the distance the peak of Cold Mountain was framed perfectly against a backdrop of clear blue sky. It was like a postcard.

"So tell me 'bout this dude playin' behind y'all," Dale said without turning around. "Was he comin' up fifteen when y'all was on sixteen?"

Jimmy and Rex stepped up beside Dale.

"That's right," Jimmy said, pointing down the fifteenth fairway. "He was walking up to the tee when we were riding down sixteen."

"He'd been behind us for a while," Rex said. "We were the last tee time today, so I was surprised when someone appeared playing behind us. And he was walking."

"He wasn't in a golf cart?" Dale asked.

"No," Rex said. "He was carrying his clubs. I first noticed him on thirteen. We were near the green, and I looked back and saw him standing in the fairway, waiting for us. I waved in our direction, indicating he could play through, but he didn't move."

"None of ya recognized him?" Dale asked.

Jimmy and Rex shook their heads.

I glanced back at Freddy, who was now sitting in a golf cart. The color had still not fully returned to his face.

"And this dude just disappears after that?" Dale asked.

"Yeah," Jimmy said. "I called 911, then me and Rex got in our carts and drove over to fifteen, but we couldn't find him. We drove all over this side but didn't see a soul. Then I went up to the Pro Shop to let them know what had happened and that an ambulance was on the way."

I imagined Jimmy and Rex taking off and leaving poor Freddy in the bunker with a dead guy. No wonder he was shaken.

"Well, I guess if I accidentally beaned somebody with a golf ball, I'd hightail it too," Dale said. "Thanks, boys. Y'all hang here for a bit. Then you can finish playin' if ya want. Shame to quit now; ya'll only got two and a half holes to go."

* * *

"Cowboy, get them boys to tell you the whole story again," Dale said to Earl when we were back next to the bunker. "And get a description of that dude they saw playin' behind 'em. We don't need Byrd thinkin' we half-assed this thing. Especially since it's Wells laid out in that litter box."

"Sheriff just called," Earl said. "Be here in half an hour."

Dale and I exchanged looks.

"I should probably get going," I said.

Dale stomped the accelerator, and I held the arm rail in a death grip as we raced across the course toward the parking lot. I asked once again, "Who's Prentiss Wells?"

"Real estate attorney, in Waynesville. Been 'round forever. He did the closin' when Daddy bought the cabin from Byrd a few years back."

Sheriff Byrd, a name that made me queasy. Byrd and I shared a mutual wariness of each other. During that thing with the three murders and the bad guys, Byrd had brought me in for questioning—he actually thought I was a killer. Of course now he'll tell you he never thought such a thing and that my being brought in was just a clever strategy to get to the bottom of the situation. But I was the one who ended up finding that situation's bottom. And that fact might still be stuck in Byrd's craw. If I were the sheriff, it would sure be stuck in mine.

We were almost to the edge of the parking lot when Dale slammed on the brakes and mumbled, "Shit." I saw it too, a news van from the local ABC affiliate in Asheville. The van's side door opened, and a petite young woman with long blond hair stepped out—Fern Matthews, one of the reporters who had interviewed me, Dale, and Dale's cousin Floppy at Graveyard Fields.

"You can walk from here," Dale said, nudging me out of the golf cart. "I ain't gettin' mixed up in that shit."

"Hang on a second. Why did you ask Earl if the shit had hit the fan?"

Dale spit a stream of brown fluid next to my shoes. "'Cause Wells' son is a big-time ambulance chaser over in Asheville. You've probably seen his billboards on I-40: 'Injured in an accident? Don't Fret, Call Brett!' Guy's a walkin' douchebag, and he's gonna be all over this like wet on rain."

With that Dale tore off back toward the golf course. For a moment I considered sneaking over to my car, but I didn't want to risk catching the eye of Fern Matthews and what I was sure would be a barrage of questions. So I spun around and followed the signs to the restaurant, where I hoped I would find a cold beer, or three.

4

When I entered the restaurant, I felt as if I'd stepped inside a luxury ski lodge: high ceilings webbed with dark wood beams, tall windows with views of the golf course and the mountains surrounding it, a large stone fireplace, and exactly what I was looking for—an inviting bar with several beer taps.

I was heading in that direction when I heard someway say, "Davis Reed?"

I turned and saw a couple sitting next to a window overlooking the golf course. The man had his hand raised, as if hailing a cab.

I shuffled over to their table.

"Davis Reed. Correct?" the man said as he stood up and shook my hand. "I'm Vance Roth. This is Lana, my wife. We recognized you from the news. Graveyard Fields. That was something. Quite impressive."

Lana offered a diamond-laden hand while Vance pulled out a chair for me.

"Please join us," he said.

I hesitated a moment, then shrugged and sat down. I looked like a bum in my jeans and sweatshirt while the Roths looked like they'd just stepped out of a Ralph Lauren ad. Vance appeared to be in his late sixties or early seventies. His head was a slick dome of suntanned skin, and his thin, navy-blue sweater was tucked into pressed white pants. The tassels on his loafers jiggled as he took his seat and crossed his legs. His wife, Lana, was at least a decade younger, if not more, and stunning. Her pink flowery top billowed around her arms and slim black capris, and her black heels weren't what anyone would refer to as "sensible." Her hair was blond and shoulder length and draped gently over the only imperfection in either one of the couple's outfits, a cream-colored neck brace.

A young woman suddenly appeared and cleared away dirty plates. The Roths had just finished a very late lunch or a very early dinner. "Can I interest you in dessert?" she asked.

Vance turned to me. "Do you like gin and tonics, Mr. Reed?"

"I like gin, and I can tolerate tonic. And call me Davis."

Vance ordered three Tanqueray and tonics, and when the server walked away, I pointed at Lana's neck brace. "I don't know what happened, but I hope you have a good attorney."

Lana winked. "I sure do. Brett Wells. He's the best."

"You're kidding," I said, pointing toward the window and lowering my voice. "His father Prentiss—"

"We just heard," Vance said. "The place is abuzz with the news."

"I was actually out there."

"Really?" Lana said. "You saw the body?"

I nodded. "My friend Dale Johnson is the head deputy with the sheriff's department. I was with him when he got the call, and we rode out together. He's still out on the course."

"Deputy Johnson," Vance said. "He was part of the Graveyard Fields matter, wasn't he? Along with the mechanic. What was his name? Dopey?"

"Floppy," I said. "That's Dale's cousin. And yeah, the three of us were all part of that mess."

"Do you work with the sheriff's department?" Lana asked. "The news reports described you as a private detective."

"No, I'm just good friends with Dale, and for some reason he seems to enjoy dragging me around to things." I leaned back and surveyed the restaurant. "This is my first time here. It's pretty nice. Do you guys live in the community?"

"Yes," Vance said. "We have a home on the eighth hole."

I glanced out the window and shook my head. "What a crazy thing today. Did you all happen to know Prentiss Wells?"

"We used Prentiss when we purchased our home here, to do the title search and closing documents," Vance said. "That's the only dealing we had with him."

"Is that how you knew about Brett? Through Prentiss?"

Vance shot Lana a quick look and then stared sharply at me. "A less generous man than I might begin to find your questions impertinent."

I straightened in my chair. "I'm sorry. I'm just—"

"Am I a suspect?"

"A *suspect*? What? No. I just came in for a beer . . ."

"You need to tread very carefully, sir," Vance said, picking up a fork and studying it as if it were a rare antiquity. Suddenly he placed the fork against his neck, the tines pressing into his tanned skin. He leaned close to me. "You have no idea who you are dealing with. No idea."

I stared at Vance and tried not to wet myself. His eyes were burning into mine. Then I noticed his lip quiver, and suddenly Lana burst out laughing. "Vance, stop it. You're going to give the man a heart attack."

Lana looked at me and rolled her eyes. "Vance thinks two months of acting classes at the Palm Beach Community Theater make him Daniel Day-Lewis."

"It was a solid performance," Vance insisted.

Lana ignored him. "We have a wonderful attorney in Florida we've used for ages. But when I got into my fender bender last week, he said Brett had a great reputation, and since he was local, it would make things a lot easier."

"Same reason we used Prentiss when we purchased our home here," Vance said. "It's often better to utilize the local professional, especially in rural areas such as this. They seem to know exactly where the strings are located and, more importantly, how to pull them."

The server returned with our drinks and Lana proposed a toast: "May all your ups and downs be under the covers."

We clinked glasses.

Lana turned to me. "Now tell us about Graveyard Fields. We want all of the gritty details."

I feigned modesty but I'd told the story so many times it was like performing a well-rehearsed monologue. Vance and Lana sat rapt as I spoke, their eyes widening when I reached the scene where me, Dale, and Floppy chased three drug dealers across the rolling hills of Graveyard Fields, one of them shooting at us and Dale returning the favor.

"That man died, didn't he?" Lana asked.

"Yeah, he did," I said. "Right then and there. The other two are now serving thirty-five years at the federal prison in Jessup, Georgia."

"What an amazing adventure," Lana said.

"And some fine detective work," Vance added, raising his glass.

I accepted the compliment even though I knew I'd solved the Graveyard Fields affair by nothing more than dumb luck. Of course whenever I told the story, I glossed over that, mainly because I was embarrassed I hadn't been able to put two and two together despite the number four staring me right in the face.

"So, what do you think about this Prentiss Wells business?" Lana asked me.

"Wrong place at the wrong time is how the medical examiner put it."

Vance raised one eyebrow. "Wrong place, wrong time. Could that not be said of all victims of murder?"

I wondered if Vance was acting again. "Murder?" I said. "You're joking."

"The odds of being accidently hit and killed by a golf ball must be extraordinarily low," Vance said.

"So's being struck by lightning. But Floppy's been struck twice. And in the same leg."

"But those were acts of God. This was an act by a man. Does your friend Deputy Johnson believe it was an accident?"

"That's the impression I got."

Vance and Lana stared at each other as if silently communicating. After a few seconds Lana nodded slightly, and Vance smiled, turned to me, and said, "Davis, I have an offer for you. Work with us to find the person or persons who murdered Prentiss Wells, and I'll pay you five thousand dollars."

I cackled, then abruptly stopped when neither Lana nor Vance joined in. They were serious.

Feeling like I'd stumbled across two people a few bricks shy of a load, I glanced at my watch, pushed my chair back, and thanked them for the drink.

"Just a moment," Vance said. He removed a slim leather wallet from his pocket and produced a business card. "Call or email when you've given the offer ample consideration. But as you are no doubt aware, in murder investigations, time is of the essence."

I headed outside, wondering if the Roths were sincere but crazy or if they were just pulling my leg. Fern Matthews was still in the parking lot, holding a microphone in front of an older man wearing khaki pants and a blue golf shirt with a name tag pinned to the chest. A cameraman stood behind Fern, slightly blocking her view of me. I tiptoed over to my car, stealthily opened the door, and climbed into the driver's seat. A moment later someone tapped hard on my window. It was Fern.

"What are you doing here?" she said when I rolled down the window.

"Having a liquid lunch."

Fern flashed her made-for-local-TV-news smile and said, "How can you relax when there's a dangerous mystery golfer on the loose?"

"No comment."

Fern rolled her eyes. "What about this: Rusty Baker was released this morning. Do you care to comment?"

I suddenly felt queasy. Rusty Baker was the son of Sindal Baker, the man Dale had shot and killed at Graveyard Fields. Both father and son had been bigwigs in a biker gang called the Steel Stooges. Rusty hadn't been involved in the Graveyard Fields incident, probably because at the time he was serving a five-year sentence for selling stolen guns. I knew who he was and where he was only because, not long after the Graveyard Fields shootout, Dale heard a rumor that Rusty had promised to avenge his father's death. And I was concerned Rusty's plan for vengeance might include yours truly.

"So?" Fern said.

I cranked the engine. "No comment."

5

Back at the cabin I grabbed a beer from the fridge, plopped down at the kitchen table, and fired up my nine-year-old laptop that was hardwired to a DSL modem. I pulled up Google and searched for *Prentiss Wells Attorney, Waynesville, NC*. Soon I was staring at the deceased lawyer's headshot at the top of his firm's website. Earlier, when he was lying in the bunker, he'd looked to be in his early to mid-seventies, but in the photo on the website he didn't look a day over sixty.

His company, Wells and Butler, included three attorneys:

Prentiss Wells—Commercial and Residential Real Estate Closing, and Contract Litigation

JoAnne Butler—Estate Planning and Probate Law

Rex Pinland—Commercial and Residential Real Estate Closing, and Commercial Leasing

Rex was wearing a blue and white seersucker suit and green bow tie in his photo. I thought about his salmon pants and green argyle golf shirt. The man's closet should be considered a crime scene.

Next I searched for *Don't Fret, Call Brett, Asheville, NC*. The first link that popped up was the firm of Brett C. Wells, attorney at law. Just as his father had done on his website, Brett had plastered his head shot front and center. He was a good-looking guy. Thick, wavy brown hair and a lantern jaw, dark brown eyes, and a clean-shaven face. I guessed him to be around fifty or so. He looked like the kind of guy you'd see hosting a home renovation show on TV. He was photogenic, fit, and had that gleam in his eye that said *"I get things done."* And he wasn't wearing a bow tie, another point in his favor.

According to the website, the firm was a one-man operation, and Brett was that man. Dale had said the guy was an ambulance chaser; the site said *Personal Injury Specialist.* "I Fight For You!" was across a banner under Brett's photo. I felt sorry for the guy. I didn't know what kind of relationship he'd had with his father, but the death of a parent—or both parents, in my case—is always traumatic, especially when it's random and unexpected, whether an auto accident or an errant golf ball.

*   *   *

Around nine PM I grabbed a book, *In the Kingdom of Ice* by Hampton Sides, and got cozy on the couch in the small living room. The cabin has a stone fireplace along one wall of the room, but Dale had ordered me never to use it. "Don't need ya burnin' down the place tryin' to get all romantic with some chick," he'd said. He didn't have to worry; I didn't know how to start a fire. Or a relationship.

I was reading about a crew of men trudging across an ice floe when I heard the squawk of a patrol car.

"What the hell you readin'?" Dale said when he waddled into the living room.

I held up the book. "It's the true story of a group of men trying to get to the North Pole in late 1870s. But their ship gets trapped in an ice floe, and they have to abandon it and walk across the ice—"

"Sorry I asked," Dale said, heading back toward the kitchen. When I joined him, he was digging around the refrigerator. "You ain't never got shit worth eatin'," he said, pulling out a slice of pizza of questionable age.

He handed me a fresh beer and grabbed one for himself, and then we both sat down at the table.

"So what happened after I left?" I asked. "Did Byrd show up?"

Dale finished the pizza in three bites and nodded. "Yep. We left Wells in that litter box so Byrd could see the body where it was. He looked at it for a minute. Told us to bow our heads, then said somethin' 'bout eternal rest and lights shinin' and Jesus doin' somethin' 'nother. Gives me the willies when he starts in on that stuff."

"Any luck finding the person who hit the ball?" I asked.

"Nah. Wells's playin' buddies said the dude who was behind 'em was wearin' an orange shirt and black pants. We drove all over that course, but there weren't many people out there. Keith and Boner found an old couple on the front nine who said they mighta seen somebody in an orange shirt. I talked to 'em, but shit, they was so old and rattled I don't think they coulda told me what *they* was wearin'."

"Any of the employees know who it might be?"

"No. Me and Tommy talked to a chick who works in the Pro Shop. She showed us the schedule, called it the tee sheet. She said Wells and his buddies had the last tee time of the day, so there shouldn't of been nobody playin' behind 'em."

I crossed my arms over my chest and leaned back. "A mystery man, huh? Who happened to kill an attorney. Sounds suspicious to me."

Dale drained his beer. "Ain't nothin' suspicious to it."

I raised my eyebrows.

"It was a freak accident," Dale yelled. "Some dude was out there and hit a bad shot and beaned Wells in the side of the head. Then the dude gets scared and runs off. Whoever it was wasn't s'posed to be out there playin'. Had to of snuck on the course somewhere without bein' seen. That's why he was walkin' and why he ain't on the schedule."

I shrugged. "Maybe Wells was a target. Maybe this mystery golfer was out there for the sole purpose of taking him out."

Dale jumped up and opened the fridge. He grabbed another beer and another slice of pizza.

"I don't know how old that pizza is," I said.

Dale examined the slice closely. "Well, it ain't got no fuzz on it, so it must be okay." He plopped back down in his seat and glared at me. "There ain't no way some dude decides to kill a man by hittin' him with a golf ball. Do you know how hard it is just to hit the damn green? Much less drill somebody in the head from god knows how far away."

I started laughing and Dale snarled. "You asshole. You don't believe none of the shit you're sayin'."

"No, I don't, but guess what? I met a couple in the restaurant today when I was trying to avoid Fern, named Vance and Lana Roth. They live at Springdale. They might be crazy but they're convinced Wells was murdered."

Dale scoffed. "I hate all this true crime bullshit that's out nowadays. Makes everybody think they're a detective."

"They recognized me from the Graveyard Fields stuff. Get this: they offered me *five grand* if I could prove Wells was murdered."

Dale laughed. "They're yankin' your chain."

I thought about Vance and his affinity for acting. "Yeah, probably," I said with a shrug. "Hey, who was that guy playing with Wells that you knew?"

"Jimmy Fletcher. He works at some mortgage company in Waynesville. We was big buddies back in junior high and high school, but I ain't really kept up with him. I know him, but I don't know him, ya know?"

"What did you call him? Double F?"

"Yeah. Fuckin' Fletcher. That's what we all called him back then."

"So what happens in a situation like this?" I asked. "I mean, whoever hit the ball that killed Wells is guilty of what? Involuntary manslaughter? Leaving the scene of an accident? Like a hit-and-run."

"I don't know what happens 'cause this type of shit ain't happened here before. We bagged the two golf balls, Wells's and one there next to his little telescope."

"It's called a rangefinder. It measures—"

"Shut up, and listen. Wells's ball is a Penfold number two. The other ball is a Kirkland brand. It's got a yellow smiley face on it."

"Kirkland? That's Costco stuff, isn't it?"

"We ain't got Costcos up here, but yeah, we googled it, it's their brand. Now we're gonna print it. But do you know how hard it is to lift prints off a golf ball? They're round, and they've got them little dimples all over 'em. And golfers wear gloves when they're playin', so even if we're able to print that ball, we probably ain't gonna find nothin'."

"Golfers only wear one glove. And most of them take it off when they're putting."

"And how do you know that?"

"I've seen it on TV."

"You don't watch TV."

"Well, not here. Your internet's so slow I have to send emails in Morse code."

Dale kicked a table leg. "Knock this shit off. This guy's gotta be scared shitless 'bout what happened. But he's not accused of manslaughter or nothin' else. It was obviously an accident, but there's insurance shit that needs to get settled and Don't Fret, Call douchebag Brett's probably gunnin' to sue the pants offa whoever hit that ball. So yeah, we're lookin' for the dude. We've put it out on the news and on Facebook and all that. We'll find the guy."

"Speaking of the news, Fern cornered me out in the parking lot. She said Rusty Baker's been released."

"Yeah, I heard that," Dale said through clenched teeth.

"Are you worried? That he might come after you?"

"I dare him to."

That statement hung in the air for a long moment. It wasn't a pleasant thought.

"Tell me something," I said. "Why did you look so shocked when you saw Wells's body today?"

"I's just surprised it was him."

"And why wouldn't Earl tell you who had died when he called? Why did he want you to see for yourself?"

"'Cause he's an asshole."

"C'mon, tell me. Do you and Wells have a history?"

Dale suddenly looked like he'd bitten into a lemon. "His son, Brett."

"Yeah, what about him?"

"I told ya Carla's a paralegal, right? Well 'bout six months 'fore she moved out, she took a job workin' for Brett over in Asheville. Things had been pretty good with us up till that point, but lo and behold, she starts workin' for douchebag Brett, and all the sudden things between me and her turn sour. Whadd'ya make of that?"

Like politics, the Second Amendment, and sports, Dale's ex-wife, Carla, was something he and I didn't discuss. As much as he loved to talk about women, Carla was more or less off limits. One of the few times he'd mentioned her, a night when he'd drunk enough beer to loosen his screws and turn him sentimental, he'd said to me, "Davis, there ain't nothin' worse than missin' a woman." Carla was Dale's Achilles heel, so I suddenly understood his feelings toward Brett Wells.

"Oh, man," I said. "I'm sorry."

Dale snorted like an angry bull. "Dickhead shows up today and starts barkin' orders at everybody like he's in charge. Acts like he don't know me. Asshole knows damn well who I am. He's lucky I didn't wring his neck."

I banged on the tabletop to stop Dale's train of thought. "Hey, do you know the difference between a lawyer and a bucket of shit?"

Dale grinned. "Yeah, the bucket."

We laughed, then Dale reached into his shirt pocket and removed a wadded-up piece of paper. "Here," he said. "Earl told me to give you this."

I unwrapped the paper and read the barely legible handwriting. "It says 'Marvin Singleton.' Who's that?"

"Earl says that guy Marvin helped search on Cold Mountain right after that bomber went down. You know they had local volunteers search for that crash 'fore the Army showed up. Earl thought Marvin could give ya some info for your book."

I looked at the paper again. "What's Sunset Seasons?"

"That's where the dude lives, it's an old folks home over in Clyde. If he helped search for that crash, the man's gotta be a hundred years old."

I threw the paper down. "I'll give it some thought."

"Davis, you lazy fuck. Go talk to the man 'fore he croaks."

"I will. Maybe next week."

"Dammit, Davis, you ain't never gonna write that book. Then you're gonna run outta money. Hell, your rent's only paid up till the end of this month anyway."

"I've got a big settlement check coming, remember?"

"Yeah, I'll believe that shit when I see it."

That was what Dale said any time I mentioned the settlement money I should be getting from the Charleston PD for getting shot by a dirty cop, not to mention a later second attempt on my life by two members of that same department. But my attorney, Allison, had yet to finalize the settlement, and as the months had rolled by, I'd started to worry that Dale might be right.

"Now here's the deal," Dale said. "Tomorrow you go talk to that Marvin feller. I get off at four thirty. Pick me up at Daddy's at five and we'll go to Boojum. There's a new bartender there. Gotta ass like an onion."

"What do you mean? Round?"

"Damn right it's round. And it'll bring tears to your eyes."

* * *

After Dale left, I cracked open a fresh beer and wondered why I'd been so stupid to tell everyone about my plans to write a book. When I'd moved to the cabin last November, my plan was to get out of Charleston and write about the B-25 bomber that had crashed into Cold Mountain in the 1940s, killing all five men aboard. The timing was perfect. I was recuperating from a gunshot wound, and since the identity of the person who had shot me was unknown, vanishing from Charleston seemed like a really good idea.

In the hospital I'd searched Craigslist for rentals with views of Cold Mountain. I lucked upon an ad for a cabin that seemed perfect, and when I dialed the number, a gruff man answered—Dale. The following day I was released, so I packed up and headed to Cruso, ready to become the next Erik Larson or David McCullough or Bill Bryson or Joan Didion.

Anyone other than Davis Reed, fledgling private detective.

But five and a half months had passed, and I hadn't written a word.

I picked up the notepaper and tried to think of an excuse not to go visit Marvin. The devils on one of my shoulders suggested spending the next day doing the usual, sitting on the deck, drinking good beer, and staring at Cold Mountain. But the lone angel on the other shoulder insisted I go see the old man, in hopes I might find a spark of inspiration and actually get down to work.

I threw the paper back onto the table and opened the laptop to look up directions to Sunset Seasons. Brett Wells's website was still on the screen. I stared at the man's face.

Dale was right: he did look like the kind of guy who could use a neck wringing.

6

Here's a little geography lesson. Haywood County covers around five hundred square miles and is home to a little over sixty thousand people. The county has four incorporated towns: Waynesville, the tourist town; Canton, home to a paper mill; Maggie Valley, a micro-sized wannabe Gatlinburg full of T-shirt shops, putt-putt courses, and mom-and-pop motels; and Clyde, a small town I still haven't been able to accurately define.

Clyde is situated halfway between Canton and Waynesville. So I headed west on 276 for a bit, then pulled into the parking lot of El Bacaratos, my go-to guacamole place. The restaurant is ten miles west of the cabin, but it's the closest place I can get cell phone coverage. On the map on my phone, I typed in *Sunset Seasons*. A minute later I was back on the road, and fifteen minutes after that I was in the middle of downtown Clyde, which is about a quarter of a mile long. I drove past a post office, a bank, and a meat-and-three restaurant that, according to its sign, had been serving locals since 1954.

I followed the map down a side street and soon spotted the sign for Sunset Seasons Retirement Village. The place looked more like an abandoned library than a village. It was a one-story, octagon-shaped brick structure that was in need of attention. In some places the red bricks had turned black, and small green shoots of weeds rose from the gutters hanging over the building's eaves.

I walked through the door into a small waiting area decorated with a few chairs and a couple of side tables covered with magazines. On the other end of the room, a woman sat behind a sliding glass window. I hobbled over and the woman slid the window to the side, as if it were one of the labors of Hercules. "Can I help you?"

"I'd like to visit with Marvin Singleton."

"He's in Memory Care. Have you visited him before?"

I said no and the woman grabbed a notebook and pushed it toward me. "Print your name here and the name of the resident you're visiting."

I did as I was told, and the woman handed me a lanyard with a green plastic key card attached to it. I put it around my neck.

"Have a seat," the woman said. "I'll get somebody to show you back there."

I took a chair and glanced at a television attached to one of the walls. It was tuned to the local news station, showing the latest high school basketball scores. I picked up a three-year-old copy of *InStyle* and was reading about the ten best moisturizers for combination skin when a young woman in scrubs, who looked barely old enough to vote, approached me.

"You're here to see Mr. Singleton?"

I stood up. "Yeah. My name's Davis Reed."

"I'm Megan. Follow me."

Megan led me through a door and into a long cinder block hallway, where the faint scent of urine caused the frozen burrito I'd had for breakfast to flip over in my stomach. On my right, a group of ten or so framed headshots adorned the wall, under a banner that read "Our Caring Administrative Staff." I shook my head. I couldn't imagine working in a rest home. Actually I couldn't imagine working anywhere.

The hallway was an obstacle course of old folks in wheelchairs or shuffling behind walkers. Doors lined both sides of the hall, each with a number on the front, like at a hotel. Under the numbers sat small nameplates etched with the names of the occupants. Most of the doors were closed, but through the open ones I could see old folks sitting in rockers or elevated in hospital-style beds, blankly staring at TVs or through windows that looked out into a world beyond their reach.

When we came to a set of closed double doors, Megan pulled a key card from her pocket and held it up to a small gray block attached to the wall. There was a short beep followed by a loud click, then one of the doors slowly swung open. We stepped through and into another identical-looking hallway lined with doors.

"This is Memory Care," Megan said. "It's a secure area."

A moment later we passed what looked like a nurses station, where an older woman with stringy gray hair and dark blue scrubs sat behind a counter and frowned at a computer monitor. When she glanced at me, I nodded and gave her my best smile. She sneered.

We continued a bit farther down the hall until we reached a door marked 312—Marvin Singleton. Megan gave it a gentle knock, then pushed it open. The room was larger than I'd expected, with a double bed, a comfortable-looking recliner, and a dresser covered with several framed photos and a couple of greeting cards. Above the dresser hung a large flat-screen TV, tuned to the same channel as the one in the waiting area, but with the sound off. In front of the only window in the room, an old man sat in a wheelchair with his back to me. Megan tapped the man on the shoulder and spoke loudly. "Mr. Singleton. This is Mr. Reed. He's come to sit for a while."

Marvin put a wrinkled hand on one of the chair's wheels and slowly spun to face me. The guy didn't look a hundred years old. He looked two hundred years old. His face was as wrinkled as a dried apple, and sprigs of white hair sprang from his scalp like weeds growing out of the cracks of a sidewalk.

Marvin squinted and it was obvious he was trying to place me. Was I someone he knew or had known? Or a total stranger?

Megan pointed at the lanyard hanging from my neck. "That'll get you back out. Have a good visit." She then walked out and closed the door behind her.

I took a seat in the recliner. "Hi, Marvin. My name's Davis. I think you know my friend Earl Pless? He's a deputy sheriff."

"Who?" Marvin said in a wet, raspy voice.

"Earl Pless. Short guy, big bushy mustache. You two used to work together at the sheriff's department."

Marvin shook his head.

"Anyway, he told me you helped search on Cold Mountain after that bomber crashed up there back in the forties. I'm writing a book about that crash, and I wondered if I could talk to you about it."

Marvin frowned. At least I think it was a frown; the guy's face was so wrinkled it was hard to tell.

"So did you find anything when you helped with the search? Did you reach the wreckage?"

Marvin didn't answer, he just glared at me with a confused look. I spent the next few minutes talking about the details of the accident, in hopes it would stir his memory, but if it did, he didn't acknowledge it.

I was staring at my shoes, wondering whether to try another tack or just give up, when Marvin said, "I let him go."

I looked up. Marvin was gazing off into space. He no longer looked confused; he looked worried. "You let him go?" I said. "Did you find someone during that search?"

Marvin kept staring at a spot somewhere over my shoulder. "That poor boy. He was so scared."

My pulse quickened. "A boy? Where was he? Was he hurt?"

Marvin raised a bony finger and pointed past me. I turned around and was staring at a dead man. Prentiss Wells's face was plastered on the TV screen, the same photo from the Wells and Butler website. I looked around for the remote, found it on the edge of Marvin's bed, and turned the sound on.

In the news studio, an anchorman behind a desk said, "Authorities are looking for any information concerning a person golfing alone at Springdale Golf Club yesterday afternoon. According to witnesses, the golfer was wearing black pants and an orange shirt, and was not authorized to be on the golf course. If you have any information regarding this matter, please contact the Haywood County Sheriff's Office at the number below." A number appeared briefly on the bottom of the screen as the reporter turned to his left. "So, Lonnie, will we need our umbrellas tomorrow?"

I hit the mute button and turned to Marvin.

"I let him go," he said. "That poor boy. He was so scared."

"Someone at the bomber crash? Or are you talking about Prentiss Wells? Did you know him?"

Marvin held my gaze and repeated what he'd just said. I wondered if he was lost in the wilderness of dementia.

"Wish we woulda found that little white horse," he said.

"Horse? What are you talking about?"

"Little white horse. Probably still out there in that field."

Marvin's eyes had an anxious look, and I got the feeling I was out of my depth. So I wished him well and headed to the nurses station, or whatever it was called. Megan was there, standing behind the counter next to the older woman who was still glowering at her computer.

"That was a short visit," Megan said.

"It was a confusing conversation."

"Yeah, this isn't one of his better days."

"Does he have a lot of visitors? Or any visitors?"

"A few. His granddaughter comes by pretty often."

A stick-thin woman with white hair slowly scooted past us with the aid of a walker with tennis balls on the ends of its legs. The older woman sitting behind the counter looked up and scowled. "Annie," she barked. "It's not time for lunch. Now get back down the hall."

The white-haired woman stopped, did a one-eighty, then headed back the way she'd come at about a half mile an hour.

I turned back to Megan. "How long has Marvin been here?"

"Probably longer than I've been alive," Megan said. She looked at the older woman. "Sheila. When did Mr. Singleton move in here?"

Sheila ignored the question.

"Does he have dementia?" I asked.

"Excuse me," Sheila barked. "We don't give out information about our residents." She turned to Megan. "And we don't answer questions about who visits our residents either. Do you understand that, missy?"

Megan nodded sheepishly.

"I'm sorry," I said to Sheila. "I didn't mean to pry. But would it be possible to leave my contact information here for Marvin's granddaughter? I'd like to talk to her about a book I'm writing and—"

"No," Sheila snapped.

I raised my hands in surrender. I didn't want to mess with Sheila. She seemed like the kind of old woman whose house children avoid on Halloween. Not because she didn't hand out candy, but because she might eat the children.

* * *

I was almost to the wall adorned with photos of the Caring Administrative Staff when I heard the squeak of tennis shoes coming up behind me. I turned around to see Megan approaching. "Hang on a minute," she said.

Megan led me down a different hall, to an open door, and I followed her into a small office with a desk and a computer. Megan plopped down and pecked at a keyboard. I looked around and wondered how anyone could work in a windowless office and retain their sanity. The only life in the room was a small potted plant on top of a filing cabinet. Next to that was a large jug of mixed nuts. I stepped closer and looked at the label: Kirkland.

"Here you go," Megan said, handing me a yellow Post-it note with a phone number and email address written on it. "Elizabeth Harper. She's Mr. Singleton's granddaughter and his emergency contact. She's real nice. I'm sure she'd be happy to talk to you about your book. Mr. Singleton's lucky. Some people here don't have any family. No visitors, nothing. It's sad."

"Thanks for this. I hope you're not going to get in trouble with Nurse Ratched back there."

Megan frowned. "Who? Oh, you mean Sheila? Ugh. I swear she rides a broom to work."

"By the way," I said, pointing at the jug of mixed nuts. "That brand is only sold at Costco, but I didn't think there were any around here."

"There's not. Callie brings stuff back for us from the one in Greenville. She's the administrative assistant here. Her parents live down there, and she goes down every couple of weeks to visit."

"Greenville, South Carolina?"

"That's right. It's only about an hour and a half from here. It's real pretty. Got a waterfall right downtown and everything."

* * *

I headed back toward Cruso and stopped at El Bacaratos for a to-go order of chips and guacamole. While sitting in the parking lot, I scrolled through the very short list of contacts on my phone. I tapped on the name of my attorney, then went through a series of prompts that led to a full minute of an instrumental version of "The Piña Colada Song."

"Nelson, Peterson, and Levine," a voice finally said.

"This is Davis Reed. I need to speak to Allison, please."

"Ms. Levine is with a client. May I take a message?"

"Yeah, please tell her I need an update on the settlement as soon as possible. Ask her to email me. I'm in the mountains and my cell service is spotty."

The voice assured me the message would be delivered, then the line went dead.

I scrolled through the apps on my phone and tapped the one for South State Bank. I logged in and gritted my teeth while I waited for my details to appear. According to the app, my checking account balance was now down to four digits, with a decimal right in the middle.

7

Twenty minutes later I was back at the cabin, sitting in front of the laptop with my first beer of the day, a bottle of my home brew I'd named Old Crab IPA in honor of Cruso's tagline: "Welcome to Cruso: Nine Miles of Friendly People Plus One Old Crab," which is on a sign along 276 as you enter the community. I typed out a quick email to Marvin's granddaughter, explaining how I'd gotten her contact information, my interest in Marvin, and that I'd visited with him briefly but thought having a family member present might lead to a more productive conversation. I hit "Send," and since chips and guacamole were now out of my price range, grabbed the last slice of leftover pizza of questionable age out of the fridge and headed to the deck.

I'd barely gotten comfortable when I heard a vehicle coming up the gravel drive. It was a car I'd never seen before, an old white Crown Victoria. I leaned over the railing and sighed when Dale's cousin Floppy dragged himself out of the car. Floppy Johnson: mechanic, local know-it-all, kleptomaniac, motormouth, martial arts expert, conspiracy theorist who doesn't trust computers or cell phones, and two-time lightning-strike-in-the-same-leg survivor. Floppy probably weighs only a hundred or so pounds soaking wet, and in his tan coveralls, splattered from hem to collar with grease and oil, he resembled a six-foot-tall dipstick.

"Hey there, Davis. You like my new car? I call her Vicky on account she's an ol' Crown Vic. I've still got Sally but I'm givin' her a rest for a while. I never thought I'd have two vehicles at the same time 'cause that seems extravagant, havin' two workin' vehicles when you're just one person. Now if you've got a family and such, then I guess it makes sense to have more than one vehicle 'cause people's gotta go in different directions sometimes, but it's just me, so havin' two vehicles don't really make a whole lotta sense, but when I saw

31

Vicky down at Ernie's Motors, I knew I had to have her. You ever get a feelin' like that? See somethin' and just have to have it, even though it don't make no sense to have it? They was this one time . . ."

"Floppy!"

"Did you ever name your Mercedes? I told you that you should name it. A car's more personal when you give it a name. I don't know any German lady names, but I guess it don't have to be German—you could name it anythin' you want, like Tabatha or Peggy or Rosanna. Hey, I used to like that Rosanna song by that band Toto. You remember them? Do you think they named that band after that dog in that *Wizard of Oz* movie? That's the one where that girl clicked her shoes together to get back home. Now it'd be real handy to have some shoes like that, wouldn't it? Just click 'em together and go back to your house whenever you want."

I waited a moment, not sure if Floppy was finished or if he'd run out of oxygen.

"What are you doing here?" I asked.

"Can I come inside?"

Floppy's unexpected visit was not all that unexpected. Once or twice a week he would show up unannounced—in his defense he doesn't have a phone or computer—and invite me to something: a car show, a flea market, a high school football game, or he'd just come inside and talk and talk and talk.

Despite being cousins, Dale had absolutely zero patience for Floppy. And truth be told, Floppy didn't have a very high opinion of Dale. Both guys were an acquired taste. I wondered what it said about me that I'd acquired it.

I nodded and Floppy quickly hopped around the side of the cabin, his bum leg dragging behind him like a broken muffler. I met him by the kitchen door, and when he stepped inside, his body odor hit me like a punch to the face.

I grabbed another Old Crab out of the fridge. Floppy looked at it and said, "Do you have any good beer in there?" I dug around the back and found a can of Coors Light left over from one of Floppy's previous visits. When I handed it to him, he grinned as if I'd just given him the title to my car.

"Last night I was eatin' at the Sagebrush, and I saw Lisa Myers. Me and her went to high school together? She was real pretty back then, but now she looks like she's been rode hard and put up wet. I guess I can't talk—I ain't no Adonis, but I take good care of myself. I was at the flea market a couple of months ago, and I saw this little marble rollin' pin thing. I thought it was for bakin' and such, but the man said if you roll it over your face, the wrinkles'll come out." Floppy raised his chin. "I think it's workin' pretty good."

"So you saw someone named Lisa," I said. "What about it?"

"Lisa works at the Springdale golf course, and she told me that Prentiss Wells got hit with a golf ball, and it kilt him. Can you believe that? He was a lawyer, but he was a nice feller. Did all the stuff when I bought my garage and trailer way back when. It's crazy. Out there playin' golf, mindin' his own business, and a golf ball comes and hits him right in the head. Killed him deader than a doornail. Now I used to play golf, but I ain't played much in a while on account of my leg. Did you know I was on the golf team back in high school? It's true, I only played 'cause you got outta school early to go to matches, but I was pretty good back then. This one time we's playin' and . . ."

I let Floppy ramble as I walked out of the kitchen, through the living room, and out to the deck. He followed without once closing his mouth.

"How fast do you think a golf ball goes?" Floppy asked when we sat down. "You know them major league pitchers can throw a ball 'bout a hundred miles an hour, but I don't know 'bout a golf ball—I bet it's faster, don't ya think? Man, I wouldn't wanna be hit in the head with one of them things. Hey, did you know they found that Prentiss man lyin' in a sand trap? That's right, Lisa told me all 'bout it at the Sagebrush. She said it was kinda weird that he was playin' that day 'cause he ain't played at that course in a long time. But there he was yesterday, dead as all get-out, layin' in that sand like he was sunnin' hisself at Daytona Beach. Hey, did you know that sand in them sand traps comes from Spruce Pine? It's true. Spruce Pine's 'bout an hour and a half northeast of here, and the sand from there's real white 'cause it's full of quartz. That fancy golf course down in Augusta, they use that same sand, 'cause it's so white and looks real good on TV. They also grow a lot of Christmas trees in Spruce Pine. I used to have a Christmas tree farm sometime back, but people started buyin' fake Christmas trees 'cause they started makin' 'em with the lights already built into 'em. Now I don't know why someone would want a fake Christmas tree, even if the lights are already on it, 'cause the nice thing 'bout a Christmas tree is the smell, and them fake trees just smell like plastic. Now why would anybody want that? I tell ya some things I just don't unnerstand."

"Hang on," I said. "Back up a minute. The Lisa person—what does she do at the golf course?"

"She works in the Pro Shop, behind the counter. She takes people's money for the golf fees. Sells 'em balls and gloves and whatnot."

I thought about Dale mentioning the woman with the Tee Sheet. "Was she working yesterday?"

"Nuh-uh. She was off yesterday, but one of her work buddies called her and told her what'd happened to that Prentiss man. Told her they was deputies swarmin' all over the place."

"And Lisa said Wells hadn't played at Springdale in a long time?"

"That's right. She's worked there over fifteen years and said it'd been at least ten since she's seen him. Said he used to golf there all the time, but then she heard he bought a membership at that golf course over in Waynesville. Hey, did you know Waynesville was named after a General called Mad Anthony Wayne? That ain't no lie. They say he . . ."

Floppy's mention of the course in Waynesville threw an image in my mind I didn't care for. There had been a woman involved in that lively adventure we'd had with the bodies and the bad guys, named Diana Ross, if you can believe that. She lives in a big house near a golf course in Waynesville. She also owns a brewery in Waynesville that, despite having the best beer in the area, I do not patronize. Diana put a knife in my heart, and I'm afraid if I run into her, she might twist it.

"Maybe it was karma," Floppy said, slapping the table and snapping me back to the present.

"Karma? What are you talking about?"

"You know—when the stuff you've done comes back to get ya?"

"Yeah, I know what it means. But what does it have to do with Prentiss Wells?"

"He hit and killed a boy with his car, way back."

"Prentiss Wells killed someone?"

"Uh-huh. They say it was an accident, but maybe it wasn't. Maybe he was speedin' or drinkin' and drivin', or just not payin' attention, and karma finally caught up with him."

"When did this happen?"

"Back in '88, I think. I's in grade school back then, but it was big talk for a while. Happened late at night, right up near his house."

I wondered what Vance and Lana Roth would think about Floppy's karma theory.

"I met a couple yesterday who think Wells was murdered."

Floppy's eyes bulged. "Murdered?"

"Yeah, they're sure of it. They offered me a heap of money to prove it."

Floppy's eyes bulged even more. "A heap of money?"

I nodded.

"Whadd'ya think?" Floppy said, scratching his head. "How could it a been done? Lisa told me somebody snuck on the golf course without payin' and hit the ball that kilt Wells. But maybe they snuck up on him when his buddies wasn't lookin' and hit him with a golf club. Or a crowbar they had hid in their golf bag. Or a billy stick. Or maybe they didn't need to sneak up on him. Maybe they hid behind a tree and used a slingshot to shoot the golf ball. Or maybe they had one of them drone things, and they flew it up in the air, and it dropped the golf ball. Or maybe they built some kind of gun that shoots golf balls, like them tater cannons you can make. Or maybe—"

"Floppy! *Floppy!* Listen to me. Forget all that. There's something important I need to talk to you about. Rusty Baker's been released from prison. He's Sindal Baker's son."

"He's the one said he's gonna kill Dale."

"That's right. But you and I were also involved in that, and we were both plastered all over the news."

"You reckon he might wanna kill us too?"

"I don't know. But it's possible the thought has crossed his mind."

Floppy jumped up and adopted a bizarre stance. "I can teach you some judo moves."

I politely declined and told Floppy I had important business I needed to take care of, but he ignored me and hopped around the kitchen like a psychotic bird.

It took twenty minutes to get him out of the cabin, and another hour for his body odor to follow suit.

8

When the air had cleared, I poured myself a bowl of Pepperidge Farm Goldfish and checked my email. I was hoping to find something from my attorney, Allison, but the only new message was from Elizabeth Harper, with the subject *Re: Marvin Singleton*.

* * *

Mr. Reed,

I'd like to learn more about your book project and possibly facilitate a discussion with my grandfather. Would you be able to meet today? Say 3:00 at Monty's Roasters in Waynesville? I apologize for the short notice, but I have a busy schedule for the remainder of the week.

Best,
EH

* * *

I emailed to accept the invitation, hopped in the Mercedes, and headed out. I stopped at the end of the drive and waited for a Jeep Wrangler to pass by on Highway 276. Trailing the Jeep were three motorcycles, which made me straighten up in my seat. The motorcycles were adventure-style BMWs, outfitted with side cases. Not exactly the type of rides preferred by biker gangs, but still, anything with two wheels and an engine made me nervous.

The Wrangler and the bikes were headed south, maybe going to the Blue Ridge Parkway, just a few twisty miles up the mountain. I had not been on the Parkway since the day Dale had shot and killed Sindal Baker at Graveyard Fields, almost six months ago. It was beautiful place—stunning actually—but to me it was now haunted. And I don't like ghosts.

* * *

I had some time to kill before I needed to be in Waynesville, so when I approached Springdale, I hung a right and drove up to the main parking lot. It was much different from the previous day—no patrol cars, no firetrucks, no ambulance. Presumably no dead bodies.

I wanted to go into the restaurant for a beer, but since my bank balance was in intensive care, I sat in the car and thought about Vance Roth's offer and wondered if he had been serious, and if so why he would offer so much money. I had no idea when—or if—my settlement check was coming, and I needed cash. I should have been proactive months earlier, but instead I'd sat at the cabin, drinking beer and not writing a book.

I've always been good at ignoring smoke right up until I'm engulfed in flames.

I pulled out of the lot and was almost back to Country Club Drive when a patrol car turned toward me. As it approached, the driver's side window lowered, and a hand extended out, the fingers covered in turquoise rings. I rolled down my window.

"Whatcha doin', Davis?" Earl said when we'd stopped our vehicles side by side. "Don't tell me you've taken up golf."

"Just wasting time," I said.

"Writer's block, huh?"

"Something like that. What are you up to?"

"It's my nephew's birthday. I'm gonna buy him a cap I saw in the shop when I was in there yesterday."

"Hey, thanks for pointing me to Marvin Singleton. I went to see him this morning, but I didn't get anywhere. I think he might have dementia."

Earl slapped his ring-covered fingers against the door of his patrol car. "Dangit, I was afraid of that. I heard he's got ol'-timers. But I thought maybe you'd catch him on a good day and get somethin' outta him."

"I've connected with his granddaughter. I'm hoping she can help me get some information about the crash search from him."

"I met her once, way back. Nice lady. And hey, if you get anythin' that helps with your book, you owe me a growler or two of your beer."

"Fair enough. So how do you know Marvin?"

"He used to be a deputy—we worked together for a few weeks. One day we were ridin' 'round, and he pointed up at Cold Mountain and said he'd helped search for that bomber when it went down, back whenever it was. And seein' Prentiss Wells out there in that sand trap made me think of Marvin. Years ago Wells hit and killed a boy with his car, and Marvin was the first one on the scene."

I suddenly heard Marvin's raspy voice in my ear: *That poor boy. He was so scared.*

"When did this happen?" I asked.

"Uh, 1988, right 'fore Marvin retired. Same year I started. The boy had just robbed a house near Wells's and was fleein' the scene when he ran out in the road. It was ruled an accident but it really tore Marvin up. Hell, I think he was more tore up 'bout it than Wells was."

Floppy is known to exaggerate, and sometimes just flat out invent things, but it seemed he was right about the possibility of Prentiss Wells having some questionable karma.

A beer delivery truck pulled into the lot and came to a stop behind Earl's patrol car—there wasn't enough room for it to pass. Earl waved to the driver, then said to me, "See ya later, Davis."

"Hold on a sec. Any leads on the mystery golfer?"

"Yeah, but nothin' solid yet. I hope we find him soon. This thing's got the big man by the short and curlies. It can't be easy havin' to deal with the asshole who stole your wife."

I nodded and left it at that. I wasn't exactly sure what Dale was having to deal with, but as head deputy he was probably catching his share of guff from Brett Wells.

I exited the lot and took a left onto Country Club Drive and headed into the residential neighborhood. The road was steep at first but leveled off after a couple of hundred yards where I began to pass some modest homes and some not-so-modest ones. I started to wonder if the road might be a dead end and if I should turn around sooner rather than later. The road was curved and narrow and bordered on both sides by thick stands of trees, homes, and the occasional drainage ditch.

I moved forward at about twenty miles per hour while trying to figure out how someone would go about sneaking onto the golf course without being seen. There wasn't room to park next to the road, and so far the course itself had only been visible a couple of times. But it appeared to me that most of the homes on my left would butt up against the course or very close to it, just like the one I'd seen by the pond on hole sixteen. Seemed to me it would be pretty easy to walk out the back door of one of those homes and onto the course without being noticed.

As I drove, I passed several people out walking, some with dogs pulling them along. I stopped by one of the walkers, an older guy with a black lab, and asked him how far the road went. He told me it was a three-mile loop that led back to the highway.

I'd gone about two miles when I saw Vance Roth power walking in my direction. He was wearing a black track suit with white piping, and bright white sneakers.

I stopped and called out, "How are you?"

"Hello, Davis," Vance said, tapping the screen of the smartwatch on his wrist. "Out for a leisurely drive? Or out investigating? My offer still stands."

I laughed. "C'mon. Are you really serious about that?"

"Oh, I'm deadly serious."

"I talked to Dale last night. The sheriff's department is convinced it was an accident."

Vance stared hard at me for a moment, then a wide smile crossed his face. "Would you be free to join us for dinner this evening? We can discuss the matter further, and if you like, I will put my offer in writing."

I weighed spending an evening drinking beer with Dale with money I didn't have against hanging out with an eccentric couple and enjoying a free meal. I didn't weigh for long.

"Why not?" I said.

9

Monty's Roasters was located in an area of Waynesville called Frog Level. Why it's called Frog Level is a mystery I haven't solved. The only clue is a large mural on the side of a brick building depicting a frog sitting atop a carpenter's level. Not a lot of nuance, if you ask me.

I'd not been to Frog Level in months, mainly because it's where Long Branch Brewery is located. Long Branch makes one of the best IPAs I've ever tasted, but the brewery is owned by Diana Ross, the woman who left the knife in my heart, so I avoid it. Unfortunately, Monty's is just a couple of doors down from the brewery, and I couldn't find a place to park that wouldn't force me to walk by it, unless I wanted to walk around the entire block—not an appealing idea with my bad leg.

I finally pulled into a space and called Dale.

"What's up, dickless?" he said by way of answering.

"I'm bailing on you. I've got a dinner date tonight."

"Bullshit."

"I'm serious. With that couple I met at the golf course yesterday. The Roths."

"The ones who offered you five grand?"

"Yep."

"How old are they?"

"I'd say the guy is late sixties give or take, and his wife is probably mid-fifties."

"I betcha they're swingers."

That thought had not occurred to me, and it made me instantly think of Lana's "ups and downs under the covers" toast. I sputtered for a moment. "No. Of course not."

40

"Is the wife hot?" Dale asked.

"*They're not swingers.* Stop it. They're just a nice couple. I need to socialize more."

"Well, don't call me when they get ya all tipsy and start strippin' down." Dale snickered, then said, "Hey, I talked to Earl a minute ago. He told me he ran into you at Springdale."

"Yeah, I was just out riding around."

"He said you went to talk to that Marvin feller 'bout your book."

"Yeah. It was a bust. If he's got anything to share, it's going to take some time to get it."

"I swear," Dale barked. "Jesus wrote the Bible faster than you're writin' your book."

"I'm not sure that's factually accurate."

"Hell yeah, it is. You've been fartin' 'round with this thing for damn near six months and ain't got shit to show for it. Now go to your swingers' party, then get back to work and finish that book so I don't have to kick you outta the cabin."

"I love you too."

Dale laughed. "Kiss my ass. Later, tater."

* * *

As I walked past Long Branch Brewery I couldn't help but glance at the large plate glass window next to the door. A short, blonde, buxom woman was on the other side of the glass wiping down a high-top table with a rag. She looked up and our eyes locked. I started to walk away, but she quickly tossed down the rag and came through the door and out onto the sidewalk.

"What's happenin', stranger? Ain't seen you in ages."

"Hey, Daiquiri. How've you been?"

"Question is how are you? I heard Sindal's boy got outta jail. What do you and that big 'un think 'bout that?"

Daiquiri, much like her boss Diana, was something of a mystery to me. Last fall Sindal Baker and some of his gang had been hanging out regularly at Long Branch, which made me concerned for Diana. But the way things ended up playing out, I now couldn't be positive whether Diana—and Daiquiri for that matter—weren't somehow involved in the gang's drug operations, or at least sympathetic to them.

"I haven't had a lot of time to think about it," I said, "so I don't know."

41

"Well, you better start thinkin' 'cause there was two of 'em in here last night. First time I've seen anybody from the Stooges in here since your fatass buddy shot Sindal."

I didn't know if Daiquiri was trying to warn me or scare me.

"Why don't you come in and have a beer?" Daiquiri said with a smirk. "Diana's in the back. I'll fetch her for ya."

"Thanks, maybe another time," I said as I started toward Monty's. *Another lifetime,* I thought.

* * *

I'd not been inside Monty's Roasters, but was expecting a "too cool for school" atmosphere. You know, heavily tattooed baristas making unpronounceable concoctions with the delicacy of chemists and the pretentiousness of royalty. But instead there was just an older guy with an elaborate combover standing behind the counter. When I approached, he handed me a one-page laminated menu.

"What will it be?" the man said.

I looked around the seating area: several wooden tables and benches, with two wingback chairs squeezed into a corner. There were five people in the place, but no one was sitting alone.

"I'm meeting someone," I said. "I'll wait until they arrive to order, if that's all right."

The man squinted. "You look familiar. Where've I seen you?"

"Maybe on the news last fall. That big drug bust at Graveyard Fields, up on the Parkway. My name's Davis Reed."

"That's it," the man said while jabbing a finger at my chest. "I saw you on the news. I'm Monty. Monty Parker. This is my place."

We shook hands.

"I followed that story pretty closely," Monty said, "since my business neighbor was involved." He jerked his head in the general direction of Long Branch Brewery. "I didn't much care to learn that undesirables were hanging out at that place. But you and that big guy, the deputy, you took care of 'em, didn't you?"

I felt my cheeks flush.

"And that skinny man, the mechanic," Monty said. "*Whoooeee.* He could talk the ears off a statue."

I nodded because it was true.

"I'll tell you what," Monty said, grabbing a paper cup and filling it from a glass pot. "Small coffee, on the house. How's that?"

I heard the door open behind me and turned to see an attractive woman walk in. She looked to be in her late fifties or early sixties. Her hair was a shimmering gray, styled straight and cut a few inches below her shoulders. As she walked toward me, she reached into a small leather handbag and pulled out a pair of black-rimmed glasses.

"Mr. Reed?" she asked, putting on her glasses. "I'm Elizabeth Harper." She offered her hand, and it took me a moment to figure out how to switch my free cup of coffee from my right hand to my left.

Elizabeth said hello to Monty, and he asked if she'd like the usual. She said yes and then politely declined my offer to pay. Which was a bit of a relief.

We found a table away from the other patrons. When we sat down, Elizabeth reached into her handbag again, pulling out a small notebook and pen.

I tried to figure out her age. She wore light makeup, and her nails were painted with clear varnish. She wasn't wearing a wedding ring but had some kind of gemstone on the middle finger of her left hand. Her hands were slightly wrinkled, as was the skin around her twinkling green eyes. I settled on late fifties. And then wondered why I cared. Maybe because when Megan had mentioned Marvin's granddaughter, I'd automatically thought of someone young. But if Marvin was almost a hundred, it was certainly possible for him to have a granddaughter who was old enough to be a grandmother.

"Thanks for meeting me," I said.

"You're welcome. And thank you for agreeing to meet on short notice."

"I have a pretty flexible schedule."

"Tell me, how did you know my grandfather assisted in the search for the wrecked plane?"

"A friend of mine. Earl Pless. He's a deputy with the sheriff's department. He worked with your grandfather for a while. Apparently Marvin mentioned searching for the crash to Earl, but didn't go into details. I'm curious if he actually found the wreckage and what the search was like."

Monty stepped up to the table and placed a steaming cup in front of Elizabeth, and she gave her cappuccino a delicate stir. "I think I remember him," she said. "I believe he came by once with a couple of other deputies to visit my grandfather when he was living with us. Short man? Thick brown mustache?"

"He's still short," I said. "But the mustache is white now."

"And a penchant for turquoise jewelry, if I recall."

I laughed. "That has not changed. I actually saw Earl just a little while ago, and he told me . . ." I hesitated, then waved away the thought. "Never mind."

"He told you what?"

"He told me your grandfather was the first on the scene the night a man named Prentiss Wells accidentally hit and killed a boy with his car. Prentiss Wells died yesterday. Hit with a golf ball."

Elizabeth's face dropped slightly, and I sensed grief in her eyes. It suddenly occurred to me that maybe she had been friends with Wells.

"I'm sorry," I said. "Did you know Prentiss Wells?"

"Not really. I knew him professionally. Waynesville is a small town. I read online about his death."

We sipped our coffees in silence for a moment. "So how is your grandfather's memory?" I said. "Earl mentioned Alzheimer's. Actually he said *old-timers*, but I think Alzheimer's is what he meant."

"Memory is a funny thing," Elizabeth said. "My grandfather is ninety-nine years old. And yes, he has Alzheimer's. At this point his mind does not create new memories. What he had for breakfast, the names of the staff who help dress and bathe him, yesterday's weather—those are all mysteries to him. And many of his past memories have faded. He doesn't know my name or that I'm his granddaughter. But he does know I'm someone special in his life."

"I'm sorry. That's gotta be tough."

"But some of my grandfather's memories, especially very old ones—his high school prom, his wedding day, the battles he fought while in the Navy—those are crystal clear. He can recall those events with astonishing detail."

The door flew open with a bang, and I jumped in my seat. I turned as a young guy in black jeans and a gray T-shirt walked in. He set a backpack down on one of the tables and took out a shiny, thin laptop that made my old notebook computer look like it should be on display in the Smithsonian.

Elizabeth asked me to tell her about my book, and I gave a long, rambling response that veered off course, with me saying that I'd been an officer with the Charleston PD, then a private detective. I didn't know why. Maybe because Elizabeth Harper, lovely, attractive, well dressed, and well spoken, was causing me to feel insecure.

"Yes," Elizabeth said. "I searched online for your name and read a couple of the news articles about you and your exploits on the Parkway. I saw your photo. That's how I recognized you when I walked in."

She was smiling now, and the grief I'd noticed in her eyes earlier had been replaced with the twinkling. I liked the twinkling much better.

"I was in Raleigh, visiting family last November when that occurred," she said. "So I missed the story when it was hot."

"To be honest, I wish I'd missed it too."

There were a few seconds of silence while Elizabeth and I both sipped our drinks. She put her cup down on the table and said, "Did you know Prentiss Wells?"

That caught me off guard. "Uh, no. But I happened to be at the golf course yesterday. My friend Dale—he's a deputy—asked me to go out there with him."

"Has anyone come forward as the person responsible?"

"Not as far as I know."

Elizabeth took the last sip of her cappuccino, then put her pen and notebook back into her bag, making me realize I hadn't said anything worth writing down. "If you'd like to speak to my grandfather again, I'd be happy to meet you at Sunset Seasons," she said.

"Thanks. I'd appreciate that." I was thinking I'd actually appreciate any opportunity to spend time with Elizabeth Harper.

Elizabeth stood up and I quickly followed. "If my grandfather has a story about searching for the plane wreckage, there's a fair chance it's still clear in his mind."

She offered her hand again, and I once again shook it.

"You have my email," she said. "I try to visit my grandfather twice a week. Let me know if you'd like to tag along sometime."

With that Elizabeth Harper gave me a pleasant smile, then strolled out the door.

* * *

When I walked out of Monty's, I noticed four motorcycles parked along the street. Not BMWs with side chests, but Harleys, and one with extended handlebars. The devils told me to stroll into Long Branch and belly up to the bar like I didn't have a care in the world. The angel suggested I shuffle around the block and avoid Long Branch altogether.

Which I did.

10

When I got back to the cabin, I grabbed a bottle of Old Crab, a handful of Goldfish, and spent an hour digging around the rabbit hole that is the internet. I discovered Elizabeth Harper had a Facebook page, but it was set to private, so I couldn't see anything other than her name and her profile picture, which looked like a professional headshot. And I found the same photo on the website of Harper and Company, CPA, LLC, along with Elizabeth's biography, which told me she had grown up in Waynesville, North Carolina; received a master's degree from Columbia University; worked for an accounting firm in Boston for several years; moved back to western North Carolina in the early 1990s; and founded Harper and Company in 1995. The company now employed thirty accountants in two offices.

It didn't tell me Elizabeth's age, or whether or not she was married. I stared at her photo and wondered why I was being such an idiot. There was no way in the world a woman most likely a decade older than me, with a master's from Columbia and who ran her own multi-office accounting firm, was going to have any interest in a guy whose idea of a good time involved drinking beer and eating stale Goldfish while stalking people on the internet.

* * *

At five thirty I showered and used my expensive stubble groomer, then spent twenty minutes trying to figure out what to wear. Despite having been somewhat of a clothes horse in Charleston, I'd been living in nothing but old jeans and wrinkled T-shirts and sweatshirts since moving to Cruso. But after digging deep through the closet, I found a pair of presentable khakis, a long-sleeve polo shirt, and a pair of brown loafers—sans tassels.

* * *

The Roths' house was a large two-story affair with a series of dormer windows jutting out from a gabled roof. The white paint looked fresh, the windows were clean, and the laurel bushes that ran along the side of the house were neatly trimmed, with small pink buds just beginning to show.

A few seconds after I rang the bell, Vance opened the door and greeted me with a wide smile. He was wearing neatly pressed cream-colored pants, a thin gray turtleneck, and a blue blazer with gold buttons. He looked like he'd just beamed down from a casino in Monte Carlo.

I was led through the foyer to an open kitchen, an enormous area gleaming with stainless appliances and a marble-topped island the size of a station wagon. The aroma was heavenly, and I noticed multiple pots steaming on a large commercial stove. Lana entered from the other direction. She grinned mischievously and offered me a hand. "Good to see you again," she said with a wink. She was dressed in tight white capris and a blue-and-pink-striped top. No neck brace.

"Neck's all better?" I asked.

Lana winked again. "I'm as right as rain."

As Vance mixed gin and tonics, Lana pointed through an open doorway large enough to roll a baby grand through. "Make yourself comfortable in the living room," she said. "We'll join you in a minute."

The room was enormous. One side was almost entirely glass and featured a view of a wide, sloping lawn beyond which a few golf holes meandered across the valley, with the mountains standing watch in the background. Across the room a large stone fireplace held several logs waiting to be lit. The back of the room was fitted with glass cabinets and shelves holding framed photos of younger versions of Vance and Lana and a bunch of people I didn't know, although one guy standing between them in one photo did look a lot like Yo-Yo Ma. The cabinets and shelves also held small bowls, statues, and other knickknacks I guessed were antiques and collectibles, as a well as some signed golf balls in small plastic cases. Another wall was a long expanse of built-in bookcases lined with books. I examined the spines and saw that almost all were mysteries and thrillers and true crime stories.

"You're welcome to borrow anything you like," Vance said as he and Lana entered the room.

"Have you read all of these?"

"Of course," Vance said, handing me a rocks glass. "We both have."

"We love a good mystery," Lana added.

Vance and Lana sat side by side on a long white sofa, and I plopped onto a black leather chair that looked like it belonged in a modern art museum.

"Tell me, Davis," Vance said, crossing his legs and giving me a glimpse of his bare ankle. "Do we have a deal? As I said, I'm happy to put the offer in writing."

I took a sip of my very strong gin and tonic and said, "I won't lie to you—I could use the money. But I'm not sure a crime's been committed. I mean, do you guys know something I don't? Like, did Wells have a lot of enemies? Was he involved in some shady stuff? Why are you so convinced he was murdered?"

Vance studied me for a moment, then said, "Davis, I'll be completely transparent with you. We have absolutely no reason to think Prentiss Wells was murdered. But, as I am sure you have concluded"—Vance pointed to the wall lined with books—"Lana and I are mystery enthusiasts. And at the risk of sounding conceited, we frequently—I dare say, generally—know the identity of the killer long before the final chapter. Yesterday, when we discovered Prentiss Wells had died after being struck by a golf ball, Lana and I began contemplating how a murderer could kill someone in such a fashion and get away with it. We both agreed it would be thrilling to pursue such a case."

Lana leaned forward. "And then you walked in."

"We immediately recognized you," Vance said, "Davis Reed, the detective who unraveled the Graveyard Fields mystery. We wondered if it was perhaps fate that had caused you to appear."

"We just think it would be fun to work with a real live private detective," Lana added, "and to be involved in a real investigation. Even if it turns out Prentiss's death was an accident."

"What happens if it really was an accident? Do I still get paid for investigating?"

"No," Vance said. "To earn the reward, you must work with us and share any and all information you uncover, and you must prove Prentiss was murdered and identify his killer. Those are the rules of the game."

Game. So that's what this was to the Roths. It seemed like a massive waste of time and I considered politely declining the offer. But the angel convinced me I had nothing to lose, and the devils pointed out I had five grand and free gin and tonics to gain.

48

"All right," I said. "How would you like to start?"

Lana clapped her hands, jumped up, and rushed out of the room. She returned a moment later with a leather-bound notebook and expensive-looking pen.

"All right, Davis," Vance said when Lana was seated, notebook open, pen at the ready. "Let's start from the moment you saw Prentiss's body."

"Um, it was in the middle of the bunker, in the fairway. He was face up and had a big red knot near his left temple. His golf ball and his rangefinder were in the bunker as well. So was another ball, the one that supposedly hit him. I didn't go into the bunker, so I didn't see it. Apparently it was almost completely covered up in the sand."

"A fried egg," Vance said.

"A *buried lie*," Lana replied.

I cocked my head.

"Golf terminology," Vance said.

"Did you notice any other marks on the body?" Lana asked.

"Like I said, I didn't get too close. But the medical examiner was there, and he didn't mention any other marks."

"What about the other players in the group?" Vance said. "Were they near the bunker?"

"No. A deputy had told them to go up to the sixteenth tee to wait for Dale to come talk to them."

I told them about that discussion, including what the three guys were wearing, and about the glue trap comment Dale had made when he and Jimmy Fletcher had shaken hands.

"Stop there," Vance said. He turned to Lana.

"Got it," Lana said, writing in the notebook. "Jimmy Fletcher."

"Do you know what he does?" Vance asked me.

"Dale said he's a mortgage broker in Waynesville. He and Dale went to school together."

Lana magically pulled a phone from somewhere out of her skin-tight pants and began tapping on the screen. Then, a moment later: "Aha. Jimmy Fletcher, senior loan originator. Eagle's Fork Financial." She turned the phone toward me.

"Yeah, that's him."

"Well done, darling," Vance said. Then to me, "The other men?"

"One guy was Freddy, uh, something with an 'S.' I think it was Sizemore."

Lana turned to Vance.

"We know a Freddy Sizemore," Vance said. "He's a real estate appraiser. He has an office in Waynesville. A few years ago the county reassessed property values. Many of the values skyrocketed, including ours. We appealed the valuation and hired Freddy to complete an appraisal of our land and home. His figure was two-thirds of the county appraisal. But it was a futile effort. They rejected the appeal."

Lana looked at her phone. "There's no photo of Freddy on his website."

"This guy's probably late forties, short with curly black hair."

"That's Freddy," Vance said. "Okay, we've identified two. Who was the third?"

"Rex Pinland, he works at Wells's law firm."

Lana tapped on her phone again. She showed it to me, and I was looking at Rex's photo on the Wells and Butler website.

"That's the guy," I said.

"What was their demeanor?" Vance asked. "Did they seem nervous or agitated?"

"Jimmy and Rex seemed fine," I said, "but Freddy was as white as a sheet. I wondered if he was in shock."

"And Freddy didn't say anything?" Vance asked.

"Other than his name, no. And he was barely able to get that out. Oh, I forgot: his shoes were caked with mud. Dale asked about it and Jimmy answered, said Freddy had gone down into the trees near the pond to relieve himself and that it was muddy down there."

"So you believe Freddy was in shock?" Vance asked.

"Jimmy and Rex said after they called 911, the two of them took off to search for the golfer they'd seen, and left Freddy in the bunker alone with Wells's body. That might have freaked him out."

"That could be the reason," Lana said. "Or maybe Freddy witnessed something horrific."

Vance raised one eyebrow. "Or *did* something horrific."

11

Dinner was served in the formal dining room. When we entered, Vance pulled out my chair as if I were at a five-star restaurant, and when I sat down, I was confronted by an elaborate place setting with multiple forks, spoons, and knives. I wondered if the Roths dined liked this every evening. I also wondered if they might enjoy drinking home-brewed beer and eating leftover pizza off paper towels while sitting on the deck of my cabin. A change of pace can be good for people.

The meal consisted of multiple courses: a small dish of ravioli in butter sauce, baked rainbow trout with lemon and capers, roasted asparagus, and a small green salad. When I took a bite of the asparagus, I thought about my steady diet of Goldfish, microwaved burritos, frozen pizza, and chips and guacamole, and wondered how my stomach was going to react when a vegetable other than avocado dropped into it.

At one point I brought up Prentiss Wells, but Vance raised a finger and said that murder talk during meals was a faux pas. Lana said it had something to do with a fictional detective named Nero Wolfe. So instead I asked the Roths what they did for a living.

"I manage my family's money," Vance said.

"And I manage Vance," Lana added with a wink.

Vance went on to tell me that the family money went back generations. Apparently, Vance's grandfather had made a modest killing in the stock market in the 1920s and pulled the money out a year before the crash, to invest in a movie studio his friend was starting, and the studio thrived during the Depression. And while a chunk of the money had been lost in the stock market crash of 1987 and another chunk in the crash of 2008, there was still enough left to have a home at Springdale and another in West Palm Beach, play lots of golf, travel extensively, putter around with various hobbies, and—most importantly—not work.

* * *

I was as full as I'd ever been when Lana offered me a small bowl containing what looked like a frozen tennis ball.

"Pistachio sorbet," Lana said. "Homemade, of course."

I wondered if it would be a faux pas to unbutton the top of my khakis.

When we'd finished dessert, I offered to help clean up but Vance and Lana shot down the suggestion and told me they'd meet me in the living room momentarily. I asked for directions to the powder room, where I spent ninety seconds praying the sound of me urinating wasn't echoing through the house.

Ten minutes later the three of us were back in the living room, sipping gin and tonics.

"The three men playing with Prentiss," Vance said. "Did you get the impression they were close friends?"

"I sorta got the feeling Jimmy and Freddy were friends, but I don't know about Rex."

Lana chuckled. "If they aren't good friends, they're at least coconspirators."

"Indeed," Vance said.

I hoped one of them would explain what they were talking about. They didn't and we sat in silence for a while before Vance stood up and stepped behind the couch. "Davis, if you'd allow, I'd like to put forth a theory of how and why the crime was committed."

I leaned back and told him to have at it.

Vance began to pace back and forth, from one end of the long couch to the other. "You have four men," he said. "One is a mortgage broker. One is a real estate appraiser. And two are real estate attorneys. These men are each in a position to help one another, not just in referrals and business growth, but in ways that can sidestep certain fiduciary rules. What if these four men were engaged in fraudulent dealings? With their various roles, I can think of a myriad of ways they could work together to swindle the public. What if this had been going on for some time, but suddenly Prentiss wanted a bigger piece of the action? Greed consumed him. It was going to be his way, or no way. So the three men concoct a plan. A friendly game of golf to show there is no ill will. But when they reach the sixteenth fairway, two of the men distract Prentiss while another swings a golf club into the man's temple. He falls down, dead. The men throw an extra golf ball into the sand. They call 911, and when law enforcement arrives, the fictional account of Prentiss's death is given as the truth."

Lana applauded while I thought again about Freddy and how he'd looked like he was about to puke when Dale was talking to him. Even if all three guys were in on the plan, it would come down to only one of them to do the deed. Was that guy Freddy? Had he drawn the short straw?

"My turn," Lana said as she and Vance exchanged positions.

"What if this crime was not premeditated?" Lana began. "What if the four men just liked playing golf together. Just four professional men enjoying a day on the course. But on hole sixteen something happened that no one was expecting. Maybe the men were playing a high-stakes money game, and someone was accused of cheating. Words were exchanged. Tempers flared. A push. A shove. A punch. A golf club to the head. Whack! And suddenly Prentiss Wells is dead. The right thing to do would be to call 911 and explain what happened. But the three men don't do the right thing. They are friends, and friends protect one another. They quickly make up a story: a mystery golfer, an errant shot, a tragic accident. And most importantly, they stick to the story because that's what friends do. All for one and one for all. The three musketeers of the sixteenth hole."

Lana took a bow and then flopped back down onto the sofa.

"I'm sure you've already considered those two scenarios," Vance said. "And probably several others. But thank you for indulging us."

I nodded and tried to come up with a fresh idea to present of what could have happened on the sixteenth hole, but all I could think of were Floppy's ridiculous theories. And I was not about to put forth the idea that Prentiss Wells was killed by a slingshot or a drone or a modified potato cannon.

"Hellooooo . . ." It was Lana, waving her hand, trying to snap me out of my daze.

"Sorry," I said. "Just got lost there for a second."

"Using your little gray cells," Vance said.

I understood the reference but only responded with a tired smile. The Roths seemed to think I was Hercule Poirot. I felt more like Barney Fife.

As we sat in silence, Lana reached down and slid off her heels, and Vance leaned in close and put his arm around her neck. I sipped my drink and tried to formulate a plan.

"Davis, would you like to share your thoughts?" Vance finally said.

"Well, it's pretty obvious that I need to talk to Jimmy, Freddy, and Rex," I said. "And separately. I don't want Jimmy answering questions meant for Freddy."

"Indeed," Vance said. "I'd be very curious to know if any detail of their story changes."

"There's a house next to hole sixteen, by the pond. When I was out on the course yesterday, it looked like someone may have been inside, watching what was going on. Do you know who lives there?"

"Oh lord, yes," Lana said. "Dot Davidson. She's probably already cruised by here in her golf cart, noticed a strange car in our driveway, and written down the description and your license plate number."

"Dot is a one-woman CIA," Vance said. "Several times a day she rides around the community in her golf cart, gathering intelligence. Who's doing what? When? And where?"

"Sounds like she needs a hobby," I said.

"She needs a man," Lana said. "You're unattached, aren't you, Davis?" Lana winked and I immediately thought of Elizabeth Harper. It then occurred to me that Lana and Elizabeth were probably about the same age, late fifties. Lana and Vance were at least ten years apart in age, most likely more, and their relationship seemed to be rock solid. Maybe I was giving too much thought about the age difference thing. Or maybe I was giving too much thought to Elizabeth Harper, a woman I'd spent all of twenty minutes with.

"I'd like to talk to this Dot Davidson," I said. "I'm curious to know what she saw. If anything."

"Then let's find out," Lana said. "Are you free tomorrow morning?"

I nodded and Lana continued, "Good. Come here at ten thirty, and we'll ride over to Dot's house together. We'll gather our own intelligence."

"So shall I put my offer in writing for you, Davis?" Vance said.

Maybe I'd had too many gin and tonics, or maybe I was just being my usual self, way too trusting. "That's all right," I said. "We can just shake on it."

Vance raised his glass. "The game is afoot!"

* * *

I was stuffed to the gills and a tiny bit tipsy when I pulled into the clearing below the cabin. That was when it occurred to me that if the Roths were swingers, they hadn't put the moves on me. I didn't know whether to be relieved or insulted.

It was almost nine and practically pitch dark. I was glad I'd left the kitchen light on so I could find my way to the door. I was digging around in my pants pocket for my key when a flash of red caught my eye. I looked down and saw a small cylinder about the size of a tube of lipstick sitting on the welcome mat. A shotgun shell, balanced on its end.

12

I stood frozen and looked through the panes of glass in the upper half of the door. The kitchen was empty, and nothing appeared disturbed. My laptop was on the table right where I'd left it. I looked back down at the shotgun shell. It wasn't a decapitated horse head on a pillow, but it sent the same message.

I spun around and hustled as quickly as I could back down to my car. Seconds later I was on 276, driving way faster than usual. Any tipsiness I'd felt had vanished. The shotgun shell was like a blast of cold water. I was fully alert. I was also terrified.

When I reached the drive leading to Dale's dad's house, I spun the Mercedes to the right and flew down the long dirt road. I came to the old stone house and was disappointed not to see Dale's patrol car out front. The only vehicle around was an old Ford Bronco parked under a leaning, wooden carport. Dale had told me it had transported Junebug to and from the paper mill in Canton five days a week for over three decades until he retired.

I banged on the front door, and Dale's dad opened it with a grunt. Junebug is a big man and was wearing what I considered to be his uniform, the only thing I'd ever seen him in: a white T-shirt under a pair of giant, faded overalls. "Whatcha want?"

"Where's Dale?"

Junebug shrugged.

"Do you know when he'll be back?"

Junebug shrugged again.

"Have you noticed anything suspicious tonight? Any sounds or lights? Like someone might be snooping around."

Junebug snorted. "I catch someone snoopin' 'round here, they'll be leavin' in a hearse."

I didn't doubt that for a second.

"Make sure all the doors and windows are locked. And stay inside. I'm going to go call Dale."

I hightailed it down the dirt drive, took a right onto 276, and drove another half mile west to El Bacaratos. The restaurant closes at eight thirty, and the parking lot was deserted.

"So how'd your threesome with the swingers turn out?" Dale said when he answered. I could hear music and people talking in the background. I guessed he was still at Boojum.

"Listen to me. This is serious. When I got back to the cabin tonight, there was a shotgun shell standing upright on the mat outside the front door. I went straight to Junebug's, looking for you. I told your dad to lock up the house and stay inside."

There was a long stretch of silence.

"Where are you?" Dale finally said.

"El Bacaratos."

"You're the only car in the lot, ain't ya?"

"Yeah."

"Get outta there. Drive up to Springdale. I'll meet ya in the parkin' lot in twenty minutes."

"What about Junebug?"

"Daddy can take care of hisself. You I ain't so sure 'bout. Now get movin'."

* * *

There were a dozen or so cars in the lot at Springdale. I figured the bar, and maybe even the kitchen, were still open. I parked and Dale showed up a few minutes later.

"What's the plan?" I said as I slid into the passenger seat of Dale's patrol car.

"Follow me up to the cabin. I wanna check it out."

I got back in the Mercedes, and Dale led the way. When he turned onto the highway, he hit the lights and siren. He wanted to be seen and heard. I couldn't keep up with him, but he was waiting for me when I reached the turn off for the gravel drive. We moved forward slowly, Dale's flashing lights casting an eerie blue glow on the thick stands of trees surrounding both sides of the narrow driveway.

The clearing below the cabin was empty. Dale and I parked side by side. Dale killed the siren but let the lights continue to flash. He got out and walked to the back of the patrol car. I met him by the trunk, which he popped open. He reached in and removed a shotgun, then pushed it toward me.

"No way," I said. "You know I hate guns."

"You used to be a cop."

"Yeah, a traffic cop—for two months. But I never carried a gun as a private detective." I glanced into the trunk. "Do you have a Taser or something?"

Dale growled, slammed the trunk closed, then gave the shotgun a pump. I followed close behind him as we slowly crept around the side of the cabin to the kitchen door. The shotgun shell was right where I'd left it.

"Is it locked?" Dale said, aiming the gun at the door.

"It should be. I didn't unlock it."

Dale twisted the knob and pushed the door open.

"Shit," I said.

"Wait here," Dale said, stepping into the kitchen.

Dale checked the cabin while I stood outside, trying to remember if I had definitely locked the kitchen door before heading out to the Roths' for dinner.

"Ain't nobody in here and ain't no sign of nobody havin' been in here," Dale said. "You sure you locked the door?"

"Pretty sure."

"How sure is pretty?"

"Seventy percent."

"Well, look 'round and see if anythin's missin' or's been moved."

I searched the cabin but didn't find any indication that someone had been inside. When I returned to the kitchen, Dale was sitting at the table, drinking an Old Crab. The shotgun shell was in a plastic evidence bag in front of him.

"Looks clean to me," I said as I grabbed a beer and took a seat across from Dale. "I probably should change the lock."

"Yeah. I'm sure nobody'll think to break one of them panes of glass and reach in and unlock the door."

Dale and I finished our beers in silence. When he stood up, I asked him how things had gone at Boojum with the bartender with the onion butt.

"She wasn't there," Dale said. "They told me she called in sick."

"Must've known you were coming."

Dale responded to that with a giant middle finger. He grabbed the evidence bag off the table and walked toward the door.

"So what are we going to do about this?" I said. "If the Stooges were trying to send a message, it came through loud and clear."

Dale opened the door and then turned to me. "I guess we're gonna watch our backs."

* * *

After Dale left, I wedged a chair under the doorknob—not that that would be all that effective—then went into the bathroom, opened the medicine cabinet, and pulled out a prescription bottle of Xanax. Up until a few months ago, I'd been taking several pills a day to calm my anxiety and quell what could occasionally be a really bad temper. But after the Graveyard Fields mess, I'd given up the pills. I'd tapered for a few weeks, then one day just quit.

But now the anxiety was back in full force. The devils on my shoulder were screaming so loud, the angel could barely be heard. I started to open the bottle but then closed my eyes and began counting backward from one hundred. I kept losing count and started over several times. When I successfully got all the way to "one," I put the bottle back in the cabinet and went to bed. The devils were livid.

slept, but it was fitful sleep. The kind you get on an airplane flying through turbulence. I made some instant coffee but didn't have any appetite for breakfast. Not even for a frozen burrito.

It was approaching ten thirty when I wheeled the Mercedes into the Roths' driveway. Lana was out front, a green garden hose in her hand.

"Good morning, dear," she called to me as she directed a stream of water into a giant pot of what looked like geraniums. "I'll be with you in two shakes."

Across the driveway, adjacent to the house, stood a three-door garage. Each door was open, so I wandered in that direction. In one bay sat a black Range Rover with a window tint so dark it had to be illegal. Another bay held a tiny red convertible Porsche. I stepped around it; the back bumper was crushed, and several long scratches ran up the panel covering the rear-mounted engine. The third bay was empty.

Lana dropped the hose and walked over. She looked dressed for golf, and her hair was pulled back in a loose ponytail. She gave me a concerned look. "Are you okay?"

"Yeah, I'm fine," I said. "Just didn't sleep well. Is Vance coming?"

"No, he's golfing this morning." Lana patted the hood of the Range Rover. "We'll take Brutus here."

I immediately thought about Floppy and his predilection for naming his vehicles.

"What do you call the Porsche?" I asked.

Lana scoffed. "Bad Luck Betty. I was driving her when I had my fender bender. We're still waiting for the collision shop in Asheville to pick it up for repairs. Some things in this part of the world move at a snail's pace."

As we pulled out of the garage, I asked Lana about her accident.

"I was really lucky. The kid who crashed into me was drunk. Nineteen years old. He was joyriding in his father's Camaro."

"Were you badly hurt?"

"Just some neck pain from the impact. I did physical therapy and wore that god-awful neck brace." Lana turned and flashed me a wink. "But now, I'm back in business."

"Did the kid get hurt?" I asked.

"No. Not a scratch."

Less than a minute later, we turned into Dot Davidson's driveway, where a beige Toyota Camry and an old blue golf cart with a ragged white top sat under an open carport.

"Is she expecting us?"

"I called her this morning and asked if I could stop by. Dot and I get along well. But I didn't mention you. She's going to love the surprise."

Lana pushed the doorbell, and a moment later a woman's voice called, "Who's out there?"

"Hello, Dot. It's Lana. I'm here with a friend."

The door slung open, and Dot's face glowed at the sight of Lana. "It's so good to see you, hon," Dot said, throwing her arms around Lana's neck.

I pegged Dot to be in her late seventies. She was tall, at least six foot, and as skinny as a rail. She wore blue jeans, a white sweatshirt that said, "Disney Cruise Line," and a pink baseball cap with the word "Gramma" bedazzled on the front.

After the hug Dot took a step back and scanned me from head to toe. "And who is this?" she asked.

"Please meet my dear friend Davis Reed," Lana said.

Dot continued to study me. "You look familiar."

"Of course he does," Lana said. "Davis is the man who solved the Graveyard Fields mystery last fall. Remember that?"

Dot grabbed my hand and jerked me into the house. When we were in the living room, she practically shoved me onto the couch. She took a seat next to me, and Lana sat across from us in a rocking chair. I could tell Lana was on the verge of laughter.

"Okay," Dot said, "tell me all about it. Leave nothing out."

I told the story for the umpteenth time, and when I finished, Dot patted my knee. "A real live private detective sitting here on my sofa. How exciting."

61

"So may I ask you a few questions, Mrs. Davidson?" I said.

Dot's eyes grew wide. "Is it about the man who died on the golf course?" she whispered. "The attorney?"

I nodded.

Dot stood and left the room for a moment. When she returned, she was holding a wire-bound notebook. She sat down, flipped through a few pages, pointed at one, and said: "Monday, March eighteenth."

Apparently Dot kept a daily log of the happenings of the community, collected during her golf cart rides and sessions staring out of the window overlooking the pond and the sixteenth fairway. Dot told us about a U-Haul that had been parked in front of the Andersons' house in the morning but was gone by noon the day of Prentiss Wells's death. About a landscape company that had mowed the Fullers' lawn and blown some of the mown grass onto Country Club Drive. About a man in khaki pants and a blue-and-white-striped shirt urinating behind a tree near the pond. And about the mass of law enforcement that had congregated around the bunker on the sixteenth fairway.

"The man you saw relieving himself is named Phil," I said. "He's the county medical examiner."

Dot huffed. "If I had a nickel for every man I've seen whip out his willie and pee in those trees, I'd have more money than Miss Priss here." Dot pointed at Lana, and the two women exchanged winks.

"What about before the deputies showed up?" I asked. "Did you see the man who got hit with the golf ball? I mean did you see him before he got hit?"

Dot shook her head. "No. And I can't believe it. For something like that to happen and me to miss it. It's irritating." Lana gave a sympathetic nod.

"I was out in my golf cart," Dot continued. "I heard sirens, and they sounded like they were getting closer. I was over past the maintenance building, and in my old cart it took me ten minutes to get back here. I wanted to listen to my scanner to find out what was happening. Then I looked out the back window and saw several officers standing in the fairway. In the bunker a tarp had been placed over something. I knew it was a body. Heart attack was my guess."

"Was everyone who was standing by the bunker law enforcement?" I asked.

Dot nodded. By then Earl had already moved Wells's playing partners up to the teeing area.

"Okay. What else did you see?"

"Not much happened for the next twenty or so minutes. Some of the deputies would get into a golf cart and leave the area, and some others would show up. But there seemed to be just a lot of standing around. Then I saw the man in the khaki slacks and striped shirt walk over into the trees by the pond. While he was doing his business, a golf cart approached the bunker from the far side. A very large man in uniform was driving, and quite fast. When he abruptly stopped the cart, you fell out." Dot smiled proudly. "I don't miss much, hon."

"Apparently not."

Dot had stayed by the window for over two hours with a pair of binoculars. She saw Dale and me get back into the golf cart and head up the fairway and out of sight, then return for a moment only to leave again. Then a few minutes later Dale returned without me. Soon after, Dot saw an older man with a droopy face arrive. She recognized him as the sheriff. Dot watched as all the deputies bowed their heads while Byrd said a few words. Then a golf cart driven by a deputy appeared, with a man in a dark blue suit.

"It was odd to see a man in a suit and tie out there," Dot said. "One of the deputies, a short man with a white mustache, walked over and talked to him for a minute. The man seemed very distressed."

I figured the man in the suit was Brett Wells. Apparently Earl had walked with him into the bunker and raised the tarp. That's when, according to Dot, Brett burst into tears.

"Did the guy in the suit seem angry at all?" I asked. "Was he yelling or did he look like he was trying to order people around?"

"Not at all," Dot said. "He looked devastated."

After an ambulance arrived, two EMTs removed the tarp covering Wells and rolled his body onto a long orange stretcher and placed it inside the ambulance. Ten minutes after that, everyone was gone and the fairway was empty.

Dot Davidson had seen a lot, but she hadn't seen the moment Wells was struck. Basically the only new information I had was that Dale's version of Brett Wells's demeanor at the golf course was not accurate. Brett hadn't bossed everyone around, as Dale had put it. According to Dot, Brett was teary-eyed and solemn. But to Dale, Brett was a jerk—anytime, anywhere.

"Could I see the view of the fairway?"

Dot hopped up like a woman a third of her age, grabbed my hand, and yanked me onto my feet. She led me to one of the tall windows that spanned the back of her living room. She pulled back a thick blue curtain and pointed toward the glass, as if I didn't know which way to look. Lana walked over to join us.

The view was nice but limited. The pond that sat below the deck was surrounded by trees to the right and left. The far side of the pond was bordered by a section of the sixteenth fairway. The sand in the bunker was blindingly bright in the morning sun. From the window I could only see about twenty or thirty yards of the fairway—the trees around the pond blocked the view of the rest of the hole. If Prentiss Wells had fallen dead anywhere besides in the fairway bunker, Dot wouldn't have seen a thing.

"Did anyone talk to you about the accident?" I asked. "Any of the deputies, I mean?"

"Yes," Dot said. "A very nice young man named Mike. He asked me if I'd happened to see anything since I have a good view of where the accident occurred. I told him everything. Except"—she waved a hand in the air—"later I saw a flashlight down by the pond. Late that night. That's all."

I cocked my head and waited.

"Since it's warmed up a little, I've been sleeping with my bedroom window open," Dot finally said. "And that night, a little after midnight, I heard something outside. I didn't turn on any lights, but I came in here to this window. I pulled back the curtain just a bit, and that's when I saw it." Dot pointed toward the edge of the pond, near the spot where I'd seen Phil, the medical examiner, emerge from the trees when I was standing in the fairway. "Right over there. Someone with a flashlight."

"Are you sure?" I asked.

Dot shot me a perturbed look. "Of course I'm sure. It's happened before."

"Could you see the person?"

"No. It was nearly pitch-black."

"How long were they out there?"

"Ten minutes or less. Then poof—they were gone."

I felt the hairs on the back of my neck stand up. I glanced at Lana; her eyes were wide.

"Did you call 911?" I asked.

Dot scoffed. "What for? I'm sure it was just one of the maintenance crew. I told you, it's happened before."

"Really?" I said. "After midnight?"

Dot pointed at the glass again. "That's the irrigation pond for the golf course. Just down below it, back in the trees, there's a pump station. That's what powers the system. All the water they use to irrigate the course comes out of that pond, and they irrigate at night. So it was probably one of the maintenance guys checking the intake pipe or something."

"And if it wasn't?" I asked.

Dot smiled and pointed to a corner of the living room where I noticed a shotgun resting against the wall. "If they'd of tried to get in here, they'd be at the bottom of that pond right now."

I thought that Dot and Junebug would make a good pair.

"Do you mind if I go down there and look around?" I asked.

Dot grabbed my arm. "Come with me."

* * *

Dot led us around the side of her house, where a narrow gravel walkway ran parallel with the building, and down a gradual slope toward the edge of the pond. I stopped and stared at the water, then began limping around the pond to the right toward where Dot had said she'd seen the flashlight. I snaked through the trees, staying about five feet away from the water's edge. Lana and Dot followed me. At one point I bent down, not exactly knowing what I was looking for. Footprints. A slingshot. Anything with the word *clue* written on it.

"What's this?" Lana said. She was just a few feet behind me, picking up something from off the ground. She straightened and held out her palm.

I shuffled over to her. The object she was holding was made of black plastic and was about the size and shape of a thimble. "It looks like some sort of knob or dial," I said.

Dot stepped up beside Lana. "Hmm," she said. "Probably belongs to one of the gadgets the maintenance crew uses."

Lana flashed me a smile. "C'mon, Davis. Let's go find out."

14

"What do you think?" Lana said.

We were back in the Range Rover, headed around Country Club Drive, toward the Roths' home.

"I think your husband's right. Dot Davidson is a one-woman CIA."

"No—about the flashlight?"

"I'm probably thinking the same thing you're thinking. If it wasn't one of the maintenance guys, then it's too big of a coincidence to ignore."

We drove past the Roths' house and continued around Country Club Drive until we were almost to the highway. Lana turned right through an open gate and pulled onto a large concrete pad near a couple of gas tanks. The maintenance building was a long wooden structure that housed multiple garage bays. Through the open bay doors, I could see all types of equipment and supplies: sprayers, spreaders, rows of shovels and rakes, hoses, weed eaters, push mowers, pallets stacked with what looked to be bags of fertilizer and seed.

Suddenly I heard a low rumbling sound, and soon a large red mower the size of a tractor passed through the gate and came to a stop in front of the building. It was followed by an identical mower, which was followed by three smaller ones, then several utility carts that looked like mini pickup trucks.

Lana stepped out of the Range Rover, and the maintenance men waved and smiled broadly at her. I stepped out and no one seemed to notice. One of the men, a middle-aged guy with a deep tan and dark wraparound sunglasses raised his hand and walked in our direction.

Lana leaned over and whispered: "That's Bill Rhinehart. He's the golf course superintendent."

"Hello, Mrs. Roth," the man said as he approached. "What can I do for you?"

"Bill, this is my friend Davis."

I shook Bill's hand; it was as rough and calloused and dirty as a freshly unearthed potato.

"We were just speaking with Dot Davidson," Lana continued. "She said she saw someone with a flashlight near the irrigation pond at around midnight this past Monday. Was one of your men around there that night?"

Bill frowned. "Monday. Whew! That was a hell of a day, wasn't it? Pardon my language."

"It sure fucking was," Lana said.

Bill cackled. "Oh lordy, Mrs. Roth. But, no, we didn't water that night."

"So you didn't have anyone working on the course that night?" I asked.

Bill shook his head. "Nope."

"Can you think of any reason someone would be out there by that pond at that time?"

"I don't know. We've got a few residents who like to go out in the evening and look for balls around the ponds and creeks. But I can't see someone doing that in the middle of the night. Could've been kids hunting night crawlers. Or night fishing in the pond. Other than that, beats me."

"That same day, the day of the accident, did you or any of your crew notice anything unusual? Out of the ordinary?"

Bill's eyes narrowed. "You helping Dale with this thing?"

I stammered for a moment. "You know Dale?"

Bill adjusted his baseball cap, and I noticed that above the dark tan on his face, his forehead was as white as the inside of a coconut. "I've known Dale since kindergarten. We graduated high school together. I don't see him much, but we catch up now and then."

I was getting the feeling everyone in Haywood County had attended high school together.

"I rent a cabin from Dale," I said. "It's just a few miles up the road."

"Oh, I know who you are. I saw you on the news, back last fall, with Dale and Floppy."

The shotgun shell on my welcome mat had made me very uncomfortable about being so recognizable.

"So if you went to high school with Dale, you probably know Jimmy Fletcher," I said. "He was playing with Prentiss Wells on Monday."

Bill looked confused, so I explained that I'd been out on the course with Dale the day Wells had died and that Dale had mentioned that he and Jimmy had gone to high school together.

"Yeah, Dale came by here that afternoon to talk to me and the crew," Bill said. "He told me Jimmy was playing in that group. And I'll tell you what I told him. Jimmy Fletcher's a no-good hustler."

At that Lana nudged me with her elbow. I waited a beat for Bill to continue, but he was silent.

"Why do you say that?" Lana asked.

The maintenance men had all disappeared inside the building, and Bill looked in that direction. I realized we were keeping him from his lunch.

"Me and my wife refinanced our house a couple of years ago when rates went down. We went to Eagle's Fork Financial; Jimmy works there. I'd seen his stuff on Facebook about refinancing. All we wanted was a new loan for what we owed at a lower rate. But Jimmy kept pressing us to increase the size of the loan. Kept saying our house was undervalued, and we could use the equity to get a bunch more money to remodel or take vacations or whatever. I told him we just wanted to refinance the amount we owed—nothing more. But he kept pressing and pressing, and finally I told him where he could stick his loan."

"Why would he pressure you to take out a bigger loan?" I asked.

"The larger the loan, the larger the fee paid to the broker," Lana said.

Bill snapped his fingers. "Yep. That's it. We ended up going down to my wife's credit union. They gave us exactly what we wanted. It was simple."

"Did you tell Dale all that?" I asked.

Bill grunted an affirmative, then glanced at the maintenance building again. "Anything else ya'll need?"

I showed Bill the plastic object Lana had found by the pond. "Any idea what this might be?"

"Looks like some kinda dial. Like off a CB radio, or maybe a metal detector or something like that."

"Could it be off of something your crew uses?"

Bill frowned and shook his head.

"Thanks for your time, Bill," Lana said.

Bill tipped his hat and started to turn around.

I cleared my throat. "Actually Bill, can I ask one more question? What do you think happened out on the sixteenth hole on Monday? Do you think someone snuck onto the golf course without paying and accidentally killed a man with a golf ball?"

Bill huffed. "I've been the golf course superintendent here for nearly twenty years. I've seen things you wouldn't believe. I've seen two stoned hippies streak, buck naked, across the fifteenth green in broad daylight. I've seen drunk golfers flip golf carts upside down and walk away like nothing happened. I've seen a thirty-five-thousand-dollar tractor sink to the bottom of the pond on number six because the operator went to take a piss and didn't set the parking brake. So somebody sneaking on the course, hitting a bad shot, and accidentally killing a lawyer don't surprise me a bit. Just another day in paradise."

Bill's eyes drilled into mine. He looked angry, and I wondered if he was upset about missing lunch or if something else was grinding his gears. "You finished with me?" he asked.

"You're a sweetheart, Bill," Lana said. "Go eat your lunch."

* * *

On the short ride back to the Roths' house, Lana asked me what I thought about Bill's opinion of Jimmy Fletcher.

"Sounds like the guy's a high-pressure salesman," I said. "But pushing someone to take out a bigger loan than they want isn't a crime. It's sort of like a car dealer talking up options and extended warranties. The real question is, does he own a metal detector with a missing knob."

15

Lana invited me to stay for lunch, but I declined and headed toward El Bacaratos. It was nearly twelve thirty when I arrived, and the parking lot was packed. I pulled into the only space available and called Dale—when it went to voicemail I just sent a text asking him to give me a call.

While I waited, I searched on my phone for Jimmy Fletcher. There was no bio of Jimmy on the Eagle's Fork Financial website or any indication that the company had ties to Wells and Butler.

I found Jimmy's Facebook page, which appeared to be completely public. Some of his posts were sales pitches: "It's a great time to refinance! Come see me!" But most were pictures of Jimmy on golf courses, beaches, cruise ships, fishing boats, motorcycles, and paddle boards. In several of the beach and cruise photos, a young woman with short black hair, probably late twenties, was standing next to Jimmy, their arms wrapped around each other's waists. Maybe Jimmy's daughter, but from the look in his eyes the odds were against it.

One picture of Jimmy that caught my eye was on a golf course, waves crashing in the distance behind him. He was fully outfitted in golf wear, with a golf club by his side, leaning on it slightly, as if it were a cane. As I stared at the photo I kept thinking, *There is something off about Jimmy Fletcher*, but I couldn't pin down what.

On to Freddy Sizemore. The website for Sizemore Appraisals was pretty sparse, with mostly stock photos of smiling families and an email address and phone number. No physical address or any information about Freddy or his qualifications. I couldn't find Freddy on Facebook.

On the Wells and Butler website, Rex Pinland's bio page said that Rex had moved to Waynesville from Teaneck, New Jersey, in 2017; joined Wells and

Butler that same year; and he enjoyed golf, jazz, and antiquing. *And dressing like a dork,* I thought.

Rex had a Facebook page, but with only his name and profile picture visible. His list of friends, his posts, and all other information was hidden.

Next I searched for *Prentiss Wells auto accident 1988.* The first link that popped up was Brett Wells's website—logical because he was a personal injury attorney. Next were links to local news outlets with reports about Wells's untimely demise courtesy of a stray golf ball, and I didn't learn anything I didn't already know.

Then I followed a link to Prentiss Wells's obituary on the website of a local funeral home in Waynesville. It said that Wells was seventy-six, had been born and raised in Waynesville, and started his law firm in 1972. His wife, Arlene, had died of heart failure in 2007, and Brett was his only child. Wells had served on several nonprofit boards and volunteered his time to various local charities, including a place called Sarge's Animal Rescue Foundation, where donations could be made in lieu of flowers.

I tried a few more searches and was scrolling through links when Dale finally called.

"What's up, numbnuts?" he said.

"I'm just wondering what you're doing today."

"Same ol' stupid shit. Me and Boner had to go up to Fines Creek this mornin'. Some asshole got in a fight with his wife and pushed her off the back porch. Hit her head on a paver. Had to get six stitches. Still wouldn't press charges. I told the dude if he touched that woman again, he'd have to deal with me, off duty."

"I don't know if that kind of chivalry is still acceptable."

"Well, if it ain't, it should be."

"What's the story on the mystery golfer? Any leads?"

"Yeah, we got a shitload of leads, but they all lead nowhere. Everybody with a bone to pick claims to know who that golfer was. Ex-husbands, ex-boyfriends, ex-bosses, bad neighbors—they're all suspects. People know it ain't them; they just want us to go shake their tree. I ain't dealin' with it no more. I put Earl and Mike in charge of it."

"Yeah, you're too busy threatening wifebeaters."

"Somebody needs to."

"But don't you think there's something weird about the whole thing? I mean, the odds of getting killed by a golf ball have to be practically zero."

"Yeah, so's gettin' stabbed in the chest and killed by a beach umbrella that's blowin' in the wind, but it happened to a dude at Myrtle Beach last year."

I thought for a moment. "Did you know Prentiss Wells hit and killed a kid with his car back in the eighties?"

"Yeah, everybody in the county knows that."

"Maybe somebody decided to get revenge?"

Dale cackled. "And kill Wells? Thirty years later? With a golf ball?"

I told Dale what I'd learned from Dot Davidson.

"So some old bat saw a flashlight 'round that pond—that don't mean shit. That pond's where all the irrigation water comes from. It was probably one of the maintenance dudes out there. They water the course at night."

"Nope. I talked to Bill, the superintendent. He said none of his men were working that night."

I could hear what sounded like Dale clicking his tongue on the roof of his mouth. After a few seconds he said, "Did you take them swingers up on that five-grand offer?"

"Yeah. I told them I'd poke around a little. See what I could find."

"You'd do just 'bout anythin' to not write that book, wouldn't you? But you're wastin' your time. This ain't Graveyard Fields, Davis. They ain't no mystery here."

"What did Phil determine Wells was hit with? Has he finished his report?"

"Yeah, I saw it this mornin'. It was a golf ball. The size and shape match the wound, and Phil even found some dimple imprints on the flesh from the ball. Wells died of that hematoma shit Phil was talkin' 'bout when we's out on the golf course. Figures the man died less than a minute after he got hit."

I didn't know what to say to that. And I didn't know if I should be embarrassed that I was imagining Floppy's theories on how to covertly shoot someone with a golf ball. I also wondered if five thousand dollars was a carrot leading me to crazy town.

"That probably settles it," I said, "but I'm going to keep poking around. Who knows? Maybe I'll find the mystery golfer. Is there a reward?"

"*You wish.* But hey, if you do find him, tell him the next time he plays golf to make sure Brett Wells is up ahead of him."

"Is Brett riding you pretty hard?"

I could hear Dale loading his mouth with tobacco. "I don't wanna talk 'bout it."

Dale was not the easiest guy to feel sorry for, but somehow I did.

"Hold on," Dale said when I started to hang up. "There's somethin' you oughta know. A buddy of mine called me this mornin'—he's Maggie Valley PD. Rusty Baker was seen at Dew-Dads last night."

I felt the air rush out of my lungs. Dew-Dads was a dive bar in the nearby town of Maggie Valley. I'd driven by it a few times but had never been inside. I love a good dive bar, but Dew-Dads had a reputation for catering to a rougher crowd than I was comfortable with.

"You wanna stay at Daddy's for a while?" Dale continued. "Or you want that shotgun?"

I didn't want either and told Dale as much.

"Well, me and Earl's goin' to Dew-Dads tonight to see if he shows up again," Dale said. "If the fucker wants to find me, I'm gonna make it easy for him."

I spent several minutes trying to convince Dale that that was a stupid idea. I was unsuccessful.

16

I pulled into the Roths' driveway at a few minutes after two. One of the three garage doors was open, and in the bay I saw Vance standing next to a workbench. When I got out of the Mercedes, he waved and yelled "Buongiorno."

I limped into the garage, where Vance was trimming a bonsai tree with a small pair of clippers. "What do you think?" he said, pointing toward the tiny tree. "My latest amusement."

"Looks tedious."

"Au contraire. It's meditative."

I looked to the other side of the workbench where a long pegboard wall was adorned with almost every tool imaginable: hammers, wrenches, screwdrivers, pliers, etcetera. Next to the pegboard stood a wide door. I pointed at it and said, "What's in there? An entire Home Depot?"

Vance chuckled and waved at the door dismissively. "Relics of past hobbies," he said.

"If you'd like to take up home brewing, I can teach you. I'm pretty good at it."

"Been there, done that. As the youngsters say. I am, however, considering trying my hand at distilling. Roths' Gin has a nice ring to it, don't you think?"

"I'm sold. Anyway, I just found out the medical examiner determined that Wells was definitely hit with a golf ball. He found dimple marks on the wound, consistent with a golf ball. Wells died almost instantly from internal bleeding."

Vance placed the clippers on the bench. "Intriguing."

"So I'm not sure where that leaves us."

"You're not giving up, are you?"

"No, I still want to talk to Jimmy, Freddy, and Rex. But the golf-ball thing seems like a step back. Not that we've made any steps forward."

"I've been thinking," Vance said. "Why don't I pay Freddy a visit? He and I know each other from the appraisal he completed of this property. I could visit under the guise of needing a new appraisal and steer the conversation to the accident and see if he reveals anything of interest."

I wondered if Vance just wanted an excuse to try out his acting chops.

"Sounds good to me," I said. "But be careful."

"Excellent. I'll change, then be on my way. And why don't you come back for dinner this evening. Say six thirty? We'll compare notes."

I agreed and Vance walked with me to my car. I was about to open the door when I blurted, "Could I bring a date tonight?"

Vance did his one-eyebrow trick.

"I mean, it might not happen," I said. "It actually probably won't happen. But I'd like to ask her if it's okay with you."

Vance flashed his perfectly straight, blindingly white smile. "Of course."

* * *

As I pulled into the clearing below the cabin, I wondered if I should have taken Dale up on his shotgun offer. At the door I stared through the glass, trying to determine if anything in the kitchen had been disturbed. When I finally unlocked the door and stepped inside, I checked the entire cabin but fortunately didn't find anyone waiting to kill me.

I popped open an Old Crab and sat down at the table to compose an email to Elizabeth Harper.

Hi. Davis here. I realize this is out of nowhere, but some friends of mine who live at Springdale Golf Club have invited me to dinner this evening at 6:30. How would you like to join me? You're not the only one who can pull the short-notice card.

As soon as I hit "Send," a knot pulled tight in my stomach. I didn't know if Elizabeth was even single. I was googling *how to unsend an email* when the laptop dinged. It was a new message.

Possibly. It depends on how the rest of my afternoon goes. Send me the address.

EH

The knot in my gut was immediately replaced with butterflies. I stared at the email in disbelief, then quickly sent Elizabeth the Roths' address.

I was sitting at the table, grinning like an idiot, when a car door slamming shut snapped me back to my senses and sent a chill up my spine. I hurried out to the deck and looked over the rail. Vicky was parked next to my Mercedes.

Back in the kitchen I unlocked the door and let Floppy inside. He immediately started rambling but I ignored him and walked back out to the deck. When we were both seated, I said, "Do me a favor. Be quiet for a minute. My nerves are shot because of this Rusty Baker business, and you showing up out of nowhere and slamming your car door scared the hell out of me."

Floppy mimed zipping his lips.

I leaned back and took a few deep breaths as a soft warm breeze blew through the trees.

"Psithurism," Floppy said. He'd stayed silent for all of twenty seconds.

"Excuse me?"

"That's the word for the sound of wind blowin' through the trees. Psithurism."

"I've never heard that before."

"It's true—you can look it up. Psithurism. It's fun to say. Try it."

I didn't try it. "How do you know all of this stuff without a computer?"

"The library. I go to the one in Waynesville. It's real nice. They got encyclopedias and atlases and all sorts of books 'bout science and nature and space and the oceans. They got fiction books too, but I ain't got no need for those 'cause true stuff's more interestin'. You can just take 'em, long as you promise to bring 'em back in a couple of weeks. They got DVDs and videos too. They even got art—can you believe that? If you're havin' company over or such, you can borrow some pictures to put on your walls. And it's all free."

The angel on my shoulder started whispering. It didn't take me long to get the message. "Do they have old newspapers at the library? The kind that are on those little filmstrips?"

"Microfilm? Oh yeah. You have to ask for 'em, and one of the librarians has to get 'em for you and help you with the machine, but all them librarians are real nice. They know me pretty well."

It was a long shot, and I didn't even know what I was hoping to find, but spending a little time looking into the 1988 Wells accident couldn't hurt. "What do I need to do to get a library card?"

"You just need to prove you live here. Driver's license, electric bill."

My driver's license was from South Carolina, and my utilities were included in my rent. I didn't want to do it, but I didn't see any other choice.

"Floppy. Would you go to the library with me?"

Floppy jumped up and did a little jig on the deck. "I only came by 'cause an oil change cancelled, and I had some time to kill, and I thought you might like to talk 'bout your book, but this'll be like a field trip. Want me to drive?"

I did not. Like his cousin Dale, Floppy drives like a maniac. But I needed to conserve gas. I also didn't want my car to smell like eau de Floppy.

When I opened Vicky's passenger door, the first thing I saw was a five-gallon bucket full of golf balls sitting on the seat with the seat belt strapped around it.

"Hang on," Floppy yelled, elbowing me out of the way. He unstrapped the bucket, put it in the back seat, and secured it. I got in and Floppy slid himself behind the wheel.

"Drive slow," I said.

Floppy cackled, then grabbed a pair of wraparound sunglasses off the dashboard and put them on. He cranked up Vicky and pumped the accelerator a couple of times. "This used to be a police car," he said. "Crown Vics were the number-one law enforcement vehicles in the United States—did you know that? This is a '93 Police Interceptor, two hundred and fifty horse power V-8 with a reinforced frame and an extra-large fuel tank. Now hold on."

With that, Floppy tore off down the gravel drive as if I were in labor and he was rushing me to the ER. When we hit 276, he spun the wheel counterclockwise and left a short patch of black rubber on the pavement.

"I don't want to puke in your car," I yelled over the growl of the engine.

Floppy slowed to around sixty. "I's just showin' ya what ol' Vicky here can do."

I rolled my window halfway down, and I was glad Floppy did the same. I needed a cross breeze to be able to breathe.

We soon passed the volunteer fire department, where three guys were washing a small fire truck. Floppy blared the horn and waved. The three guys waved back with enthusiasm. A minute later we came to the straightaway by the golf course, and I thought about the bucket of golf balls sitting behind me.

"Hey," I said, pointing out the window toward the course. "Didn't you tell me that you used to sneak out there at night and scuba dive in the ponds to look for golf balls?"

"Yessir. Them balls is like white gold. They sell for a quarter apiece at the flea market. Can you believe that?" Floppy jerked his thumb toward the back seat. "I bought that bucket from my buddy Cecil. He didn't tell me where he got all them balls and I didn't ask, but he sold me that whole bucket for ten dollars. They's gotta be at least a hundred balls in there."

A thought made its way to the surface. "Do you still have your scuba equipment?"

"Uh-huh. But I don't use it much no more on account I got some bad air one time, and it made me real dizzy and such, like I'd been huffin' paint thinner."

I was formulating a plan. It was a ridiculous plan, but better than no plan at all.

*　*　*

When we reached the library, Floppy led the way inside and up to the counter. An older woman in a blue sweatshirt with a teddy bear on the front gave us a pleasant smile as we approached.

"Hello, Floppy," the woman said. "How are you coming with *A Brief History of Time*?"

"Did you know nothin' can escape from a black hole?" Floppy said. "Not even light. Ain't that crazy? I wouldn't wanna get close to one of them. Be like bein' sucked up by a giant vacuum cleaner. Hey, this is my buddy Davis. He wants to look at some old newspapers, but he ain't got a library card. Can he look at 'em usin' my card?"

The woman introduced herself as Ruth. I told her I was interested in local papers from 1988.

Ruth led us to a room in the back of the library, where a microfilm machine sat on a small metal table. "Make yourself comfortable," she said. "I'll be back in a minute."

Floppy excused himself to go browse the shelves, and I sat alone, wondering if I was wasting my time. I also wondered if Vance was having any luck with Freddy Sizemore.

Ruth returned, holding a small box containing several film spindles. She took one spindle and slowly loaded it into the machine, going over each step so I could do the others on my own. "This is the *Waynesville Mountaineer*, January third, 1988." She pointed to the spindles in the box. "The paper was published three days a week. The entire year of '88 is here."

I thanked Ruth and she left me to my work. I texted Dale and asked him if he remembered the month of the Prentiss Wells auto accident. A few seconds later my phone buzzed.

"The hell are you doin'?"

"I'm at the library," I whispered. "I'm looking for news articles about the Wells accident from '88. When I ran into Earl, he told me that guy Marvin was the one who investigated that accident. He was the first one on the scene."

"Good god, them swingers've got you chasin' your tail."

"When was the accident? Do you remember? It was in 1988."

"Hang on, let me think. Uh, I was in ninth grade. I think it was right after school started for the year."

"Great. Thanks. I gotta go."

I hung up before Dale could argue.

I removed the spool Ruth had loaded for me and inserted the one containing issues from August and September.

It was tedious business, made even more tedious by my wandering eye. Instead of focusing on the top stories, which I figured the Wells accident might be, I found myself drawn to the old advertisements for clothing stores, record shops, restaurants, and car dealerships. I found a couple of ads for Springdale Golf Club, eighteen holes with cart, twelve dollars, no coupon needed.

Forty-five minutes later I hit on what I was searching for in the September 8 issue. The headline was on the first page, below the fold.

Waynesville Man Killed in Tragic Auto Accident

A young Waynesville man was killed late Tuesday night when he was struck by a vehicle on Fosters Road. Authorities say 19-year-old Adam Ritter was running across a field adjacent to Fosters Road when he suddenly darted out in front of a 1978 Buick Estate Wagon being driven by Waynesville Attorney Prentiss Wells. Ritter was killed instantly.

Deputy Marvin Singleton of the Haywood County Sheriff's Office arrived on the scene only minutes after the tragedy occurred.

Singleton was in the area, responding to a burglary reported at a home on Dutch Elm Road, which intersects with Fosters Road near North Lake Baptist Church.

The accident occurred at approximately 11:55 p.m. and less than 300 yards from Mr. Wells's residence. Mr. Wells declined to comment at the scene.

Deputy Singleton discovered a bag near Mr. Ritter's body that contained bottles of prescription medications, a power drill, a power jigsaw, and a Colt .38 Special snub nose revolver.

Mr. Ritter was pronounced dead at the scene by Haywood County Medical Examiner Edwin Fisher. The Sheriff's Office has ruled Mr. Ritter's death an accident. Sheriff J. B. Bryant issued the following statement: "Prentiss Wells is an upstanding member of this community. This was a tragic accident, but Mr. Wells did nothing wrong, and based on the evidence collected and examined at the scene, he could have done nothing differently to have changed the outcome."

* * *

Between the headline and the article, a photo showed a station wagon on what looked to be a dirt road. A man in a deputy's uniform knelt by the vehicle's grill. He was the only person in the photo. The caption underneath read: "Haywood County Deputy Marvin Singleton inspects the Buick Estate Wagon driven by Prentiss Wells."

I looked around and saw a printer sitting near the microfilm machine. It took me some time, but I finally figured out how to print the section of the paper with the Wells article.

I searched through the next several issues of the paper, to see if anything else had been written about the accident, but came up empty handed.

As I approached the front counter, I saw Floppy talking with Ruth. A stack of books sat between them.

"Did you find what you were looking for?" Ruth asked me.

I waved the piece of paper in the air. "Yeah, thanks for your help. What do I owe you for this?"

Ruth smiled. "I'll put it on Floppy's tab. You know, it's funny. Those old newspaper microfilms have been collecting dust as long as I've been here, and that's for more years than I care to admit. But you're the second person to ask for them in the past month."

"The same newspaper? From the same year?"

Ruth nodded. "Isn't that odd?"

Floppy started to say something, but I quickly cut him off. "Who asked for it?"

Ruth glanced around uncomfortably. "We don't share information about our patrons. I'm sorry."

I turned to Floppy and looked deep into his eyes, trying to send a telepathic message. "I'll meet you at the car."

I went outside and leaned against Vicky's trunk. A few minutes later the library door opened, and Floppy emerged, carrying an armful of books. I opened the rear passenger door, and he gently set the books next to the bucket of golf balls. When we were both in the car, he turned to me and said, "Ruth told me who looked at them old newspapers."

I stiffened in my seat. "Who was it?"

"I told you them librarians like me a whole lot. I've been comin' here since I was a young'un. I even volunteered here back when I was in high school."

"Tell me the name."

Floppy put on his wraparound sunglasses. "Some dude named Rex Pinland."

17

I didn't know what to make of that, but I knew I didn't like it.

I pulled out my phone and searched the maps app for Wells and Butler. When the address appeared, I showed the screen to Floppy. "Let's go here."

"That's the place I went to sign all the papers when I bought my garage and trailer," Floppy said. "That's Prentiss Wells' office. What's goin' on?"

"Remember the couple I told you about? I met them at Springdale a couple of days ago?"

"The ones who said they'd pay you a heap of money if you could prove Prentiss Wells was murdered?"

I nodded.

"You took 'em up on it?"

I nodded again.

"Who are they?"

"Vance and Lana Roth. They live at Springdale. They're rich and they love murder mysteries. I thought they were crazy when they said Wells had been murdered, but who knows? Maybe he was."

"So this is a murder mystery?"

"I'm not sure yet. But there's a chance it might be."

"And we're tryin' to catch the bad guys?"

"If they exist, yes."

"Whoo-ee," Floppy said, stomping on the accelerator. "You're the Green Hornet and I'm Kato."

* * *

Wells and Butler was located a mile and a half south of the library. Floppy pulled into a small lot next to the building, a blue, two-story Craftsman-style

home, and parked Vicky between a gray Honda Civic and a white Range
Rover. "Wait here," I said. "But if I'm not back in fifteen minutes, come in and
find me." I handed Floppy the printout from the library. "Read this while I'm
gone."

When I opened the door to the firm, I expected to see a reception desk,
but the foyer was empty. To my right was a small sitting room, what I guessed
used to be the home's parlor. To my left was a hallway, and in front of me a
stairway led up into darkness. I stepped into the hall. The first door I came
to had a nameplate attached to it that read "J. BUTLER." I kept moving. The
nameplate on the next door read "R. PINLAND." I took a deep breath, then
gave the door a few sturdy raps. A moment later it opened, and Rex Pinland
eyed me with a mix of recognition and confusion. I glanced over his shoulder
and saw a desk. A young Hispanic couple, both with pens in their hands, sat
in front of it.

"May I help you?" Rex said.

"I don't have an appointment, but I was hoping you might be able to spare
some time."

Several slow seconds passed, then Rex smiled and said, "Of course. I
should be finished here soon. Have a seat in the lobby."

Lobby was a generous term for the sitting area. I took a seat on a saggy
sofa and ignored the stacks of magazines atop a wooden coffee table. I was
trying to figure out what I was going to say to Rex, when the young couple I'd
seen in his office appeared in the foyer. They were both beaming. The woman
was carrying a tan file folder with legal papers sticking out from both sides. I
wondered if they had just closed on their first home.

The couple had barely closed the front door behind them when Rex
stepped up to me. He was wearing a powder-blue suit, white dress shirt, and
pink bow tie. He offered me his hand, and I stood up and shook it. "Nice to
see you again," he said. "Please follow me."

I sat down. "Can we talk out here?" I did not want to be in Rex's office.
I wanted to be near the door and within limping distance of Floppy, just in
case. In case of what I wasn't sure. But better safe than sorry.

"Certainly," Rex said, taking a seat in a wingback chair on the other side
of the coffee table. "What brings you in?"

Possible answers spun around my head like numbers on a roulette wheel.
"Do you know who I am?" I finally blurted out.

"I recognize you from Springdale. You were with Deputy Johnson."

"My name's Davis Reed. I'm a private detective."

Rex nodded but didn't say anything.

"I've been hired to look into Prentiss Wells's death."

Rex appeared appropriately surprised. "I see. By whom, may I ask?"

"The identity of my client is confidential."

Rex shrugged. "Well, you were there when we told Deputy Johnson what happened. I can't imagine what I could add that would help in your inquiry."

"Can you tell me whose idea it was to play at Springdale that day?"

"Oh, that was Prentiss's idea. He set up the game. The four of us often golfed together."

"But Mr. Wells was a member at the golf course here in Waynesville. So why would he set up a game at Springdale? It's twelve miles away."

"I'm a member at Waynesville as well, as are Jimmy and Freddy. But we play other courses occasionally. For variety."

I nodded—it seemed to make sense. "If I remember correctly, you said you didn't actually see the ball hit Mr. Wells. Is that right?"

"That's correct. Prentiss and I were riding together. I dropped him off by the bunker, then drove over and parked in the rough."

"To check your voicemail."

"That's correct."

"And where was Freddy at that time?" I asked.

"He had gone to relieve himself."

"In the trees by the pond?"

"That's correct."

"You saw him go into the trees?"

Rex thought for a moment. "I saw him get out of the cart and walk in that direction. Then I was focused on my phone."

"And then a little later Jimmy yelled your name?"

Rex nodded.

"How much time would you say passed between when you started checking your voicemail and when Jimmy yelled for you?"

"Perhaps a minute, ninety seconds. It's hard to say."

The front door opened and I turned, expecting to see Floppy. Instead, a woman walked in, holding the hand of a young girl of about four or five. The woman was painfully thin, with a scarf with a bright floral pattern wrapped around her head. I immediately wondered if she was undergoing chemo. The little girl yelled "Daddy," and bolting, from the woman's grip, ran directly into Rex's waiting arms. The pair hugged for a moment before Rex gently pushed the little girl away.

"Go into my office with Mommy," he said. "I'll be there soon."

When they were gone, Rex turned to me. "Where were we?"

"Just a couple more things," I said. "Your group had the last tee time of the day? Is that right?"

"Yes. That's why I was surprised to see someone playing behind us."

"Other than you and Jimmy and Freddy, who would have known that Mr. Wells would be playing golf at Springdale that afternoon?"

Rex balked. "I really couldn't say." He glared at me for a beat, then asked, "Is this pertinent?"

"It could be. Tell me, did Mr. Wells have any enemies?"

"Excuse me?"

"Enemies," I repeated. "Anyone who might want to harm him."

"We're real estate attorneys, Mr. Reed, not criminal prosecutors."

I shrugged.

"If I may," Rex said. "Are you suggesting the person who hit the ball that killed Prentiss did so on purpose?"

"I'm looking at every angle."

"You do realize not even Tiger Woods could hit such a target from that distance."

"I'm not sure the person was at that distance."

Rex cocked his head.

"I mean I don't believe the person you saw on the fifteenth tee, just before Mr. Wells collapsed, is the person who hit him," I said.

Rex's face looked like he'd just caught a whiff of something stale. "Mr. Reed, I'm not sure I follow."

"I think there's a possibility a second person was out there," I said. "A person working with the golfer you saw playing behind your group. I think this person was much closer in distance to Mr. Wells. Maybe hiding behind one of the tall trees that run between the fifteenth and sixteenth fairways."

"And this person hit a golf ball toward Prentiss in hopes it would kill him?" Rex asked.

"No, I don't think they hit a golf ball. I think they were armed with something capable of accurately shooting a golf ball."

Rex clinched his teeth, and I couldn't tell if he was stifling a laugh or was pained by the scenario I was painting.

"So again," I continued. "Did Mr. Wells have any enemies?"

Rex sat up straight and relaxed his face. "No. Prentiss was a saint. He served on the boards of several nonprofits. He raised money. He donated money. He volunteered at an animal rescue and adoption facility. And the work he did here was in no way adversarial. He was well respected in the community."

"Did you know about his car accident years ago that resulted in a fatality?"

"Yes," Rex said. "Prentiss told me about that not long after I started working here. He said in a small county such as Haywood, people tend to know other people's business, even business that goes back decades, and that he would rather I hear the story from him than from someone else."

"And that was the end of it?"

"Yes. Prentiss told me what happened and that was it." Rex paused and his face dropped slightly. "It was an accident, but I think Prentiss always carried that guilt with him. To have taken a life has to weigh heavily on a person. Don't you think?"

"I wouldn't know."

I heard a commotion outside, then the front door flew open and Floppy stepped in. When he saw me, he waved. "It's been fifteen minutes," he said.

I stood up and Rex did the same. We shook hands over the coffee table. "Thanks for your time," I said.

Rex reached inside his suit coat and pulled a business card out of the breast pocket. "If you need anything else, please feel free to call."

* * *

Floppy and I hobbled across the lot. The Civic was gone, but the white Range Rover was still there. Next to it now sat a Volvo SUV that I assumed belonged to Rex's wife. It made me wonder how much a small-town real estate attorney pulled down a year.

When we got in and closed Vicky's doors, Floppy asked me what had happened.

"That was Rex Pinland, the guy who requested the same microfilms I looked at. He's a real estate attorney, and one of the three guys who was playing golf with Prentiss Wells the day Wells died."

"Do you think he did it?"

"I don't have any reason to think he did it. Actually, I don't have any reason to think anybody did it. Yet."

"So why did ya wanna talk to him?"

"I wanted him to know that I'm investigating Wells's death and that I don't think it was an accident. But I didn't want him to think I suspect him, so I gave him a crazy story about how someone may have hidden behind a tree and shot Wells with a gun built to fire golf balls."

"Hey, it ain't crazy. You could do it. But what 'bout what I said 'bout somebody sneakin' up on him and hittin' him with a golf club or a crowbar?"

"Nope. The medical examiner determined Wells was hit with a golf ball."

As we pulled out onto the street, Floppy started listing off various ways to launch a golf ball toward someone's head.

"Floppy. Hush for a second. I want to make a call."

I pulled up the website for Jimmy Fletcher's mortgage company and tapped the phone number link. The woman who answered said Mr. Fletcher was out for the rest of the day. I left my name and number.

When we cruised past the library, I looked at the printout and read the article again. On my phone I located North Lake Baptist Church. I showed the screen to Floppy. "Let's go here."

"Whatcha wanna go there for?" Floppy said. "Church ain't goin' on right now."

"I want to find the location where Wells hit that kid."

Floppy nodded and gunned Vicky. I clenched my teeth. And my butt cheeks.

18

The parking lot of North Lake Baptist Church was empty except for a small blue and white van with the church's name written across its side. We were on Dutch Elm Road, looking for the intersection of Fosters Road. Not long after we passed the church, we came to a four-way stop.

"This is it," Floppy said. "Which way?"

"I don't know," I said while staring at my phone. "I can't find an address for anyone named Wells on Fosters Road. He probably moved. I guess take a left."

Fosters Road was a narrow two-lane surrounded by open fields. It had been paved at some point since 1988 but was in dire need of attention. The asphalt at the shoulders was crumbling like the edge of a pie crust. I'd thought Cruso was rural, but we seemed to have entered another world. We'd driven at least a half a mile before the first house came into view, atop a small knoll in one of the fields.

We weren't far from the house when I spotted a small wooden cross standing next to the road. Floppy pulled Vicky up beside it and we both got out.

The cross was painted white, and three stick-on letters, the kind you put on a mailbox, were affixed at the point where the two pieces of wood intersected: "A L R."

"This is where it happened," Floppy said.

Next to the cross the land rose up steeply for five or so feet, then leveled off into a large field covered in tall grass. According to the newspaper article, Ritter had run out in front of Wells's vehicle, but I couldn't help but wonder if he had fallen and tumbled down the slope and onto the road.

Floppy and I got back in Vicky and continued forward toward the house. A mailbox sat next to the driveway, and Floppy pulled up close to it. The name Evans was on the side—it seemed Prentiss Wells had moved.

I asked Floppy to turn around and head back to the intersection, where I told him to turn left, back onto Dutch Elm Road.

We'd driven maybe a quarter of a mile before a large brick house appeared on our left. "Pull in there," I said, pointing at the driveway.

Floppy pulled up behind a blue Kia sedan and turned off the engine. "What're we doin' here?" he asked.

"I'm wondering if this is the house that Adam Ritter robbed."

We got out, and I stared over the top of the Kia. Behind the house the field of tall grass stretched far and wide. The Evans' house was visible in the distance.

Floppy followed me to the front door, and I rang the bell. A sharp voice said, "Who is it?"

"My name's Davis Reed. I'm a private detective. I'm wondering if I could have just a minute of your time."

The door swung open, revealing a small elderly woman dressed in a white and purple track suit. She eyed me suspiciously for a moment, then looked at Floppy and started laughing. "I recognize you. From the news."

"Yes, ma'am," Floppy said. "That's me."

"My name's Davis Reed," I said again. "I'm a private detective. Did you happen to live here in 1988?"

"No, my sister and her husband lived here then. I inherited the house after they passed."

"Do you know if the house was robbed that year? Eighty-eight?"

The woman grimaced for a moment, then took a step back and smiled. "Why don't you fellers come in and sit down."

A few minutes later the woman, who introduced herself as Susan Wallace, was sitting on her sofa, sipping on a bottle of Ensure. Floppy and I sat across from her with the cans of off-brand cola she'd offered us.

"Does this have anything to do with Prentiss Wells?" Susan asked. "I saw on the news that he died."

"In a way, yes," I said. "I've been hired to look into Mr. Wells's death, and I'm curious about the accident he was involved with in '88."

"I guess you know he lived in that house across the field over there," Susan said. "He sold it not long after the accident. I can't say I blame him. If I killed somebody, I wouldn't want to drive by where it happened every day."

"And your sister and her husband were living here at that time?" I asked.

"Yes. They moved in here in '75, I believe."

"And this is the house the man robbed just before he was hit by Mr. Wells's car?"

Susan nodded solemnly. "My brother-in-law, Frank, he thought it was justice. He said the boy got what he deserved. But my sister Greta was so upset."

"Did she talk to you about the robbery? What exactly happened?"

"She said her and Frank were in bed. He was asleep, she was reading. She heard a noise downstairs and thought maybe the cat had knocked something over. When she started down, she heard what sounded like drawers being opened and closed. She ran back to the bedroom and woke up Frank and told him what was happening. He got a pistol out of the nightstand and went to the top of the stairs and yelled, *'I'm calling the police.'* Then Greta heard the screen door on the back of the house slam shut. Two deputies showed up about an hour later to investigate. They said a boy had been hit and killed by a car on Fosters Road."

"Did Frank or Greta see anyone in the house?" I asked. "Or see anyone running away?"

"No. But that boy had a backpack on him when he was killed. All the stuff he'd taken from here was in it. Frank's pain pills. Some tools. A little gun Frank kept in a bureau in a back room. The only thing they didn't recover was my sister's horse."

I stiffened. "Horse?"

"A small white ceramic horse," Susan said. "Greta always loved horses, even as a little girl. Our daddy gave it to her for her birthday one year. She kept it on top of that same bureau where Frank hid the gun. It's probably still out there. Somewhere in that field between here and where the accident happened."

"Has anyone talked to you about this recently? I mean, asked you the same kinds of questions I have?"

"No, and honestly I haven't thought about it in years. Not until I saw Prentiss Wells's picture on the news a couple of days ago. Just think. He killed someone by accident, and someone killed him by accident. Crazy world, isn't it?"

"Yes, ma'am," Floppy said.

* * *

"What kind of person would steal a little ceramic horse?" Floppy asked once we were back in Vicky, headed toward Cruso.

"You know you have a tendency to help yourself to things that don't belong to you," I pointed out.

"Just things people ain't got no more use for. Stuff I can fix up and repurpose. It's a shame to let things go to waste."

Floppy rambled about repurposing junk all the way back to the cabin. When we pulled into the clearing, I told him about the plan that I'd begun to formulate earlier.

"You wanna do it tonight?" Floppy asked.

"Tonight's not good," I said. "Maybe tomorrow night. I'll find out and stop by the garage tomorrow and let you know. In the meantime I've got a job for you. You know half the people in this county, so see if you can find out if Adam Ritter's family is still around here. I'd like to talk to them."

Floppy puffed out his chest. "I'm on it, chief."

"And hey, thanks for chauffeuring me around today."

"Just call me Kato."

"Well then, Kato. Would you mind going inside the cabin first to see if Rusty Baker's in there?"

19

After Floppy left, I nuked a burrito and checked my email. Nothing new. I was beginning to wonder if my attorney Allison was avoiding me. It was not a comforting thought.

I spent the rest of the afternoon on the deck, sipping beer, staring at Cold Mountain, and taking turns between thinking about Prentiss Wells and Elizabeth Harper.

At six thirty I pulled in to the Roths' driveway. When I rang the bell, Lana swung the door open with a whoosh. "Hello, darling," she said. She was wearing tight black capris and a snug, lavender V-neck sweater that looked as soft as a cloud. She held her gin and tonic out to the side as she leaned forward and kissed my cheek. "Ooh," she said putting her hand to her mouth. "I shouldn't do that in front of your date. She might get the wrong idea." Lana looked past me. "So where is this young lady with impeccable taste?"

"I'm not sure she's coming. She said *possibly*."

"Well, it's her loss if she doesn't," Lana said, threading her arm through mine and pulling me inside.

"Is that Detective Davis Reed?" I heard Vance say as we approached the kitchen. When we entered, he was standing at the cooktop, his back to me, the strings of an apron knotted in a bow just above his belt. He twisted his head to look at me. "Buona sera."

Lana made me a gin and tonic and we clinked our glasses together.

"You two go sit," Vance said. "I'll join you in a minute."

"So what's the latest?" Lana asked when we were in the living room sitting on the couch.

"I talked to Rex Pinland today."

"Vance," Lana yelled. "Davis talked to Rex today."

A moment later Vance hurried into the room, holding a glass in one hand while untying his apron with the other. He took a seat across from us. "Proceed," he said.

I took a long sip, then a deep breath. "Okay. In 1988 Prentiss Wells hit a young man named Adam Ritter with his car and killed him. The sheriff's department ruled it an accident. It happened late at night, very close to where Wells was living at the time. Ritter had just robbed a nearby house and was running away when he darted out in front of Wells's car."

"How dreadful," Vance said.

"I went to the library today to look at microfilms of old newspapers to see if I could find more information about the accident." I pulled the printout from my pocket and handed it to Lana. She read it, then passed it to Vance. "According to the librarian only one other person besides me has recently asked to look at those specific microfilms."

"Who?" Lana asked.

I raised my eyebrows but didn't speak. After a few seconds Vance said, "The drumroll is unnecessary."

"Rex Pinland," I said.

Lana turned to Vance. "What do you think that means?"

"Hang on, there's more." I told the Roths about my conversation with Susan Wallace. "I was hoping to find something that might cast some suspicion on the official story of the accident but her story, or at least the story she got from her sister, matches the one in the newspaper. Really, the only interesting thing I learned is that a small, white ceramic horse was stolen during the robbery, and it's the only item that was not recovered. Well, as it happens, I met this man yesterday." I pointed to the photo on the printout. "His name's Marvin Singleton, and he lives at a rest home in Clyde. I went to see him about some other matter, but when I was talking to him, a news report about Wells's death came on the TV. A photo of Wells popped up, and Marvin started repeating three phrases: *'That poor boy. He was so scared. I let him go.'* And after that he started rambling on about a little white horse."

"The one that was stolen but not recovered," Lana said.

I nodded. "Yeah, he was obviously remembering the Wells accident from '88."

"'*That poor boy,*'" Vance said. "Perhaps the newspaper reporting is inaccurate, and Adam was not killed instantly. Perhaps he was hanging on to life when Marvin arrived and Marvin witnessed his final moments."

I nodded again. "It's a possibility."

"Perhaps Marvin comforted the young man during those moments," Vance said.

"'*I let him go*,'" Lana said. "So Marvin was talking about comforting Adam as he died."

Now I shook my head. "No. I don't think so. When Marvin says, '*I let him go*,' I think he's talking about Prentiss Wells."

Lana's eyes widened. "Prentiss was guilty of something."

"Could be," I said. "Maybe he was drunk or speeding or somehow at fault, and Marvin let him get away with it. Maybe Wells paid Marvin off."

"You believe Rex discovered this?" Vance asked.

"It's a pretty big coincidence Rex would be looking at newspaper microfilms from that year. So let's assume he was researching the Wells accident. He found the article and then kept digging around and somehow learned the truth, whatever that truth is. Then he confronted Wells with it and demanded money."

"But blackmailers don't kill the person they're blackmailing," Lana said.

"Did you confront Rex with this information?" Vance asked.

I shook my head, and gave the Roths a blow-by-blow of my conversation with Rex. Then I asked Vance if he'd talked to Freddy.

"He wasn't at his office," Vance said. "The door was locked. A vehicle was parked in the drive, a black BMW seven series. I called his number and was directed to voicemail."

"Okay," I said. "I'll go by there tomorrow and see if I can catch him."

"How did you leave things with Rex?" Lana asked. "Did he seem concerned that you were investigating?"

"Curious more than concerned," I said. "He admitted knowing about the old accident. He said Wells told him about it sometime back. That's why I didn't ask him about the newspaper thing. If there is something to that, I didn't want to show my hand. I told him my theory was that the golfer they'd seen on the fifteenth tee may have had an accomplice positioned closer to Wells. And that Wells may have been shot with some sort of golf-ball gun."

Lana looked at Vance and giggled. "A golf-ball gun. Now there's a theory worth investigating."

The doorbell rang and the butterflies in my stomach took flight.

Vance left the room, and I stood up and brushed myself off.

Lana gave me a sweet smile. "You look just fine, dear."

A moment later I heard laughing. Then suddenly Vance and Elizabeth entered the living room, arm in arm. Lana jumped up and shouted, "Oh my God!"

Elizabeth went over and the two women hugged tightly. "Davis," Lana said, her chin resting on Elizabeth's shoulder, "why didn't you tell us?"

"You guys know each other?" I asked.

"Quite the detective," Vance said.

The reunion went on until Vance left to get Elizabeth a drink. Lana and Elizabeth sat side by side on the couch, and I tried to appear comfortable in the modern art chair.

"So how do you know each other?" I asked.

"Zumba!" they said in unison.

"When was that?" Lana asked. "Four years ago?"

"Five," Elizabeth said.

"I only lasted three classes," Lana said to me. "But Elizabeth and I have been friends ever since."

Vance entered and handed Elizabeth a glass of white wine. He sat down on the couch and asked how Elizabeth and I had met.

"Are you on one of those online dating sites?" Lana asked Elizabeth.

"Oh lord, no," Elizabeth said. "It's not like that at all. As I'm sure you know, Davis is writing a book about the bomber that crashed on Cold Mountain in the 1940s. He heard my grandfather was one of the volunteers who searched for the wreckage. He got in touch to see if I could facilitate an interview."

"I wasn't aware you were writing a book," Vance said.

"It's in the very early stages. I'm just doing research." Which was another way of saying *I haven't started yet and might not ever.*

"I mentioned your project to a colleague today," Elizabeth said. "They were curious if you'd uncovered any mention of gold bullion being on that plane? And if so, where it might be now?"

I tried to laugh naturally, but it probably sounded forced. "That rumor's been circulating for decades. A guy I know named Floppy swears that his grandfather found a chest of gold near where that bomber crashed, and that not long after it was stolen from him and has been hidden ever since. For a while I was obsessed with finding it. But I'm not sure there was ever any gold to begin with. So I've given up searching for lost treasure."

"What's the title of your book?" Lana asked.

"I haven't gotten that far yet," I said.

"Not the best title I've heard," Vance said with a laugh.

I didn't want to talk about my nonexistent book, so I turned to Elizabeth and casually said, "I'm investigating the murder of Prentiss Wells."

"Really?" Elizabeth said. "I thought the death was an accident."

Lana grabbed Elizabeth's knee. "It was murder, plain and simple. One of the men playing with Wells did it, and the other two are helping to cover it up."

"Or," Vance said with a smirk, "someone hid behind a tree and shot Wells with a device designed to discharge golf balls."

Elizabeth glanced at the bookshelves stuffed with who-done-its. "You two love a good mystery, don't you?"

The Roths nodded in agreement.

"Believe it or not," I said, "Elizabeth's grandfather is Marvin Singleton."

"You're kidding," Lana said. "This gets more fun by the minute."

Elizabeth looked puzzled, so I explained that during my investigation I'd found an old news article about the Prentiss Wells accident, the accident I'd mentioned to her at Monty's Roasters. I handed Elizabeth the article, and she read it quickly.

"Do you believe this is tied to Prentiss's death?" she asked.

I didn't want to suggest to Elizabeth that her grandfather might have done something dishonest, so I just said, "I don't know. I'm gathering all the information I can." Vance and Lana didn't add anything, and I got the feeling the three of us were on the same page about not throwing Marvin under the bus in Elizabeth's presence.

We sipped our drinks, and I went over some of the details of the case. Elizabeth listened intently, and I was captivated by her. She was dressed in skinny-legged blue jeans and a black boatneck sweater. Her shimmering gray hair was pulled back in a ponytail.

Close to an hour or so had passed when Vance looked at his watch. He then stood and said, "And now I shall prepare the finest gnocchi the mountains of western North Carolina have ever witnessed. Darling, do you mind?"

Lana hopped up and rolled her eyes. "It's my recipe." She stepped past Elizabeth and said, "You two stay put. I'll come get you when we're ready."

A moment later Elizabeth and I were alone. She sipped her wine while I tried to think of something to say. She broke the ice—unfortunately. "Are you under the impression this is a date?"

I tried not to look wounded. "I was kinda hoping it was."

Elizabeth smiled, then seemed to force her face to harden. "How do you know Lana and Vance?"

"I just met them a couple of days ago. I'm hoping they'll adopt me."

"They're incredibly sweet, if a bit quirky. Did you meet at the golf course?"

"Yeah, at the restaurant. They recognized me from the Graveyard Fields stuff."

"Do you live in Cruso?"

"Uh-huh. But not here—at the golf course, I mean. Up the road a few miles. I rent a cabin."

Elizabeth nodded but didn't say anything else. We sat in silence for a few moments.

"Why did you accept?" I blurted. "It was a last-minute invite."

Elizabeth stared into her glass. "To be perfectly honest I wasn't going to. I wasn't tempted to spend an evening with a strange man and his two friends."

"When you say 'a strange man,' do you mean a man who is a stranger, or a man who is strange?"

"Perhaps both. Anyway I was about to politely decline, then I saw the address, and thought, why not? I haven't seen Lana and Vance in a while."

"But it's not a date?"

Elizabeth hesitated before answering. "It's drinks and dinner with friends and a strange man."

I sheepishly admitted to Elizabeth that I'd looked her up on the internet and knew she owned an accounting firm. I also admitted I didn't know anything about accounting except that it sounded boring. That prompted Elizabeth to tell me about her work, which was anything but boring to her.

"Why did you come back?" I asked.

"I beg your pardon?"

"I read your biography on your company's website. It said that after college you worked for several years at a firm in Boston. So why did you decide to come back to Waynesville?"

"I got pregnant," Elizabeth said without hesitation or emotion. "And the father, my boyfriend at the time, wanted me to terminate the pregnancy. I was not about to do that, so he immediately became my ex-boyfriend. I knew if I was going to have a child, I would need help. So I moved back here, back in with my parents. I took a job at a small accounting firm, making a quarter of what I'd earned in Boston. I gave birth to my daughter. And my mother and father, and Marvin too, were there every step of the way to support me, not only as a mother but also as an entrepreneur. When Chloe started kindergarten, I opened my own firm. That was almost twenty-five years ago. I've made a lot of sacrifices, but it's paid off."

Elizabeth said that last sentence with a hint of remorse, and as soon as the words were out, her eyes dropped down to the carpet.

I waited a few seconds, then said, "So, do you still live with your folks?"

Elizabeth cackled and quickly put her hand in front of her mouth. I was glad she took it as a joke—some of my attempts don't land all that well.

"No, I have my own place now, thank you. So does my daughter; she's married, and has a six-month-old son."

So Elizabeth was a grandmother.

"Did you ever marry?" I asked.

"No. I raised my daughter and raised my business. I had little time for anything else. What about you?"

"Get married? No. Not even close."

We both stared into our glasses for a moment, then Elizabeth said, "Do you like Cruso?"

"I love it. Despite all the stuff that happened right after I arrived, I've never felt calmer. You know, at peace." I grimaced. "I don't mean that in a hippie-dippie way. I mean, I just used to be angry a lot of the time, and since I've moved here, that's shifted. I can't explain why. Something in the air I guess."

Elizabeth smiled. "I understand what you mean."

We kept chatting until Lana came in to announce dinner. In the dining room Vance poured the wine, and Lana served the salad. This time the table held two tapered candlesticks. I watched the flames reflect in Elizabeth's eyes. The angel on my shoulder swooned. The devils stuck their fingers down their throats.

I barely said three sentences during the entire meal, which was fine with me. Vance and Lana talked about Italy and their trips to Venice, Florence, and some place called Cinque Terre, and Elizabeth interjected with details about a trip she had taken to Rome and Pompeii. I thought about mentioning that my parents had taken me and my sister to EPCOT once, but decided against it.

A few times during dinner, I caught Elizabeth's gaze, and each time she smiled sweetly at me. I probably read way too much into that.

When we'd polished off the tiramisu, Lana suggested we retire to the living room. Elizabeth politely declined, saying she needed to get home. Vance and Lana begged Elizabeth to stay, but she was adamant, so we all walked with her to the front door, where she and Lana hugged, then chatted for a minute, then hugged again, then chatted for another minute.

"Goodbyes are usually more effective when someone actually leaves," Vance said with a chuckle.

Lana jabbed Vance's shoulder, and Elizabeth waved and walked toward her car, a white Lexus SUV parked behind my Mercedes. When she reached it, she stopped and looked back at me.

Lana put her hand on my back and pushed me forward. "Time for a goodnight kiss," she whispered.

A moment later I was standing close to Elizabeth. The moonlight turned her shimmering gray hair a pale shade of blue. We gazed at each other for a moment, then both turned toward the front door, where the Roths stood arm in arm, staring at us as if we were exhibits in a museum.

"Goodnight," Elizabeth yelled.

Vance and Lana got the hint and went inside.

Elizabeth turned to me and stared into my eyes. The butterflies had returned to my stomach. I tried to remember how to initiate a kiss. A slight head tilt? A slow lean in?

"Do you really believe Prentiss Wells was murdered?" Elizabeth said.

I took a step back. Elizabeth did not look like she was in the mood for a kiss. She looked like she was about to audit my taxes.

"Lana and Vance are amateur sleuths who've read too many mysteries," Elizabeth continued, "but you're a professional detective. So tell me the truth: Do you believe Prentiss Wells was murdered, or are you just indulging the Roths?"

"I'm not a hundred percent certain," I said, "but I think the odds are pretty good that what happened to Prentiss Wells was not an accident."

Elizabeth studied me closely, then reached into the back pocket of her jeans and handed me a small card.

"Come to my Asheville office tomorrow. Eleven o'clock."

"Why? What's going on?"

"If Prentiss was murdered, I might know why. My office. Eleven o'clock. I have something to show you."

When I nodded, Elizabeth quickly got inside her vehicle and cranked the engine. She gave me a brief wave as she backed out.

So much for the kiss I didn't know how to initiate.

I went back inside the house and told the Roths what Elizabeth had just said and about the plan involving Floppy that I'd devised. I thought Lana was going to burst with excitement.

"Excellent idea," Vance said.

"I'll call Dot in the morning, but I'm sure it will be fine," Lana said. "She's going to love it."

* * *

When I reached the stop sign at the intersection of Country Club Drive and 276, I stopped and let the Mercedes idle. It was almost nine, and I was not looking forward to going back to the cabin, even though I'd turned on every light in the place and double-checked the front door lock before I'd left.

I sat there for a good five minutes trying to decide what to do. Not a single car passed by. Cruso, especially at night, can seem like a ghost town.

I finally made a decision and headed toward Maggie Valley.

20

A sodium light attached to the top of a telephone pole illuminated the parking lot of Dew-Dads. I cruised through but didn't see a patrol car, just several motorcycles along with a handful of pickups and SUVs. I found a spot at the rear of the lot that faced the front door. Once parked, I sent Dale a text—I didn't want to go in if he wasn't inside.

As I waited for Dale to respond, two motorcycles rolled in, big Harleys with black saddlebags hanging off the sides; they circled the lot, then parked near the door. I was watching the riders dismount and remove their helmets when the door opened, and Earl appeared, wearing snakeskin cowboy boots, carpenter jeans, and a Western shirt with shiny silver buttons. A silver belt buckle the size of a coaster glistened on his waist. He took a few steps away from the door and lit a cigarette.

I got out of my car, and when I slammed the door, the bikers jerked their heads toward me. Earl noticed me too, and as I limped toward him, he raised his hand like a gun. A pretend shot fired, and I jerked to the side to dodge the imaginary bullet.

"What's the good news, Davis?" Earl said.

"You tell me. What's going on in there?"

"Not much. The big man's spent the last half hour tryin' to get the bartender's phone number. She's a cutie."

The bikers started toward the door. They exchanged nods with Earl as they passed. I eyed them closely.

"Any trouble?" I asked.

"I don't believe anybody in there's with the Stooges. Nobody's given us a second look."

Earl pointed to the two motorcycles adorned with saddlebags. "Road Kings," he said. "I've got a 2005 Street Glide. I love to take it up on the Parkway on a clear day. Ain't nothin' like it." Earl shot me a look. "Not every biker's a threat, Davis."

I waited for Earl to finish his smoke before we stepped inside. The place was only about half full, but it was loud. "Ain't Talkin' 'Bout Love" by Van Halen blasted from the sound system. I immediately saw Dale's enormous orange back. He was sitting at the bar, wearing his going-out outfit: jeans and a size four-XL University of Tennessee sweatshirt. There was an empty stool on both sides of him, and when Earl and I climbed on them, Dale glanced at me and scoffed. "The fuck you doin' here? You never stay out past nine o'clock."

"I told you. I'm trying to be more social. So how is it?"

Dale grabbed a plastic menu and slid it in front of me. "The beer selection's shit, but the music's good."

The bartender approached. She was probably late thirties, overly tan, a little heavy, buxom, and with dirty-blond hair that came down just past her shoulders. She was wearing a tight black T-shirt with a skull and crossbones stamped on the chest. Both of her arms were covered in tattoos.

I ordered a Coors, Banquet not Light, and when the bartender turned around, I read the back of her T-shirt: "I'm The Bitch That Fell Off."

"Charming place," I said to Dale.

"I like it," he said, leaning in close. "That bartender's got curves in places I ain't never seen before."

"Speaking of such, I ran into Daiquiri yesterday. I was on my way to the coffeeshop next to Long Branch, and she saw me walk past."

Dale scowled. "What's that psycho up to?"

When Dale and I first visited Long Branch last fall, Daiquiri was our server. As soon as she walked up to our table and introduced herself, Dale was smitten. When he asked if she was named after the drink, she said, "Yeah. I'm a little bit sweet, a little bit sour. And too much of me will make your head spin." Dale then flew right past smitten all the way to head over heels in love. But the pair only went on one date, and Dale's been reluctant to tell me what happened. All I know is that there is a mutual disdain between the two.

"She wanted to know what we thought about Rusty Baker's release," I said.

Dale snarled like a wild dog. "I oughta go there tomorrow night. Tell her myself what I think."

I left it at that.

We drank and listened to good eighties rock 'n' roll for about an hour. Dale took turns staring at the bartender and surveying the crowd. I watched the crowd pretty closely myself. But no one approached us, and no one caused any trouble. And most importantly, Rusty Baker didn't show up.

At ten thirty Earl said he needed to get going, so we called over the bartender and settled up. My beer was three bucks.

Earl and I got up to leave, but Dale kept his seat and chatted with the bartender for a minute. Then she disappeared, only to return a moment later holding a folded piece of paper. She grabbed Dale's hand and placed the paper in his palm, then slowly pushed his hand closed and brushed her fingers across his knuckles. Dale's face was bright red.

Outside by the passenger door of a black pickup, Dale stood grinning like a kindergartner on school picture day. "I still got it," he said, holding up his fist.

"Let me see that," I said.

Dale unfolded the paper. As he read it, his nostrils flared. He wadded it up and tossed it across the hood of the truck. "Let's go," he said.

Earl shot me again with his finger gun, and then he and Dale climbed in the truck and took off.

I limped over and picked up the paper Dale had thrown. It read: *If I wanted to fuck a pig, I'd go to a farm.* I laughed until I turned toward my car. My front right tire was flat.

*   *   *

It turned out all four tires were flat. I called Dale, and a minute later Earl's truck swung back into the lot and pulled up next to the Mercedes. Dale got out and stomped over to me.

"Nails," I said. "There's at least three or four in every tire."

"Motherfuckers," Dale said. He turned to Earl, who was stepping out of the truck. "Cowboy, go in there . . ."

"Yeah, yeah, yeah," Earl said. "I'm goin'. I'm goin'."

Earl headed off, and I asked Dale what we should do.

"I doubt anybody in there saw anythin'. And if they did see somethin', they ain't gonna admit it. So there ain't much we can do."

"Earl said he didn't think anybody in there was associated with the Stooges."

"Who knows? It ain't like at Walmart—they don't wear uniforms."

I leaned against Earl's truck. "I can't afford four new tires."

"Where's your big check?"

"I don't know. I can't get a hold of my lawyer. I'm starting to worry there's not going to be a check." I forced a laugh. "Guess I'm just going to have to solve the Wells case for that five grand."

"Yeah, 'bout that," Dale said. "Some woman called in to the sheriff's office late this afternoon. Said she knows the man who snuck on the golf course and accidentally hit Wells."

"Another person with a bone to pick?"

"I don't think so. She said the man told her what happened, and she gave us details most people don't know. Like how he was on the fifteenth tee when he hit the ball."

"But those three guys have probably told the story a hundred times by now. Everybody in the county probably knows every little detail."

Dale shrugged.

"Did she give you his name?" I asked.

"Nope. She wanted to know if there was any type of reward and what would happen to the man if she could convince him to turn hisself in."

"What would happen? What would he be charged with?"

"I don't know. Trespassin'. Leavin' the scene of an accident. Byrd's gonna call douchebag Brett and see if he wants to offer a reward. The woman said she'd call back tomorrow afternoon."

I looked up at the stars and tried to think.

Dale punched my arm. "Guess there goes your five grand, buddy." He then walked around the Mercedes, bending down to check each tire. When he'd finished, he leaned against the truck next to me and pulled a tin of Copenhagen out of his pocket. "We'll drop you off at Peckerhead's. Maybe he's got some tires that'll fit."

Earl strolled out of Dew-Dads a few minutes later.

"Well?" Dale yelled to Earl as he approached.

"What do you think?" Earl said.

"That's what I figured." Dale jabbed me with an elbow. "Climb in the bed. Let's get out of here."

I turned and looked through the truck window. "Can't we all fit in the front?"

Earl laughed.

* * *

I was windburned and almost frozen when we pulled up next to Floppy's garage. Earl laid down on the horn, and a moment later Floppy appeared around the corner of the cinder block building. He was holding a shotgun.

"Put that down 'fore you hurt yerself," Dale yelled.

I climbed out of the truck, limped over to Floppy, and explained what had happened. When I finished, he waved at Dale and yelled, "I got it under control."

With that Earl and Dale took off.

"So do you have some tires that will fit?" I asked.

"Nuh-uh," Floppy said. "But I can find some. Might take a few days, but I'll get ya up and runnin'. I can go get your car in the mornin'. I'll borrow my buddy's rollback. It'll be safe here."

I wondered how safe it would be overnight at Dew-Dads.

"I'm going to need to borrow a car," I said. "Does that old Bronco at Junebug's still run?"

"That thing ain't moved in years. I wish Junebug would sell it to me. I keep askin' but he always says no. I don't know why he won't. I could get that thing runnin' again and make it real nice. It's a shame to just let it sit there. A car's s'posed to be driven, not sit 'round like a statue." Floppy's eyes suddenly bulged. "Sally," he yelled.

"What?"

"You can borrow Sally. Ya know I never thought I'd have two workin' vehicles at the same time, but now I do, and look: it worked out real good 'cause you need somethin' to get 'round in."

"No. No, no, no, no, no."

"It's fine, she's just sittin' back there 'cause I'm drivin' Vicky. It'd be good for Sally to get drove a bit. She's used to goin' fast, but . . ."

Sally was a beat-up brown Volkswagen Rabbit that ran on cooking grease Floppy collected from local fast-food restaurants. He'd done some other interesting modifications to the vehicle, including replacing the passenger seat with a fifty-quart Igloo cooler. I'd taken one terrifying ride while strapped atop that cooler. It had been a five-minute-long panic attack.

Floppy kept talking while I tried to think of other options, but I was too exhausted to think.

"Okay, okay," I said. "I'll take Sally. Thank you."

Floppy grinned and disappeared inside his garage. A moment later the entire area was illuminated by floodlights. Floppy returned and I followed him around to the back of the building, where Vicky and Sally were parked side by side. I could see Floppy's green trailer fifty or so yards in the distance. It was surrounded by all sorts of rusty appliances, dented water heaters, and other junkyard staples.

Floppy opened Sally's door like a valet, and I slid inside. It smelled like a giant bag of Doritos.

"You can drive a straight, right?"

Floppy pulled a stubby screwdriver out of his coveralls, then reached across me and shoved it into a hole in the steering column. "If she starts stallin' on ya, just pump the gas like all get out."

I pressed the clutch and twisted the screwdriver. The car came to life with a roar. I gave the accelerator a couple of gentle taps, and Sally shook like a clothes dryer on spin. A plume of dark smoke rose from the exhaust. I grabbed the eight-ball gear shift and worked it into what I hoped was first. Floppy slammed the door and gave me a thumbs-up through the window. I rolled it down and yelled over the sound of the engine, "I need another favor. Do you have a Taser?"

21

The next morning I woke up with a sore right arm. Fighting with Sally's transmission had left me feeling like I'd played ten sets of tennis. I reached over to the nightstand for my phone and accidentally knocked over the bottle of bear spray Floppy had loaned me in lieu of a Taser. I grabbed the phone and looked at the time: 9:47. I needed to get a move on.

I threw on some clothes and walked into the kitchen, where I almost had a stroke. Floppy was standing on the other side of the kitchen door, grinning at me through the panes of glass.

"Are you trying to kill me?" I said when I opened the door.

"I didn't wanna knock and wake ya up if you's still sleepin'."

I offered Floppy a cup of instant coffee, but he declined and pulled a large silver thermos from somewhere out of his greasy coveralls. "I don't drink coffee—it's toxic. I drink green tea. Did you know green tea is good for all sorts of things? It's fulla antioxidants. Now I don't exactly know what them things do, but I talked to a guy down at that health food store in Waynesville, and he said green tea is good for your skin and makes you smarter and cures diabetes, I don't have diabetes, but I don't want 'em, and it helps you lose weight."

"Floppy!" I yelled as I stuck a frozen burrito into the microwave. "I'm in a hurry. I've got to be in Asheville in an hour. What do you need?"

"Are we gonna do that thing tonight?"

"Maybe. I don't know yet. I have to talk to some people first."

Floppy sat down at the table and unscrewed his thermos. "You know you asked me to find out if that Ritter feller that Wells killed had any family 'round here? I found out where his sister lives. I got the address. It's in Candler."

"You're kidding? How'd you do it so fast?"

Floppy poured himself a cup of green tea. "Well, I started first thing this mornin' with my buddy Cecil. He teaches weldin' at Pisgah—that's the high school in Canton. I thought that Ritter feller mighta gone there. Cecil checked the records, and sure 'nuff, he did go there. Graduated in '87. His address was on his school records, a place on the north side of Canton, so I rode over there and talked to the man who came to the door. He said he bought the house from the Ritters back in '99, but that a couple years back, a man and woman came by wantin' to look at the house. The woman said she'd grown up there and wanted to see it again for sentimental reasons and such. Said her name was Roberta Ritter Allen. So I thanked him and drove over to the tag office and asked my buddy Paul to look up the woman's name. He ain't s'posed to do stuff like that, but there weren't nobody else in there, so he said it was okay." Floppy pulled a small piece of paper out of his coveralls and placed it on the table. "So there ya go."

"You did all of that this morning?"

"I don't diddle-daddle. I'm gonna get the rollback right now and go pick up your car."

I patted Floppy on the shoulder. "You could run circles around Kato."

* * *

I'd used the laptop to look up directions to Elizabeth's office in Asheville, and according to Google Maps, it would take me forty-five minutes to get there from the cabin. It was more like sixty-five. Asheville has more traffic than it needs, and that, along with Sally's obstinate transmission, had me fuming at 11:25, the time I finally pulled into the parking lot at Harper and Co. I limped at top speed across the parking lot and was huffing when I stumbled inside and approached the reception desk. A young woman in a white shirt and black blazer smiled at me patiently as I tried to catch my breath. "Davis Reed. Elizabeth Harper. Eleven o'clock."

The woman tapped the screen of an iPad then looked up and said, "You are in conference room C. Up one floor. Take a left, last room on your right." She pointed over my shoulder. "Elevators are just there."

Somehow I managed to find the right room; the big letter "C" painted on the door helped. When I pushed it open, I saw a long conference table surrounded by about twenty chairs, all empty except the one at the far end of the table.

"Was there some confusion about the time?" Elizabeth said, not looking up from the laptop in front of her.

"Sorry. Asheville traffic is always horrible."

"Then you should anticipate it and leave earlier."

I hurried across the room and pulled out a chair.

"Just giving you a hard time," Elizabeth said. "Thank you for coming. I know it's a long drive from Cruso."

I sat down and yelped as something jabbed into my groin. I reached into my pocket and pulled out the stubby screwdriver that doubles as Sally's key and placed it on the conference table. Elizabeth glanced at it, then at me.

"Don't ask," I said. "You look lovely, by the way."

"We don't have time for that," Elizabeth said. "I have a lunch meeting at noon. So let's get down to business. In early February, Prentiss Wells called me. I'd never met him before, but he told me he was familiar with our firm and our reputation. He asked to set up a consultation. I suggested he speak to one of my colleagues who specializes in trusts and real estate, but Prentiss insisted on meeting with me, and only me. He refused to give any information over the phone and wanted to meet at this office, not Waynesville."

"Okay. So what happened?"

"We met a few days later. He came here, to this very room." Elizabeth stood up and walked to a corner of the room, where a small wet bar was installed. She opened a mini refrigerator and pulled out two bottled waters. "Do you know what an escrow account is?" she asked as she came back to the table and handed me one of the bottles.

"Isn't it like a holding account?"

"In the most simplistic terms, yes. In real estate, if you made an offer to purchase a house, you would be asked to put up earnest money. That's a deposit that goes against the price of the home. And you get that money credited back to you at closing. But in the meantime, that money is placed in an escrow account, managed by either the real estate brokerage or the law firm handling the closing."

I nodded while trying to unscrew the cap of my water bottle. Elizabeth watched me struggle for a few seconds, then grabbed the bottle out of my hand and opened it with ease. "Sorry, my hands are clammy," I said as she passed the bottle back to me.

"The point about escrow accounts is this," Elizabeth said. "The money in those accounts does not belong to the real estate brokerage or the law firm—it belongs to the client. And the manager of an escrow account has a fiduciary duty to ensure the account is managed properly and that there is no commingling of funds. Meaning the escrow account remains completely independent from the firm's operating account."

"So Wells wanted to meet with you about his escrow account? Why?"

Elizabeth raised her eyebrows. "You might not believe it, but even a small real estate law firm like Prentiss's could have one or two million dollars in its escrow account at any one time. Especially if the firm is handling commercial transactions. For some people, access to that kind of money can present enormous temptation."

I sipped my water and wondered what I'd do if I had the combination to a safe containing two million dollars. The angel and devils had conflicting answers to that question.

"Prentiss told me he was planning to retire in a couple of months," Elizabeth said, "and had begun to turn over responsibilities to Rex Pinland. Last night you said Rex may have been blackmailing Prentiss with something he had discovered regarding the accident in 1988, which may have ultimately led to Prentiss's death. But there's another possible motive. Prentiss was concerned Rex may have been stealing from the firm's escrow account."

"Why did he think that?"

"All he said was that he had an uncomfortable feeling. And he admitted that feeling might be due to his impending retirement and his difficulty ceding control of the firm."

"So he had no proof?"

"No. But when he met with me, he brought along a thumb drive." Elizabeth turned the laptop to where we could both see the screen. I noticed a small black portable drive sticking out of one of the ports. "He said he wasn't technologically savvy but that he'd tried to download the firm's escrow account data from the cloud for the previous twelve months. When I viewed the contents of the drive, I discovered Prentiss had not just downloaded the escrow account data but many of the firm's files—contracts, closing statements, HUD disclosures, indemnity agreements—for the twelve months prior to our meeting." Elizabeth clicked on a folder icon, which opened to reveal rows and rows of more folders. "This was a good thing because, as I told Prentiss that day, to find any irregularities in the escrow account, I would need to compare the account with the contracts and closing statements."

"Because that would show when deposits were made and when they were paid out?" I wanted Elizabeth to know that I was keeping up.

"Exactly. I also told Prentiss such an analysis would take time—and money. He audibly gulped when I quoted the figure."

"So he didn't hire you to look into it?"

"He told me to keep the thumb drive and that he'd get back to me within the week if he wanted me to proceed. I never heard from him again."

"Did Wells say why he was turning over his responsibilities to Rex? There's another attorney at the firm, Butler."

Elizabeth typed on the laptop's keyboard. A moment later we were looking at the Wells and Butler website. She clicked on the name JoAnne Butler, and a new page appeared, showing a photo of a woman who looked to be at least seventy. A short paragraph stated that JoAnne had retired but was occasionally available to provide legal assistance on a pro bono basis to local nonprofits.

"Prentiss told me JoAnne retired in January," Elizabeth said. "Evidently JoAnne had managed the escrow account for years, and with her departure Prentiss turned that responsibility over to Rex."

"But Wells never called you back," I said. "And he obviously didn't fire Rex. So he must have decided everything was on the level."

"Yes, perhaps Rex wasn't embezzling. Or perhaps he got better at covering his tracks."

"Vance floated a theory about Wells and the three guys he was golfing with all being involved in some kind of scam. He said he could think of many ways four guys in their positions could commit fraud."

"Remind me what the other two men do again."

"Jimmy Fletcher is a mortgage broker and Freddy Sizemore is a real estate appraiser."

Elizabeth leaned back and crossed her arms over her chest. "Just off the top of my head I can think of several: mortgage fraud, loan modification fraud, equity skimming, illegal flipping. However, if they were working some sort of scam, I don't believe Prentiss was involved. If he were, he wouldn't have contacted me about his escrow account. And he certainly wouldn't have provided me with a year's worth of his firm's transactions."

"He might if the scam didn't involve his firm."

Elizabeth considered that point, then shrugged. "Possibly. But I still don't think Prentiss would want to bring attention to himself, even if he was involved in a crime and believed one of his coconspirators was taking advantage of him."

I was liking Elizabeth more and more with each passing moment. She was beautiful and elegant and well spoken—and smart as a whip. And for some reason I found her all-business attitude attractive. I could picture us sitting on the deck of the cabin, her with a glass of wine, me with an Old Crab, our chairs side by side, holding hands as we watched the sun dip below the mountains.

"Have you entered a fugue state?" Elizabeth said.

I snapped back to reality. "Just processing what you've told me. Listen, be completely honest with me, okay?"

Elizabeth frowned. "I'm always completely honest."

"Okay, so tell me this. When we had coffee together and I mentioned Prentiss Wells, you immediately looked distraught. Was it because of this escrow stuff?"

"Yes, of course. When I first heard Prentiss had died, I immediately thought of our meeting. It was less than six weeks ago. And when I learned of the details, of him being accidentally killed by a golf ball, it sounded suspicious, and I considered the possibility that his death might be tied to his concerns regarding his firm's escrow account."

I pointed at the laptop. "Have you looked at any of those files?"

"Only briefly, and in Prentiss's presence. Since he claimed to be a Luddite, I wanted to see exactly what data were on the drive. But I will go through them if you think it might prove worthwhile."

"The best I can say is it might, and it might not."

"That's not very reassuring," Elizabeth said, glancing at her watch. "I'm sorry, but I have to ask you to leave. I need to prepare for my next meeting." She extended her hand and I shook it.

I tried to think of some smooth, suave line to lay on Elizabeth before I left, but decided to act as the strong, silent type. I simply stood up and confidently strolled toward the door. I was about to open it when I heard Elizabeth clear her throat. I turned around to look—she was holding up the screwdriver.

22

Before I cranked up Sally, I called Vance. Lana answered.

"Hold on a minute, I'll go get him," she said. "He's ironing his pajamas."

"Is that a euphemism?"

Lana giggled. "You're adorable. Now hold on."

A moment later both Vance and Lana were on speakerphone, and I gave them a rundown of my meeting with Elizabeth.

"If there's anything fishy in those files, Elizabeth will find it," Lana said. "She's tenacious with a capital 'T.'"

"What's next on your agenda?" Vance asked.

"I thought, since I'm in Asheville, I'd take a chance and see if I could get a few minutes with Brett Wells. I'm curious if he's at all suspicious about what happened to his dad. And what he remembers from the accident in '88."

"Excellent idea. I'll call his office and inquire, if you'd like?"

"That would be great. Listen, I'm also going to try to talk to Adam Ritter's sister today. Floppy located her address. I want to get her take on that accident."

"Davis," Lana said. "We're all set for tonight. We have dinner plans with some friends but should be back home by nine."

"Okay. I'll tell Floppy nine thirty just to be safe. And hey, I've got some news. I talked to Dale last night. He said someone called the sheriff's department late yesterday afternoon, claiming to know the person that hit the ball that killed Wells. They had some details about the accident that probably aren't widely known."

"Phooey!" Vance barked.

"Yes, phooey," Lana said. "Keep digging, Davis. You'll get to the truth. And oh, by the way, we have a present for you. It arrived today. You're going to look smashing."

* * *

I checked the map app on my phone for directions to Brett's office, then fought with Sally down Hendersonville Road, past the entrance to the Biltmore Estate, and on into downtown Asheville. I found a parking space near Malaprops Bookstore and was lucky enough to find seventy-five cents in Sally's ashtray for the meter.

I walked a block and a half to the entrance of an office building and examined the directory next to the elevator. Brett's office was on the third floor.

I was in the elevator when my phone rang. It was Vance calling to tell me that he'd spoken to Brett and that he'd said he could see me either immediately or the following afternoon.

"I'll be there in thirty seconds," I said.

* * *

When I walked in, an older woman with curly brown hair was sitting at a desk, typing on a computer. I gave her my name, and she picked up a phone and spoke into it briefly. Then she stood and asked me to follow her.

I did, across the room to where a doorway opened into a long hall. We passed a couple of closed doors and one open one. Through it I saw a small room full of file cabinets. A blonde woman was on her tiptoes, peering into one of the file cabinet's top drawers. *Carla,* I thought. My heart hurt for Dale.

We turned a corner, and the hallway ended at a door. The older woman knocked on it, then opened it. "Davis Reed," she said as I walked in behind her. Brett was sitting behind a giant wooden desk that probably wouldn't have fit in my kitchen. Behind him a large rectangular window offered a view of downtown Asheville. Brett stood and I suddenly realized he was a big guy, not fat, just stout and sturdy, like a bouncer. He came around the desk and nodded at the woman, who left and closed the door behind her. Brett was wearing dark blue suit pants and a white dress shirt; a green tie hung loose around his neck. As we shook hands, I studied his face. He looked as though he'd been crying. He pointed to an armchair, one of two, that were positioned in front of his desk. Brett returned to his seat, and looking across the giant desk at him, I felt like he was in a different time zone.

"I just got off the phone with Vance Roth," Brett said. "You got here fast."

"I was in the neighborhood."

"When Vance said your name, I recognized it immediately. I'm familiar with the Graveyard Fields story. Did you know Dale Johnson's ex-wife works here? She's a paralegal. Invaluable. I don't know what I'd do without her."

I didn't have anything to say to that other than "Hmm."

"But Vance didn't tell me why you wanted to see me. Have you been injured? I noticed you limp."

"No. I mean yes. But that's not why I'm here. I just wanted to stop by and offer my condolences. I was with Dale when he got the call about your dad, and I went with him to the golf course."

Brett's eyes began to water, and he quickly opened a desk drawer and pulled out a small box of tissues. He used one to wipe his eyes, then gave me a weak smile. "Sorry," he said. "I'm quick to tears these days."

"My parents died in an accident several years ago," I said. "I know what it's like to suddenly lose people you care about."

Brett hesitated for a few seconds. "What happened? If I may ask."

"Car accident." As soon as I said it, I felt own eyes get misty. "They were on their way to my sister's house for dinner. My dad was driving. The car went off the road and into a concrete pylon. The impact killed both of them instantly."

"Christ," Brett said in what amounted to a whisper.

"It was later determined my dad had suffered a stroke just before the crash. It was a minor stroke but enough to cause him to lose control and veer off the road. So if they hadn't been in the car at the time . . ." My voice trailed off, and the next thing I knew Brett was in the chair next to mine, offering me the tissue box. I snatched one and put it to use.

"How did you deal with the pain?" Brett asked.

"With a lot of beer."

"How long did it take?"

"What do you mean?"

"For you to feel better."

I held up the tissue. "This should tell you."

Brett put his elbows on his knees and his head in his hands. "Christ," he whispered again.

"I'm sorry," I said. "I didn't mean to . . ."

Brett stood and began to pace around his office. It reminded me of Vance pacing back and forth behind his sofa while offering up a murder theory, which in turn reminded me why I was in Brett Wells's office in the first place.

"You were obviously very close to your father," I said.

"I was," Brett said, continuing to pace. "He was my best friend. We spoke every day."

"Is he the reason you became an attorney?"

"One hundred percent. I wouldn't have amounted to anything without him believing in me and pushing me."

"My parents tried to push me, but all I did was push back."

Brett sat down in his desk chair. "Oh, I did my share of pushing back. I was a wild child. But my parents never gave up on me." Brett looked away and wiped his eyes again. "They both sacrificed a lot for me."

I hadn't meant for my talk with Brett to turn into a group therapy session, but here we were. Two grown men talking about personal loss, dabbing their eyes with Kleenex.

"So what changed?" I asked.

"I beg your pardon?" Brett said.

"You said you were a wild child. What changed that?"

"My dad put his foot down. He told me it was not my destiny to be a failure." Brett looked away for a moment, then straightened in his chair. "So, you were out on the golf course. I don't recall seeing you."

"I was only there for half an hour or so. I left right after Dale talked to the guys who were golfing with your dad."

Brett shook his head. "I feel terrible for them. To witness something like that."

"Do you know them?"

"I know Jimmy and Freddy. I've known them for years. Great guys. Met them at some charity golf event my dad and I played in. I don't know Rex very well. He only moved to this area a couple of years ago." Brett exhaled. "God, what he's dealing with now."

"You mean with the law firm?"

"Uh, no, personally. His wife. Stage four colorectal cancer. It's to the point they're now trying experimental treatments."

"Oh, I'm sorry to hear that. I happened to run into Rex yesterday in Waynesville. He seems like a good guy."

"I'm so glad Dad hired him. He needed someone to take some of the load off. He was working himself into an early . . ." Brett closed his eyes tight.

I let a respectable amount of time pass, then said, "Sounds like your dad's work was very important to him. Did he ever talk about retiring?"

"He talked about it, but talking and doing are separate things. Last spring Dad made a grand announcement that he was going to work for one more year, then retire and play golf five days a week. I knew it would never happen, Dad's work was his life—he'd go stir crazy without it. And sure enough, as the months passed, he began hedging. We had dinner together a few weeks ago, and he casually announced he was going to work for maybe two more years and then retire. When he told me that, I said, 'Dad, we both know you're going to work until the day you die.'" Brett forced out a tiny chuckle. "You know, I think if he could have chosen where he would die, he would have said a golf course. I guess I should take some comfort in that."

"I know the sheriff's department's working hard to try to find the person who hit the ball."

Brett scowled. "To be responsible for something like that and then run away. It boggles my mind." He gestured at some papers on his desk. "I've dealt with it for years. But the negligence people are capable of never ceases to amaze me." Brett pointed toward my bad leg. "Was that caused by someone's negligence?"

"I'm not really allowed to talk about it. I signed an NDA."

Brett nodded as if he understood perfectly. "I hope you were adequately compensated. Because when something is taken from you due to the negligence of another, the scales need to be balanced. That's what I do for my clients: I balance the scales." Brett closed his eyes tight. "The scales are so out of balance right now."

Even though the guy was responsible for the breakup of my best friend's marriage, it was impossible not to feel sorry for him. "Dale told me they're running down some leads. I'm sure they'll find the person."

"A Deputy Pless keeps me abreast of the investigation. I have faith."

"Speaking of Deputy Pless—that day on the golf course he said something about an accident your dad was involved with back in the eighties."

Brett looked confused, or maybe just surprised. I understood why. As far as segues go, it was a terrible one.

"A horrible thing," Brett said. "A young man ran in front of my dad's vehicle. There was no time to react. The man was killed instantly."

"Deputy Pless said the man had just robbed a nearby house."

Brett nodded. I waited a moment, but he didn't speak.

"Do you mind telling me what happened?" I said. "I'm just curious."

Brett looked away, and when he didn't say anything, I began to stand up. "No, it's okay," Brett said, gesturing for me to stay put. "I'm happy to talk about it. I'm just emotional right now, and that was a very difficult time for my family."

"It's all right. I'm sorry I . . ."

"It happened late at night, basically right in front of our home. Our dog, Peanut, had gotten loose and run off. Mom was hysterical, so Dad went out driving around to look for him. Dad was on his way home when it happened. The man had just broken into a house a half or so mile away and was fleeing the scene when for some reason he jumped out into the road. Thankfully, my mom and I were behind the house, so we didn't see it. But Dad was badly shaken by it. It wasn't his fault—he wasn't negligent—but it ate at him, and the way people talked . . ."

Brett told the story the same way I told the tale of Graveyard Fields, like it had been repeated a thousand times, which it probably had been. I felt a little guilty for asking him to tell it.

"The man who was killed, did you or your parents know him?"

"No. None of us had any connection with him. He was a couple of years older than me. He had graduated from Pisgah High in Canton. I was at Tuscola in Waynesville." Brett raised a palm. "I'd just started my senior year, and let me tell you it's not easy to have your classmates call your dad a murderer behind your back."

When Brett didn't say anything else, I glanced at my watch, then pushed myself up. "I've taken up too much of your time."

Brett stood and came around his desk. "Not at all. Sorry for being such a mess."

"It gets better," I said. "Slowly. But it does get better."

We walked to the door, where Brett offered me his hand. "It was kind of you to stop by," he said.

As we shook, I glanced at a shelf near the door, where some books and a few framed photographs were displayed. One photo showed Brett and another man standing on a beach, dressed in swim trunks and tank tops. They had their arms around each other's shoulders and were smiling broadly at the camera. I pointed at the photo. "That kind of looks like Folly Beach. My sister lives there."

"Close," Brett said. "Kiawah Island. That's me and my partner, Todd."

"Your business partner?"

Brett smiled. "No. My partner." He pointed at the photo. "That was last summer, when we got engaged. We're getting married this June."

"Congratulations" was all I could think to say.

23

Before leaving Asheville, I sat in Sally and pulled up Facebook on my phone. I searched for Brett Wells and when I spotted him, saw that his profile was private, so I tapped the "Add Friend" icon. I then switched over to my mapping app and entered the address of Adam Ritter's sister.

Roberta Ritter Allen lived in Candler, a suburb west of Asheville, an area I'd pass through on my way back to Cruso.

The house was in a small residential neighborhood near a middle school. I pulled onto the concrete drive and parked behind a gray Ford F-150.

I was almost to the home's front porch when the door swung open, and a man stepped out and gave me a cautious look. He glanced at Sally, then back to me. "Help you?" he said. He was a big guy, probably in his mid-forties and wearing baggy black shorts and a brown T-shirt with a drawing of some sort of fish hanging from a hook on the front.

"My name's Davis Reed. I'm a private detective. I'm looking into the death of a man named Prentiss Wells. He was a real estate attorney over in Waynesville."

"Oh, I know who Prentiss Wells is. Or was."

"Are you Mr. Allen?"

"That's right."

"I'm wondering if it would be possible to speak to Mrs. Allen? It should only take a few minutes."

"Looking into his death? I thought Wells was killed by a golf ball. That's what it said on the news."

I took a few steps forward. "You might have seen me on the news as well. Right before Thanksgiving last year. That big drug bust on the Parkway, up at Graveyard Fields."

The man's eyes narrowed, then he pointed at me and started laughing. "I remember that. That skinny guy had that reporter in a tizzy. That's the best thing I've seen on the local news in years."

It's worth explaining that a couple of hours after the Graveyard Fields fiasco, and just before Dale, Floppy, and I were to be interviewed by Fern Matthews from the local ABC affiliate, Dale had said he would do the talking and that Floppy and I were not to say anything unless asked a direct question. But when the cameraman started filming, and Fern shoved her microphone close to Dale's face, he turned as white as a sheet and became as still and as mute as a mannequin in a department store. After a few uncomfortable seconds, Floppy grabbed the microphone, and you can image how things went from there. Fern was not happy. My laughing probably didn't help.

"So, is Mrs. Allen home?" I asked.

The man thought for a moment. "Yeah, all right. C'mon in."

* * *

The house was fairly small and felt cozy. The living room was furnished with an overstuffed sofa and two overstuffed chairs. The walls were covered with family photos, needlepoint works, and wall art featuring inspirational quotes. A small upright piano sat along one wall.

The man introduced himself as Chris Allen, and I waited in the living room, as instructed, while he went upstairs to get his wife. A minute later Roberta Allen walked into the room alongside her husband. She had wavy brown hair and was dressed in jeans and a navy polo shirt with the logo of some restaurant embroidered on the chest. She appeared to be about the same age as her husband, forty-five, give or take a year or two. I introduced myself to her and everyone sat down.

"Is this about Adam?" she said.

"Yeah. I'm sorry to drudge it up."

"What's he got to do with Prentiss Wells dying?"

"I'll be honest with you, Mrs. Allen: I don't know. Probably nothing. But some people hired me to look into Mr. Wells's death, and I'm following a bunch of threads to see if any of them unravel."

Chris and Roberta exchanged glances; then Chris turned to me with a hard look. "You think we mighta had—"

I raised my hands. "No, no, no, no, I do not. Not at all. I've just not been able to find out much about the accident. The deputy who handled it is almost a hundred and has Alzheimer's."

"I still don't see what this has to do with Prentiss Wells getting killed by a golf ball," Chris said.

"There's a possibility that someone was blackmailing Mr. Wells about the accident that killed Adam," I said.

"Are you saying Prentiss Wells was murdered?" Chris asked. "'Cause on the news they keep saying it was an accident." Chris turned to Roberta. "I'm telling you, you can't trust the media for nothing. All they do's lie."

Roberta ignored her husband and focused on me. "What do you want to know?"

"Is there anything you remember about the accident that seems odd or suspicious?"

"Yeah—who drove him out there? Same question I've been asking for thirty years."

"What? You mean who drove Adam out to the house he robbed?"

Roberta's face stiffened, and she emphasized every word: "Yes, to the house he robbed."

I raised my hands again. Roberta took a deep breath, and her face relaxed. "It's just, I haven't had anybody ask me about Adam in a long time, that's all."

"Were you close to your brother?"

"We got along. But we weren't what you'd call close. Adam was eight years older than me. That's a big age difference when you're kids."

"So you were, what, eleven at the time of the accident?"

Roberta nodded.

"Was Adam still living at home?" I asked.

"Uh-huh. He was working at the Pizza Hut in Canton, saving money to get his own place."

"So he had a car?"

"Yeah, a little Honda CR-X."

"But he didn't drive it out to that house that night?"

"No. It was still parked behind the Pizza Hut the next morning. My daddy went and picked it up. Sold it the next week."

"So what do you remember about that night, exactly?"

Roberta let out a long breath. "Adam drove to work—I don't remember what time, but he worked evenings. After his shift he called Momma from the pay phone there and said he wouldn't be back 'til late. He was nineteen, didn't have a curfew, but he always called Momma if he was going to be out after midnight."

I slid to the edge of my overstuffed chair. "And you have no idea who might have been with him that night?"

"No," Roberta said. "Law enforcement asked around. My family asked around. No one ever 'fessed up."

"Did he have a girlfriend?"

Roberta shook her head. "No."

"Do you remember any of his friends? People he hung out with?"

"No. He didn't bring friends to the house. I didn't neither. Our daddy was a drunk. By five PM he'd either be passed out in his recliner or stomping around the house screaming about Reagan. So Adam and me didn't really have people over."

"Was Adam in trouble a lot?" I asked.

"Never," Roberta said. "That's another reason I'd like to know who drove him out to that house. Whoever it was must've dared him to break into it." Roberta turned away, and I could tell she was working hard to hold back tears. "He was a good person, kind."

"So he was working at Pizza Hut. What else did he do?"

"He liked drawing and painting and music," Roberta said. "Played the guitar. He was very talented. He could've been a professional musician. Said he was going to move to New York when he got enough money saved." Roberta shook her head and scowled. "Daddy told him there was nothing but freaks and fairies in New York."

"So back then," I said, "do you remember Adam ever mentioning the name Jimmy Fletcher?"

Roberta shook her head.

"What about Freddy Sizemore?"

Roberta shook her head again. "No."

I waited for a few seconds, hoping the angel would whisper something useful in my ear.

In the silence Chris leaned forward and said, "So what would someone have to blackmail Wells with? Do you think Wells hit Adam on purpose?"

Roberta looked down and mumbled, "Stop it."

"Or that maybe he was drunk?" Chris said.

Another whisper, "Stop."

"Or stoned or something?"

Roberta turned to her husband. "Enough, I said."

I glanced at a needlepoint quote on the wall: *The Past is Heavy. Put it Down.* It was good advice, and I wondered if I should get one for the cabin.

"Look, I don't know exactly what happened that night," Roberta said. "But I do know Mr. Wells felt horrible about it. He came to our house with the deputy that morning."

"You mean when you were first informed?"

Roberta nodded. "It takes a big man to do that."

"Hang on a second," I said as I dug into my back pocket and removed the newspaper article. I handed it to Roberta. "That man in the photo. Is he the deputy who came to your house?"

Roberta stared at the paper and slowly nodded. "I believe so. Singleton. Yeah." Roberta grimaced. "I'll never forget that morning. We were all standing in the living room, and the deputy was explaining what had happened. When he said Adam was dead, Momma collapsed. Just fell to the floor."

"And your dad?"

Roberta scoffed. "Daddy was just angry. I'd never seen him so hot."

"I can imagine."

"No. Not at Mr. Wells. He was angry at Adam. He said now all his boy would be remembered for was robbing a house." Roberta paused. "Anyway. Like I said, Mr. Wells was a big man to show up and take responsibility. He offered to pay for Adam's funeral but Daddy wouldn't have it. Later on we found out Mr. Wells donated two thousand dollars to my parents' church in Adam's name. Then a few years after that, the checks started coming."

"Roberta," Chris said.

"Oh, hush," Roberta snapped. "You deposit those checks before the ink can dry. You're just mad they're gonna stop."

Chris stood up, walked over to an open doorway. He crossed his arms over his chest and leaned against the jamb.

"What checks?" I asked.

"A few years after the accident, Daddy got a check in the mail for five hundred dollars," Roberta said.

"From Mr. Wells?"

Roberta nodded.

"Why did you say they were going to stop? Have there been other checks?"

Roberta nodded again. "After that first one, Daddy got an identical check every month. And after Daddy died, the checks were payable to Momma. And when Momma died three years ago, the checks started coming here, in my name."

"Do you happen to have a canceled check I could look at?"

Roberta hesitated a moment, then stood up and left the room. In her absence I avoided Chris's gaze, but I sure felt it. When Roberta returned, she was holding an iPad. She tapped on the screen for a few seconds, then handed the tablet to me. The screen showed a banking app, and in the center of the screen was a window showing the scan of a check. The account holder was Philos Adelphos Dikaios LLC, with the address listed as a PO box in Waynesville. The check was typed, and the memo line read: *In memory of Adam Ritter.* The signature was an illegible scribble.

I pulled out my phone. "Do you mind if I take a photo of this?"

Chris started to say something, but Roberta interrupted. "Yeah, that's fine."

I snapped a picture and handed Roberta her iPad. "And you said the checks didn't start right after the accident? It was some time later?"

"Yeah, years later. I think I'd just started college when the first one showed up. So eight or nine years after the accident." Roberta shook her head. "Daddy drank the first couple of those checks. Then Momma started taking them and depositing them in a new savings account she opened without him knowing. That money's been a godsend to our family."

I looked over at Chris. His face told me I should wrap things up. Which I did.

*   *   *

I climbed into Sally and called Vance. Again, Lana answered.

"He's in the shower," she said. "I was just getting ready to join him."

"I didn't need to know that. But listen, I talked to Brett. He's pretty shaken up about his dad's death. But he doesn't suspect anything other than that it was an accident. He said he's friends with Jimmy and Freddy but doesn't know Rex all that well. And I just talked to Adam Ritter's sister. It seems Adam might not have been alone the night he was killed. If someone was with him, they may have seen exactly what happened. And maybe what happened wasn't an accident."

"Any idea who this person might be?" Lana asked.

"The sister didn't know who Adam hung out with. She's eight years younger. But I know Adam graduated from Pisgah, the high school in Canton, a few years before Jimmy Fletcher, so there's a chance they might have known each other. The sister didn't recognize his name, or Freddy's name. Anyway, I'm going to go into Waynesville and see if Freddy's at his office. And I left a message yesterday with Jimmy's office but haven't heard back. I may stop by unannounced and see if I can speak to him. Then I'm going to stop by Floppy's to make sure he's set for tonight."

"Look at you go," Lana said. "Now be safe, darling. See you soon."

I sat in Sally for another minute and stared at the tailgate of the gray Ford in front of me. The devils started whispering that I was a time-wasting fool. Riding around western North Carolina in a fryer grease–fueled deathtrap, bugging people about their dead relatives when I could be sitting on the deck of the cabin, drinking good beer and ignoring the world. A part of me was inclined to agree with them.

Then the angel cut through the noise and told me to stay focused. So I closed my eyes and thought of everyone involved in my brief investigation and which one of them could have had a connection with Adam Ritter. It was most likely someone who was close in age to Adam when he died. If it wasn't Jimmy or Freddy, maybe it was someone connected to them. Maybe somebody I'd already talked to. Somebody I had an odd feeling about.

I hopped out and limped back up to the Allen's front door. I knocked and Roberta opened it only wide enough for me to see her face. "Sorry," I said. "I asked you if you remember Adam ever talking about a guy named Jimmy Fletcher or Freddy Sizemore."

"Yeah. I don't remember him ever saying those names. But it was a long time ago."

"What about this name?" I said. "Bill Rhinehart."

24

headed West out of Candler while wondering what it meant that Bill Rhinehart had known Adam Ritter. It was another coincidence I wasn't comfortable with.

Near Canton I picked up Interstate 40 toward Waynesville. I'd driven a couple of miles when I saw a billboard advertising Brett Wells's law firm. The board read: "Injured In An Accident? Don't Fret, Call Brett!" Under that was "I MAKE THEM PAY!" followed by an 800 number. There was also a head-shot of Brett, his face contorted into a menacing scowl. It looked nothing like the teary-eyed guy I'd talked to.

I called Dale but got his voicemail, then called Vance and got his voicemail too.

Ten minutes later I turned onto US 74. Ten minutes after that I took the Waynesville exit and pulled into a Publix parking lot. I glanced over at the Igloo cooler that doubled for Sally's passenger seat and wondered if I should pick up a couple of six packs and a bag of ice. Then I remembered my bank balance.

I called my attorney, Allison, and left another pleading message with the receptionist. Then I tapped the mapping app and pulled up directions for Sizemore Appraisals. According to the map, it was eight minutes away.

* * *

Freddy's office was in an area that looked similar to where Wells and Butler was located, a street mixed with residential and commercial buildings. Right across the street from Freddy's sat Ernie's Motors, the lot where Floppy had said he'd purchased Vicky. It made me wonder if Floppy had retrieved my car from Dew-Dads and if he was making any progress with the search for tires.

I pulled into the concrete driveway next to Freddy's office. There was one other car in the drive, a black BMW 740e. Like Rex's Range Rover, not inexpensive. The car's trunk and roof were covered in bird droppings. Past the vehicle sat a small one-car garage.

I was about to step out of Sally when my phone buzzed. It was Dale calling.

"I need Earl's number," I said.

"Why?"

"Just text it to me. I need to talk to him."

"Jesus Christ. Is this got somethin' to do with that wild goose chase them swingers've got you on?"

"Just send it to me."

I hung up and a few seconds later my phone buzzed again, a text with Earl's number.

I stepped out of Sally and hobbled up onto the front porch. An etched wooden sign next to the door read "Sizemore Appraisals Est. 1997." I gave the knob a turn, but the door was locked. I knocked hard and waited. I let thirty seconds pass, then did it again. And then again, just for good measure. The upper half of the door was paned with frosted glass. I pressed my nose against one of the panes but couldn't see inside.

I went around to the back of the building, in hopes of finding another way in. I stepped across the backyard, which needed mowing, and up three steps to a door, a slab of solid wood. I tried the knob—locked. I knocked a few times, even though I knew it was probably pointless. There was a window just to the right of the door, and I stretched over to look through it. The room I was looking into was a small kitchen, and I wondered if this was Freddy's home as well as his office. I banged on the glass and waited. No one appeared.

On my phone I used the browser app to pull up the Sizemore Appraisals website and clicked the phone-number link at the bottom of the page. After a few rings a robotic voice came on the line: *The voicemail of the person you are trying to reach is full. Please try again later.*

I left Freddy's and drove to Main Street, where I found a single parking spot and tried to parallel park. An older couple on the sidewalk watched in horror as I ground Sally's gears while trying to maneuver into the space. After a minute I gave up and drove to a side street, where I found three empty spots in a row.

I limped up the sidewalk to Main Street and turned the corner. I glanced in some of the shops and wondered for the hundredth time how many enamel mugs and cinnamon brooms you had to sell a month in order to pay the rent.

When I stepped into Eagle's Fork Financial, I was greeted by a smiling young man in khakis and a white button-down shirt one size too large for him. He lurched toward me and held out his hand, saying his name so quickly that I didn't catch it, not that I needed to.

"I'd like to speak with Jimmy Fletcher," I said.

The man sucked air through his teeth. "He's out for lunch. I'm not sure when he'll be back."

"Does he eat around here? On Main Street? Or does he go home for lunch?"

"I don't know. Sorry."

I thanked the guy and stepped back out onto the sidewalk. I was contemplating my next move when the door to Eagle's Fork swung open, and an older, balding man with a red face stepped out. He was dressed like the guy I'd just spoken to, but his white shirt was stretched tight against an impressive beer belly.

"Do you work here?" I asked.

"Sure do. Can I help you?"

"I'm Davis Reed. I'm a private detective. I need to talk to Jimmy Fletcher, and they said he's out to lunch. I've got some information he requested, and it's time sensitive, but he's not answering his phone. I'm wondering if he's a regular at one of the restaurants around here."

"Odds are he's over at Waynesville Country Club."

I gave the man a thumbs-up. "Thanks. I'll check there."

"Not the restaurant," the man said. "The driving range."

I thanked the man again, started off, then spun around. "One more thing," I said. "Do you know a Freddy Sizemore? He's an appraiser here in town."

The man laughed. "Yeah, I know Friday Sizemore."

"Friday?"

The man laughed again. "That's what some of us here call him," he said, gesturing toward the Eagle's Fork door. "Freddy is Jimmy's guy Friday. Picks up his dry cleaning. Chauffeurs him to the airport. House-sits when Jimmy's out of town." The man rolled his eyes. "Probably tees up Jimmy's golf balls for him. I wish I could find me a Friday Sizemore."

129

Me too, I thought.

* * *

It took less than ten minutes to get to the entrance of Waynesville Country Club. I parked in the main lot and followed the signs for the Pro Shop, where a friendly woman gave me directions to the driving range.

There were three people on the range when I arrived. Jimmy was on the far-right side of the hitting area. I watched him hit a few balls. His swing was controlled and fluid.

Between each shot he would step away and pause for a moment before using the head of his club to roll another ball into position. Then he'd stand behind the ball and stare down the range. Finally he'd nod, then address the ball and take his swing. It was a disciplined, graceful routine.

I was about fifteen feet from Jimmy, moving along slowly in his direction, when he noticed me. If he was surprised to see me, it didn't show.

"Davis Reed in the flesh," he said, extending his arm.

"You know my name," I said as we shook hands.

"Of course I do. I saw you on the news last fall. They must have showed that clip a dozen times. You know it's on YouTube, right? God, Dale looked like he'd been tasered. And Floppy, bless his soul, he can't be anything other than himself."

I nodded in agreement.

"How did you know I'd be here?" Jimmy asked.

"A guy at your office tipped me off."

Jimmy laughed. "Well, it's no secret. If it's not raining and it's above forty degrees, this is where I spend my lunch break."

I started to speak but Jimmy interrupted. "I got your message," he said. "Sorry I haven't called. I would say I've been too busy." Jimmy looked over at his bucket of range balls and frowned. "But I don't guess you'd buy that, would you? Truth is, I've just been trying to stay occupied. What happened to Prentiss hit me pretty hard."

"Were you and Mr. Wells close?"

"I guess you could say that. I knew him for years. He was a lot older than me, so we didn't really hang out—you know, go to bars and stuff. But we played a lot of golf together. He was a pretty good stick for his age. Seventy-six years old with a twelve handicap is nothing to sneeze at. Whole lot better than Freddy. That guy hits more trees than a blind Tarzan."

"What's your handicap?"

"I'm a two. But if we're playing for money, I'm a ten." Jimmy winked, then took off his golf glove and put it in his back pocket. "So Rex Pinland tells me you've been hired to look into Prentiss's death."

"That's right."

"And you won't say who hired you."

"That's right again."

"Hmm," Jimmy said. "Rex told me your theory, but would you mind repeating it? I think he must've gotten it wrong."

"It is just a theory. But it's possible the golfer you saw playing behind you, the person in the black pants and orange shirt, was working with an accomplice who was hiding behind a tree farther up the fairway, closer to the bunker where Mr. Wells was standing, and the accomplice used some sort of modified gun to fire a golf ball at Mr. Wells's head. And during the initial confusion, the golfer and the accomplice escaped from the area without being seen."

Jimmy pushed out his bottom lip. "Huh," he said. "I guess Rex did get it right."

I started to speak but Jimmy interrupted again. "But what's the motive?" he said.

"That's what I'm trying to piece together. I think it might have to do with something in Mr. Wells's past."

"Like what?" Jimmy asked.

"Are you aware of the incident Mr. Wells was involved in in 1988?"

"Yeah. Prentiss hit a kid with his car. The kid died. Well, not a kid—he was in his early twenties I think."

"Adam Ritter. He was nineteen. Did Mr. Wells ever speak to you about it?"

"No. But this is a small county. It was even smaller back then. Everybody knew about that accident."

"Adam Ritter graduated from Pisgah in '87. Did you and he ever cross paths?"

"Not that I remember. I was still in junior high then."

"But what about around town? You just said it was a small county."

"Don't you remember how it was back then? No cell phones. No internet. No social media. You had a small group of friends you went to school with, and if you were lucky, your parents would let you call them on the land line once in a while. It wasn't like today, where kids are constantly connected to everybody. Point is I didn't know the guy. Now, c'mon. Are you really convinced Prentiss was murdered? That somebody shot him with a golf-ball gun?"

"I'm being paid to look into it, so that's what I'm doing."

Jimmy held my gaze for a moment, then raised his arm and looked at his watch. "Listen, I've got to get back to the office. But let's get a beer sometime. I'll tell you some stories about me and Dale back when we were teenagers."

I nodded and pointed at Jimmy's wrist. "Nice watch."

Jimmy moved the watch close to my face. "Rolex Daytona. Practically impossible to get a new one. I had to buy this on the gray market. Paul Newman wore one, a 1968 model. It sold at auction last year for over fifteen million."

"So what time do you have?"

Jimmy twisted his wrist. "Two thirty-eight."

I looked at my twenty-year-old Timex. "Whadd'ya know. Me too."

25

Back in Sally, I texted Earl and asked him to give me a call, then headed toward Floppy's garage. Twenty minutes later I was passing an area known as Lake Logan when my phone buzzed. It was Earl.

"What's up, Davis? How did you get my number?"

"Dale," I replied.

"What can I do you for?"

"That accident Prentiss Wells was involved in back in '88, what else can you tell me about that?"

"Hell, I don't know. Like I told ya, it was ruled an accident pretty quick. Wells wasn't charged."

"I've been poking around a little, and I found out that the guy who Wells hit was named Adam Ritter and that he didn't have a vehicle anywhere near the scene. I drove out to where it happened. It's basically the middle of nowhere. Did you guys ever determine how he got all the way out there without a vehicle?"

Earl didn't respond. I waited a few more seconds, then said, "Earl? You still there?"

"Yeah, yeah, I'm here. Look, Davis, I didn't work that accident. That was Marvin's. He handled it."

"I understand, but do you remember hearing anything about someone else being with that guy that night? I mean, someone had to drive him to that house he robbed. He worked at a Pizza Hut in Canton, and his car was found parked there the morning after the accident."

"Dale told me some couple's gonna pay you five grand if you can prove Wells was murdered. Is that what this is 'bout?"

"Yeah. I've been looking for any loose ends regarding Wells, and the more I poke around into that '88 accident, the looser it gets."

"Well, I've told ya all I know. You could try askin' Marvin."

"What about the guy who was sheriff back then? Bryant."

"He died ten or so years ago."

"Is there anyone else who might know something? Another deputy who worked back then?"

"I don't know. Let me think on it and get back to ya."

I hung up and rounded the curve near Floppy's garage. Then I started crying.

* * *

My Mercedes sat just out from one of the open garage bays. It looked like it had been in a riot. Every window was smashed, and the door panels and hood were covered in dents.

"Looks like somebody used it for battin' practice," Floppy said as he emerged from the garage.

"What happened?" I asked.

"It was like that this mornin' when I pulled into Dew-Dads. It was the only vehicle there. The bar was locked up, weren't nobody there. You got insurance, don't ya?"

"Yeah." I pulled out my phone and called Dale, no answer. I called Earl, no answer. "I got to go, Floppy. I need to file a report on this. Don't do anything to it until I can get someone from the insurance company to look at it."

"Don't you worry," Floppy said. "I'll put her in the garage, keep her safe and dry."

"Thanks," I said. Then I used my phone to take photos of the damage.

I was about to head out when Floppy said, "Hang on a minute. I got somethin' to show you. Wait right there."

Floppy disappeared inside the garage and then reappeared a moment later carrying a U-shaped device that appeared to be made out of various pieces of black plastic pipe.

"What is that?" I said.

"You'll see. Now what I did is I took some old pipe I had layin' 'round, some straight pipe, these elbows here, a couple of reducers here, this end cap here, and connected them all with PVC cement. Then I got an old bar-b-que grill sparker I had and mounted it here." Floppy pointed to a red button peeking out of one of the pieces of pipe. "Now c'mon, follow me."

We walked around to the back of the garage to where Vicky was parked near a wooden picnic table. On top of the table sat a can of hairspray, a long iron rod, and a piece of black pipe about two feet long and maybe an inch and a half in diameter. Floppy picked up the pipe, and I could see it was threaded on one end. He screwed it onto the other device, which made it now resemble a "J" rather than a "U." He then reached into his coveralls and pulled out a golf ball.

"You've got to be joking," I said.

Floppy grinned as he shoved the golf ball into the open end of the long piece of pipe. He grabbed the iron rod off the table and tamped the golf ball down deep into what I now realized was the barrel. Then he unscrewed the cap on the short end of the device and sprayed the inside of the short section of pipe with the hairspray. He quickly recapped it, then held the contraption like a rifle and aimed it toward a rusty water heater that sat thirty or so yards in the distance. He pushed the red button and there was a low thump, then a loud clang as the golf ball crashed into the side of the water heater.

Floppy looked at me and nodded. "Told ya it weren't crazy. It ain't all that accurate, but give me some time with it, and I bet I could knock a beer can off a fence post at fifty paces."

I felt numb. I didn't know if I was still in shock from seeing my car or if Floppy's invention was making me reassess my theories regarding the death of Prentiss Wells.

Floppy demonstrated the golf-ball gun a couple of more times, and then I asked if he'd drive me to the sheriff's department. My head was spinning, and I'd fought with Sally's transmission enough for the day.

"Kato at your service," Floppy said.

After Floppy rolled my Mercedes into the garage and locked up, we piled into Vicky and took off toward Waynesville.

"So did you go talk to that Ritter man's sister at the address I got for ya?" Floppy asked.

I gave him a full rundown, maybe because I needed to go over things again or maybe because I didn't want to hear about golf-ball guns for the entire twenty-five-minute drive.

By the time I finished, we were pulling into the parking lot of the Haywood County Sheriff's Office. When we parked, Floppy turned to me and said, "What if that rich couple did it?"

"What are you talking about?"

"That rich couple that hired you to find out who killed Prentiss Wells. What if they's the ones who killed him?"

"Floppy, that's ridiculous. They're helping me investigate. They're going to pay me five grand if I find who did it."

Floppy raised a finger. "I saw this movie once 'bout this real rich man who thought he was smarter than everybody else. He thought he could pull off the perfect murder and not get caught. So he killed a man and made it look like an accident. He didn't have no reason to kill him other than to see if he could do it and get away with it. And he did. But that weren't 'nuff for him—he wanted to outsmart the police. So he killed another man and was sure to make it look like murder this time so the police would have to investigate. They couldn't figure it out, so the man started sendin' anonymous letters to the police, tauntin' them with clues they'd missed and such. It was just a game to him. But he slipped up, and they ended up catchin' him. Now who played in that? I think it was that man played in that funny movie where Bigfoot moved in with a family and they all got along. Or maybe it was that one where—"

"Floppy. Stop. The Roths did not murder Prentiss Wells. I'm still not a hundred percent sure anyone murdered him. It could have happened just like the guys who were golfing with him said. It could have been an accident."

Floppy shrugged. "Are we gonna do that thing tonight?"

"Yes, at nine thirty. Now wait here. I'll be back soon."

* * *

I entered the lobby and saw a blueish-gray bouffant hovering over the counter. It belonged to Barbara, the sheriff's department gatekeeper. When I approached, she gave me a thin smile and asked if I'd read her latest blog entry. I'd looked at Barbara's food blog exactly one time, for all of two minutes, and that was more than enough. Recipes for chicken 'n' dumplings and broccoli casserole and country fried steak were not my thing.

"I'll check it out when I get home," I said. "Is Dale around?"

"He's out on patrol."

"What about Earl?"

"He's on patrol too."

I'd taken a chance one of them would be there. I really didn't want to talk to any of the other deputies about my car. I thanked Barbara and turned to leave.

"Hold on just a second," Barbara said as she picked up a telephone receiver and put it to her ear. She pushed a button on the phone console, and a moment later said, "Sheriff Byrd. You told me to let you know if Mr. Reed ever came in."

I waved my hand quickly in front of Barbara's face. "No. No, no, no, no, no. No."

"Well, he's here. Standing in front of me. He was looking for Dale or Earl." Barbara stared at me as her thin smile evolved into an ear-to-ear grin. "Yes, sir." Barbara replaced the phone receiver. "The sheriff will see you now."

"Thanks a lot," I said.

"You know the way, don't you?"

I did, so I walked around the counter and through a door marked "Private." I strolled down a long hallway, past a couple of conference rooms, then saw Sheriff Byrd's door standing wide open. The old man was sitting behind his desk, gazing at a computer monitor. He'd always reminded me of a basset hound. Droopy eyes, droopy ears, droopy jowls. His white hair was cut short and parted to the side, and even from the hallway I could see the comb marks in it. When Byrd noticed me, he pointed to a chair on the other side of his desk.

"How are you, son?" he said as I took a seat.

"Don't call me 'son,' and I won't call you 'Royce.'"

Byrd grinned. "Why are you here?"

"My vehicle was vandalized last night. It's practically totaled. I need to file a report."

"Any idea who did it?"

"Yeah, the Steel Stooges. They put a shotgun shell on my welcome mat a couple of nights ago."

Byrd's grin evaporated, and his jowls dropped below the top of his shirt collar. "I'm not happy those people have returned to this area."

"That makes two of us."

"You know, maybe you should head back down to the Lowcountry, and lay low, as it were."

"You know I've got some enemies down there as well."

Byrd scoffed. "Who? Oh you mean the entire Charleston Police Department? You uncovered a drug ring run by dirty cops. You'd think they'd be thankful."

"Law enforcement organizations don't like to be embarrassed."

Byrd held a pained smile. He knew I wasn't just referring to Charleston. "So what's this I hear about you investigating the death of Prentiss Wells?" He pointed a finger at me. "If you have information that a crime has been committed, you are obligated to share that information."

"I have no such information. But you shouldn't worry. Dale told me someone called here yesterday who knows the identity of the mystery golfer."

Byrd stared hard at me. I knew he hated that Dale kept me in the loop about departmental affairs. "That person is looking for a reward. Mr. Wells's son has refused to offer one. So, if that's what you're after . . ."

"Do you remember the accident Wells was involved with in '88?"

Byrd leaned back in his chair. "I do. But I wasn't sheriff at the time."

"There's something weird about that accident. I think Wells might have been at fault, and I think somebody knows that."

Byrd sat silent. "Thirty years is a long time to wait for revenge," he finally said.

Through Byrd's office window I could see the parking lot. Floppy was sitting on Vicky's hood.

"But then again," Byrd continued, "you've always had an overactive imagination."

I smiled. "You don't believe I'm still searching for lost gold, do you, Sheriff?"

Byrd didn't respond, and we stared at each other for an uncomfortable moment. Finally I said, "I don't guess you'd let me look at the paperwork regarding that accident."

"You guessed right. Now you bring me some evidence of malfeasance regarding the matter, and I'll review the paperwork myself. But it's going to take more than you having a hunch."

I started to speak, but Byrd abruptly turned toward the window. Floppy was standing just on the other side of it.

"Hey, Sheriff," Floppy said, his voice muffled by the glass.

Byrd raised a hand, then Floppy looked at me and said, "I gotta get back. I got an oil change in thirty minutes."

I stood up and looked down at Byrd. "Always a pleasure, Sheriff."

I was stepping through the doorway when Byrd said, "Hold on. That accident, from '88? I was elected the following spring, and the deputy who worked that incident retired just before I started." Byrd paused. "Funny thing is he wasn't scheduled to retire for another two years."

I heard Earl's voice in my head. *"That accident really tore Marvin up. He seemed more upset about it than Wells did."*

"Why are you telling me this?" I asked.

Byrd grinned. "Just some fodder for your overactive imagination."

* * *

We were almost back to Floppy's garage when my phone buzzed.

"What's up, dickless?" Dale said when I answered.

"My car is totaled," I said.

"What are you talkin' 'bout? The tires are flat."

"Floppy picked it up from Dew-Dads this morning. Somebody went to town on it last night after we left." I gave Dale a rundown of the damage.

"Shit," he said. "I'll make the report and get ya a copy for insurance."

"What are we going to do about this? This is crazy."

"Well, until we catch 'em doin' somethin', we're just gonna have to try and catch 'em doin' somethin'. Does Peckerhead have anythin' you can drive?"

"Yeah. Sally."

Dale laughed so hard I had to hold the phone away from my ear.

"Listen, meet me at Bearwaters in Canton at six," Dale said. "I'll buy. Even the food."

26

Bearwaters is a small brewery and taproom located right next to the Pigeon River in downtown Canton. I arrived at a few minutes after six. Dale's patrol car was in the parking lot next to a shiny gray Mercedes S-Class sedan. I walked around to the front of the building, which faces the river, and immediately noticed Dale's giant orange sweatshirt. He was sitting at a table on the patio. Jimmy Fletcher was sitting across from him.

I acknowledged them with a wave, then stepped inside. At the counter I ordered a Papertown Pilsner and told the guy who poured it to put it on the tab of the man sitting outside who resembled a giant pumpkin. He knew exactly who I was talking about.

When I joined Dale and Jimmy at their table, Jimmy raised his half-full beer glass and tapped it against mine.

"We were just talking about the time Dale and I grew our own pot with some seeds a buddy gave me," Jimmy said. "How old were we? Sixteen? Seventeen?"

Dale laughed.

"We finally grew one plant," Jimmy continued. "We cared for that thing like it was a newborn baby. But we didn't let it grow for very long. Once a few leaves popped out, we took them and dried them out on the roof of Junebug's carport. Our buddy Craig came over, and Dale made a bong out of an empty Coke can. We smoked every bit of that pot and didn't feel a thing. Except for Craig—he was stoned out of his gourd."

Dale was still chuckling. He looked at me. "We found out later it was fuckin' hibiscus."

Jimmy slapped me hard on the back, then drained his beer and stood up. "Another round?"

Dale handed Jimmy his empty glass.

"I'm good," I said.

Jimmy walked across the patio. When he stepped inside the taproom, I turned to Dale and said, "What's he doing here?"

"He messaged me on Facebook sayin' we should catch up. So here we are. He told me you talked to him at the golf course in Waynesville this afternoon."

"Yeah, I'm telling you, there's something weird going on with this Wells thing. Last month Wells suspected Rex Pinland of taking money from the firm's escrow account."

"Really?"

"Yeah, Wells went to an accounting firm to see what they would charge to audit the books. But then he never went back."

"I guess he was wrong. If Pinland was stealin', he'd of fired him."

"Not if Pinland had something to hold over him."

Dale's face scrunched. "Like what?"

"I'm not sure, but it might have to do with that accident way back Wells was involved in."

The door to Bearwaters opened, and Jimmy appeared, holding two beers. For the next hour or so we drank and shared baskets of fries covered in chili and cheese while I listened to Jimmy and Dale exchange stories from their teenage years.

When Jimmy finished off his third beer, he turned to me and said, "So, having any luck finding that sniper armed with a golf-ball gun?" He laughed and Dale gave me a curious look.

"What do you think about that?" Jimmy said to Dale, his words just a tiny bit slurred.

"I think you've turned into a lightweight since high school. Three's your limit."

"No," Jimmy said. "Not that. This crazy idea that Prentiss was murdered."

Dale chuckled. "Yeah, I think it's pretty crazy."

My two beers had given me a little courage. I turned to Jimmy and looked him dead in the eye. "I'm going to find out who did it." I then pointed to Dale. "And then he's going to arrest them."

Jimmy started giggling. "I'm just messing around," he said. "Don't take me seriously after three beers." Jimmy glanced at his Rolex, then stood up and gave Dale's shoulder a squeeze. "I love ya, buddy," he said. "Let's do this again soon."

Dale slapped Jimmy's arm. "Be safe, Double F."

Jimmy gave me a nod then walked toward the parking lot. It was nearly dark and getting a little chilly.

"What's he talkin' 'bout?" Dale said. "Golf-ball gun?"

"I'm just trying to stir things up. See what happens. The golf-ball gun thing was kind of a joke, but Floppy's made one. He showed it to me today. Put a big dent in a water heater with it."

Dale rolled his eyes.

"What about the person who called yesterday saying they knew the identity of the mystery golfer?" I asked.

"They called back today and talked to Byrd. Douchebag Brett won't offer a reward, said it'd bring all kinds of people out of the woodwork looking to cash in. But that ain't the reason—he's just a cheap fuck. But they said they'd talk to the person anyway and try to convince him to turn hisself in."

A low rumble suddenly went through the air, and Dale and I both turned toward the bridge that crosses the river. Three motorcycles were headed in our direction. We watched them closely as they passed Bearwaters and vanished around the side of the building. A moment later we could hear the rumble coming from the parking lot. Not long after that three guys in jeans and black T-shirts approached the patio. The guys had tattoos on their arms and necks. One guy was bald, and the other two looked like they used the same hairstylist who specialized in the long and stringy look.

Dale stood up and walked over to them. I kept my seat. It would take a lot more than two beers to give me enough bravado to confront guys like that. Although back in my Xanax-popping days, I might have gone over and punched them in the face.

Dale's conversation with the bikers seemed intense but controlled. After a couple of minutes, Dale took a step back and spread his arms. The bikers all nodded at him as if an understanding had been reached, then walked into the taproom.

"Well," I said when Dale wiggled himself back into his seat.

"They claim they ain't with the Stooges. But I told them if they happen to run into anyone from that gang, to give 'em a message from me."

"What message?"

"You don't wanna know."

"You're going to get us all killed."

Dale finished his beer and slammed the glass down on the table. "I'm beatin' the ground to startle the snakes. That's whatcha do. Now c'mon—let's go over to Long Branch, see if any of them fuckers are there tonight."

I didn't want to go to Long Branch, for multiple reasons. "I can't," I said. "I've got plans."

"You hangin' out with them swingers again?"

"Yeah. Now listen, how well do you know Bill Rhinehart?"

"The superintendent at Springdale?"

"Yeah, he said he's known you since kindergarten."

"We went to school together. But we didn't really hang out. We're buddies on Facebook, but that's 'bout it? Why?"

"I don't know. It's probably nothing. But I found out Bill Rhinehart knew Adam Ritter, the guy Wells hit and killed back in '88. Well, actually I'm not sure if they knew each other, but I do know they met once."

"So? Most of the people in this town have probably met at least once."

I shrugged. "I know. Small town. Probably just a coincidence."

My phone buzzed, but it wasn't a call; it was a Facebook notification, something I almost never receive. I tapped the screen and saw that Brett Wells had accepted my friend request. I scrolled though his photos and found the one I was looking for. I zoomed in, then turned the screen toward Dale, who sneered at the sight of Brett. "What do I wanna see this shit for?" he barked.

"That's Brett and his partner," I said.

"Whadd'ya mean?"

"His romantic partner. They're getting married this summer."

Dale stared at the screen like it was a crystal ball showing him the past as well as the future. After a few seconds of silence, he turned to me and said, "No shit."

* * *

Dale went inside to pay while I sipped the last of my beer. I still had my phone in my hand, so I tapped on the email icon. There was one unread message.

Davis,

Sorry for the delayed response and sorry to be the bearer of bad news. It doesn't look like the CPD is going to settle. Dealing with them is slow going. When I know more, I'll pass it along. Again, I'm sorry. But don't give up hope. I'll be in touch soon.

Allison

I hate when people use the word *literally* to refer to something that didn't literally happen, as in *"My head literally exploded."* But sitting there on that patio, staring at that email, I knew I was literally screwed. I had no money, no idea how to get any money, and I had bills coming due, not the least of which was a rent payment to an ornery deputy.

I glanced up and saw Dale step through the door and out onto the patio. He gave me a wave and headed off toward the parking lot. I pulled out my wallet and dug a small plastic bag out from behind my debit card. The emergency Xanax. I stared through the plastic at the little white pill and knew if I swallowed it, I would soon be enveloped in a comforting numbness. I also knew I'd go back to the cabin and take another one. And then another. And the chain I'd broken would quickly become reattached. A chain I might not be able to break again.

* * *

I went inside to use the restroom. I peed, washed my hands, and checked myself in the mirror. I looked exhausted, which I was.

The door handle rattled, and when I opened it, one of the stringy-haired bikers was staring at me. I froze for a moment, then stepped by him and hobbled outside. On the patio the other two bikers were sitting at a table near the river. They didn't seem to notice me.

Out in the parking lot, I saw the three motorcycles, but Dale's patrol car was gone, as was the silver Mercedes, which I now figured belonged to Jimmy. I opened Sally's door and bent down to retrieve the screwdriver from under the driver's seat. After the incident in Elizabeth's office, I'd learned not to keep it in my pocket. I grabbed the screwdriver just as something crashed into my back. It was as if a telephone pole had fallen on me. Another crash followed, and all of the air in my lungs flew out of my mouth. An arm reached around my neck, and I was jerked up onto my feet. Whoever had me was strong. The arm was like a thick vine around my neck. The pressure increased, and I knew I only had a few seconds before I would be out. I reached up and thrust the screwdriver behind my head. I did it again and again, jabbing as quickly as I could. It finally hit something soft, and there was a loud howl, and then the pressure released. I dropped down to my knees, then onto my face.

27

When I woke up, I was lying on a stretcher in the back of an ambulance. The doors were open, and I could see we were in the Bearwaters parking lot.

"How you feelin'?" a young EMT asked.

"I'm not sure yet," I said.

"Looks like you just got the wind knocked out of you. You'll be okay."

"What about the other guy?"

The EMT shrugged.

I sat up and felt a dull pain in the middle of my back. "Can I go?" I asked.

"Help yourself."

I stepped out and saw two patrol cars, lights flashing. Several people were standing on the patio, beers in hand, enjoying the unexpected entertainment. I looked around the parking lot. The motorcycles were gone.

I was limping toward the patio when Deputy Mike appeared out of the crowd. "You okay?" he asked.

"I think so. Did you catch the guy?"

"No. No one saw it happen. One of the workers went out to the lot to smoke and saw you laying in the dirt. Called 911. Is anything missing?"

I reached in my pockets. My phone, wallet, and cabin key were where they should be. I didn't bother opening the wallet to see if my cash was still there. If someone needed three dollars that bad, they were welcome to it.

"Dale and Earl are inside interviewing people," Mike said. "Dale's in a mood."

We reached the door to the taproom, and Mike opened it for me. Inside I saw Earl sitting at the table talking to the guy who'd poured my beer earlier. Dale was on the other side of the room, talking to a young couple. When he saw me, he came over.

"The fuck?" he said.

"This has got to end, man, or I'm going to have to go back to Charleston and hide."

"Oh, it's gonna end. I guarantee your ass that. Now tell me what happened."

I told Dale about going into the bathroom and the biker standing at the door when I came out. "The other two were sitting at a table on the patio when I left."

"We've talked to everybody here. No one can say for sure that all three of them bikers were in view durin' the time you were attacked. But they sure left soon after."

"I hurt the guy," I said. "I had a screwdriver in my hand when he grabbed me."

"A screwdriver? Why?"

"To start Sally."

Dale rolled his eyes. "Jesus Christ."

"I'm certain I stabbed the guy with it. Maybe in the face or the neck, but I got him."

"Good," Dale said.

I looked at my watch. "I've gotta go."

"Well don't go back to the cabin. Stay at Daddy's."

"No. It's okay. I'll ask the Roths if I can stay at their place tonight."

Dale raised his eyebrows.

"They're not swingers," I shouted.

* * *

Dale said he'd drive me, and when we got in his patrol car, I pointed at Sally and said, "You think it'll be safe here overnight? I don't want it to get vandalized like my car did."

Dale scoffed. "Vandalized? How would you be able to fuckin' tell?"

We were pulling out of the Bearwaters parking lot just as a large white van pulled in. Fern Matthews was in the passenger seat. Her eyes widened when she saw us. I waved as Dale punched the accelerator. Fifteen minutes later we pulled into the Roths' driveway, and Dale squawked the siren.

"Is that necessary?" I said.

The front door of the house opened, and Vance appeared in the doorway. As usual, he looked a million bucks, now sporting a slim gray suit over a black turtleneck. A second later Lana joined him. She had on a short green dress and white heels. Her legs seemed a mile long.

"Holy shit," Dale said. "No wonder you're up here all the time."

"Wait here a minute." I got out and shuffled over to the Roths. They both looked concerned.

"You're moving a little slower than usual," Vance said.

I heard a door slam and turned to see Dale approaching. When he was standing next to me, I introduced him.

"It is a pleasure to meet you," Vance said with an enthusiastic shake of Dale's hand.

When Dale shook Lana's hand, she said, "My, aren't you a big one."

Dale blushed but thankfully didn't respond.

"Perhaps you would care to join us for dinner one evening," Vance said. "Lana and I would love to hear your version of the Graveyard Fields story."

Before Dale could answer, I jumped in. "Listen. Something happened tonight." I explained what was going on with Rusty Baker and the Steel Stooges. "I hate to impose, but I was wondering if I could stay here for a night or two? Just until the sheriff's department can get a handle on this thing."

Vance and Lana looked at each other for a few seconds before Lana gave Vance a tiny nod.

"Of course," Vance said to me. "We have a top-notch security system. You'll be safe here."

I thanked the Roths and told them I'd be back soon.

* * *

Dale and I flew up 276 as AC/DC's "Hell's Bells" poured out of the stereo.

"So what do you think about the Roths?" I asked.

"The wife is hot, but why's the man gotta be so snooty? I hate when people talk the way he does."

"What do you mean?"

Dale sat up straight and pursed his lips. "*Perhaps you would care to join us for dinner*'? Why ya gotta say *perhaps*? Just say fuckin' *maybe*."

* * *

In the clearing below the cabin, we repeated the act of two nights prior. Dale got the shotgun out of the trunk, and I followed closely behind him to the kitchen door. I stayed put while Dale gave the cabin a check. When he announced it was clear, I grabbed a duffel bag and stuffed it with some clothes and toiletries and the bottle of Xanax from the medicine cabinet. In the living room I unplugged the laptop from the modem and put it and the charging cable into the duffel.

"Ready?" Dale asked.

I looked around. I didn't have much else to take.

I was headed for the door when I abruptly spun around and limped quickly into the bedroom and on into the bathroom. I pulled the Xanax bottle out of the duffel bag and poured the contents into the toilet. I did the same with the emergency pill from my wallet, then flushed. Not the best way to dispose of pharmaceuticals, but effective when you're fighting temptation.

* * *

When we arrived back at the Roths', I asked Dale what he was going to do.

"I told ya, I'm beatin' the ground to startle the snakes," he said.

"Well, try not to get bit in the process. Okay?"

Dale nodded and I hopped out and made my way slowly up to the door. Vance opened it just as Dale was peeling out of the driveway.

"Welcome home," Vance said as he glanced at my duffel bag.

"I really wouldn't mind a stiff G and T," I said.

In the living room, with said gin and tonic, I gave the Roths a more detailed account of what had happened at Bearwaters. "I really appreciate you letting me stay here. Right now the cabin's a bit too secluded for my comfort level."

I proceeded to give the Roths a full account of my conversations with Brett Wells and Roberta Allen, including Roberta's revelation that Bill Rhinehart and her brother Adam knew each other.

"Interesting," Vance said. "You should talk with Bill again."

"I will. Tomorrow. I'm also going to dig around and see what I can find out about the LLC Prentiss was using to send the Ritters' checks. Oh, here—I took a photo of one." I pulled out my phone and showed the Roths the picture of the canceled check.

"Philos Adelphos Dikaios," Lana said. "'Love of humanity and justice for all.'"

"You speak Latin?"

Lana shrugged. "I know a few phrases."

"Maybe whoever was with Adam that night saw what happened. And maybe saw that Wells was at fault. I spoke to the sheriff today. He said Marvin retired not long after that accident, even though he still had another two years left to work."

I gave the Roths a rundown of my conversation with Jimmy Fletcher.

"Now, Davis, I believe it is imperative you speak with Freddy," Vance said.

"It's imperative I do a lot of stuff," I said, a bit louder than I intended. "Sorry. Just a long day, and it's still going. And I'm frustrated. I've got a lot of information but can't figure out how it fits together. Or even if it's supposed to. I mean, the medical examiner says Wells was hit and killed by a golf ball. So are we just spinning our wheels?"

"If this were a mystery novel, I'd say we'd be approaching the third act," Vance said. "Have patience, Davis. All will become clear. It always does."

Lana tapped the screen of her phone and turned to Vance. "We should get changed."

After they left, I stood up and paced around the living room, then wandered over to the cabinets and shelves that lined one wall. I tried to decipher some of the signatures on the encased golf balls and picked up one of the framed photos of the Roths. They were sitting on a sun-kissed patio, the Eiffel Tower off in the distance. I smiled at imagining me and Elizabeth in a similar scenario.

I moved over to the wall of books and ran my finger over some of the spines. I wondered for a moment if pulling on a particular book would cause the wall to swing open and reveal a hidden passage to some secret lair. I grabbed a Harlan Coben novel, but the wall didn't budge. I was looking at the author photo on the back of the book and wondering how much hair I'd have to lose before I threw in the towel and just shaved my head, when the Roths walked into the room, decked out in cargo pants, hiking boots, flannel shirts over turtlenecks, and thin black jackets with Gore-Tex logos on the sleeves.

"We're ready," Lana said.

I followed the Roths into the kitchen, where Lana pulled three plastic tumblers out of a cabinet. "Roadies," she said.

Armed with gin and tonics, the three of us climbed into Brutus and headed out.

* * *

Dot Davidson greeted us like long-lost family, giving each of us a powerful hug. "This is so exciting," she said. When she noticed our drinks, she clapped her hands. "Ooh, I'll join you."

The Roths and I took seats in the living room, and a moment later Dot entered, holding a plastic wineglass full of what looked like rosé.

At 9:35 the doorbell rang. When I opened the door, I almost burst out laughing. Floppy was wearing a skin-tight black wetsuit that came all the way up over his head. His face was framed in a tight oval of black neoprene; he was wearing thick goggles, and above those a headlamp stuck out from his forehead like the eye of a cyclops. An air tank was attached to his back, and the regulator dangled from a tube draped across his shoulder. In one hand he held a pair of flippers, and in the other a white mesh sack.

"I'm ready," he said with a big grin.

I heard someone clear their throat, and I turned to see Vance, Lana, and Dot standing behind me. I made the introductions and was grateful Floppy said nothing more than "Howdy."

Dot slipped on a pair of garden clogs sitting by the door, and said, "Shall we go?"

She led us around the side of her house, where she stopped, pulled out her phone, and tapped the screen a few times. Suddenly a series of floodlights secured to the corners of the house clicked on, illuminating the narrow gravel walkway. It was a clear night with a half-moon, and the water in the pond rippled in an eerie blue hue.

Floppy sat down by the pond's edge and reached into the mesh sack. He pulled out two yellow walkie-talkies, both labeled waterproof. He turned them both on and handed one to me. "Good thinking," I said.

"Now what is it I'm lookin' for?" Floppy said as he wrangled the flippers onto his feet.

"Anything that doesn't belong. Anything curious. Anything out of the ordinary." I pointed across the water near the point where Dot had seen the flashlight and where Lana had found the plastic knob. "Focus on that section over there first."

A few seconds later we watched Floppy slip into the murky water and slowly disappear under the surface. I could just make out the light from his headlamp traveling through the water. Then the light vanished. An anxious couple of minutes passed before Floppy's head poked out in the dead center of the pond. The walkie-talkie in my hand crackled to life: "This is Floppy. Come back."

I pushed the transmit button. "What is it? Did you find something?"

"They's a buttload of golf balls in here. This place is a gold mine."

"Forget the golf balls. Go over to the section I pointed out. Search there. Grab anything that doesn't belong. Except golf balls."

"Ten-four."

With that, Floppy disappeared again. I glanced at Lana. She was grinning wildly. "I love this," she said.

We waited. And waited. And then waited some more. As the minutes passed, I became convinced my plan was nothing more than a fool's errand. But at least Vance, Lana, and Dot seemed to be enjoying themselves.

Suddenly, a short, high-pitched wail rang out somewhere in the trees below the pond. The sound quickly deepened into a low rumble. "That's the pump station kicking on," Dot said. "They must be irrigating the course tonight. Tell your man to stay away from the intake pipe."

I sent Floppy the message over the walkie-talkie, but when he didn't respond, I realized he couldn't hear me while he was submerged. There was a splash, and when I looked across the water, I saw Floppy's headlamp shining in my direction.

"Hooooeeeeey!" Floppy said over the walkie-talkie. "They's a big ol' pipe down there almost sucked my flipper in. Good thing it's got a grate over it."

"That's the intake pipe for the irrigation pumps," I said. "Stay away from it."

"Ten-four."

The headlamp disappeared under the water, and the waiting began anew. I didn't like that someone was out irrigating the golf course. If they happened to stop by the pond, we would all have some explaining to do since we were all trespassing.

Ten minutes passed and no one said a word. We sipped our drinks and stared hypnotically at the shimmering pond. I was to the point of telling Floppy to give up the next time he broke the surface.

"Uh-oh," Dot said.

I turned to her. "What is it?"

She cupped her hand behind her ear and listened intently. I couldn't hear anything except the rumbling from the pumps. "Golf cart," she said. "Someone must be coming to check the pump station."

The four of us hustled up the gravel path, then leaned back against the house. Dot used her phone to turn off the floodlights, and the shadow from the house wrapped us in almost complete darkness. We all kept our eyes on the pond, and I tried to send Floppy a message via ESP: *Stay under the water. Stay under the water.*

A golf cart with two bright headlights appeared in the section of the sixteenth fairway visible between the clearing in the trees. It was headed in our direction, and the headlights shone over the top of the water. The cart turned, then disappeared behind the trees, but we stayed put. A minute or two passed, and the sounds of the irrigation pumps died. A moment later they cranked up again.

I started to head back toward the pond, but Dot grabbed my shoulder. "Wait a minute, hon," she said.

Soon the golf cart reappeared in the fairway. It passed by the bunker, then turned away from us and kept moving. I followed the lights until they were out of sight.

"Now it's safe," Dot said, raising her phone close to her face.

"Leave the floodlights off," I whispered. "Just in case."

"I'll get a flashlight out of Brutus," Vance said.

Lana, Dot, and I used the lights on our phones to illuminate the way back to our position at the edge of the pond. Vance soon joined us, holding a black foot-long metal Maglite.

I started worrying about Floppy. I didn't know how long he'd been submerged. Then I worried he might have gotten tied up in the intake pipe when the pumps stopped, then quickly restarted.

Suddenly Floppy's headlamp appeared on the far side of the pond. He wasn't in the section I'd asked him to search. He was directly in front of the clearing in the trees. I could see the outline of the fairway bunker behind him.

My walkie-talkie hissed. "Found somethin'," Floppy said. "It's pretty out of the ordinary if ya ask me."

"Okay. Bring it in."

Vance, Lana, Dot, and myself all exchanged excited looks. Vance patted me on the back, and Lana clinked my plastic tumbler against hers. But I didn't want to get too optimistic. I wasn't sure what Floppy's idea of 'out of the ordinary' was. He might emerge from the pond holding a dead turtle or a broken fishing rod.

Floppy swam across the pond toward us. When he got close to the edge of the water, I extended a hand, but Floppy waved it away. He plopped down in the shallow water and pulled off his flippers. When he stood up, he held the mesh bag high above him. It sagged with the weight of whatever was in it. "I got fifty-four golf balls—can you believe that? And I betcha there's a hundred more in there."

"I told you to ignore the golf balls," I said.

"I figured since I was already geared up and in the water, I might as well multitask."

I bit my tongue. "What else did you find?"

Floppy lowered the bag and reached inside it. Then, with his other hand, he tugged on a thin cord threaded around the bag's opening, basically cinching his right hand inside. He stepped over and held the bag in front of us. Vance trained his flashlight on it. Floppy opened the bag a tiny bit and slowly began pushing a golf ball out of the small, cinched hole in the bag's top. When half of the ball was visible Floppy stopped. It was like he was a magician performing a trick and being careful not to reveal its secret.

"Okay," I said. "It's a golf ball. What's out of the ordinary about it?"

Floppy grinned and held us in suspense for a few seconds. I wondered if the golf ball had a smiley face on it and what that would mean, if anything.

Suddenly Floppy jerked his hand out of the bag. He was holding a carpenter's hammer. It had a rubber grip, and a claw for removing nails. But the hammer's face had been modified. It was covered with a golf ball. We all stared at it, dumbfounded.

"That's the murder weapon," I said.

Lana turned to me and smiled. "No shit, Sherlock."

Vance put his hand on my shoulder. "Welcome to the third act, Detective."

28

In Dot's driveway I made her promise not to say anything to anyone about what had just happened. She promised to keep it under wraps, but the smile she gave me while she said it didn't fill me with confidence. She went inside her house and returned with two clean hand towels. Floppy took one and wiped off his face. I took the other and pulled Floppy aside. "You go to flea markets and thrift stores; have you ever seen something like this?" I said, holding up the hammer.

Floppy shook his head.

"Can you think of any reason this hammer would be in that pond?"

"Ya mean besides somebody throwin' it in there after hittin' that Prentiss man with it?"

I nodded and Floppy scratched his neoprene-covered head. "I guess it could be a joke thing somebody made. Like a funny trophy or a gag gift. Give it to somebody who likes gettin' hammered while playin' golf. Get it? Hammered? Like gettin' drunk?" Floppy punched my arm. "That's a good one, ain't it?"

"How would somebody make something like this?"

"Well, they bored a hole in the golf ball, and then they probably used some kinda high-strength adhesive to secure it over the hammer's face. If you look real close right there, you can see a clear seam 'round where the ball's attached. That's some sort of adhesive. The hardest part would be borin' a hole in the ball big 'nuff to put the hammer's face into it. Probably need a drill press to do somethin' like that. But I guess you could do it if you just had a sturdy vise and a good drill with a big ol' bit. But it'd be a whole lot easier with a drill press."

"What is that? A drill press?"

"You've seen the one in my shop, in the back by the plasma cutter. It's skinny, yellow, 'bout as tall as I am."

I had a vague idea of the machine Floppy was referring to. "Okay. Listen, good job finding this, but don't tell a soul about it until I can get it to Dale."

Floppy again mimed zipping his lips. Then he said, "Hey, as long as I'm here, I'm gonna get the rest of them golf balls. It's like free money."

Before leaving, I told Floppy what had happened to me at Bearwaters and that Sally was still in the parking lot. He seemed equally concerned for both me and Sally.

The Roths and I said goodnight to Floppy and Dot and then climbed into Brutus. I sat in the back, the towel-covered hammer in the seat next to me.

Lana spun around to face me. "When did you first realize there might be something in that pond? Was it when you found that plastic knob?"

"You found that, remember?" I said. "I must've walked right over it."

Lana giggled. "That's right. Good thing I was there."

* * *

Back at the Roths' house, Vance and Lana wanted to a have a gin and tonic-fueled debriefing session, but I told them I just wanted a cold glass of water, a hot shower, and a warm bed. I grabbed my duffel bag, and Vance led me upstairs to a guest bedroom that was bigger than the cabin's kitchen, living room, and deck put together.

"Bathroom is through there," Vance said, pointing across a king-size four-poster bed to a doorway that opened into a room full of marble and chrome. "You'll find fresh towels as well as a variety of toiletries."

Lana entered and slinked her arm around Vance's waist. "There are some robes in the closet," she said. "Help yourself."

"Fine work today," Vance said with a solemn nod. "Damn fine work."

"Oh," Lana said. "The gift. I almost forgot."

"I'll fetch it," Vance said as he turned and hurried out of the room. A moment later he returned, carrying a large package wrapped in silver paper, with an elaborate white bow on the top. He handed it to me.

Lana clapped her hands. "Open it."

I removed the wrapping to reveal a brown box with the word *Burberry* stamped on the top. I suddenly felt nauseous. Inside the box was what I feared, a tan trench coat with belt, epaulets, and tortoiseshell buttons.

"Try it on," Lana said.

"I should probably shower before putting this on," I said. "But thanks. This is great."

Vance pointed at my chest. "You're a fine detective, Davis."

Lana pulled Vance toward the door. They stepped through, and as Lana leaned in to close it, she winked and said, "Sweet dreams."

Whatever the Roths were used to paying for water each month, I probably increased it by twenty percent. I stood in the enormous marble shower and let the hot water cover my body until my skin was the color and texture of an overcooked hot dog.

A wide shelf built into the shower held an array of small unopened bottles, just like at a hotel. I used everything.

I put on underwear and a T-shirt and slipped on my new, expensive trench coat. I stepped back into the bathroom and stared at myself in the full-length mirror. I didn't know whether to laugh or cry.

* * *

The next morning I awoke to a gentle tapping on the guest room door. I pulled the sheets all the way up to just under my chin and said, "Come in."

"Good morning dear," Lana said as she pushed the door open and stuck her head in. "Breakfast in thirty minutes. Vance and I have an appointment in Asheville this morning."

I showered to try to loosen the muscles in my back and again used every shampoo, conditioner, body wash, body oil, and moisturizer available. I threw on some clothes and went downstairs, where I found Vance sitting at the kitchen island, drinking an espresso and working on a crossword on his iPad. The top button of his pale blue dress shirt was undone, and a green paisley ascot billowed out from his neck like a psychedelic cloud.

"Hello, handsome," Lana said, entering the kitchen. She kissed me on the cheek, then sniffed my neck. "You smell like you just robbed a Sephora." She laughed and stepped over to an expensive-looking machine sitting on one of the kitchen counters. "What kind of coffee would you like?"

"Black and weak, if you have it," I said.

Shortly, the three of us sat around the island, eating bowls of fresh fruit and yogurt.

"That hammer proves the murder was premeditated," Vance said. "What happened to Prentiss was not an impulsive act. And I'm sorry, Davis, but I believe the hammer negates your golf-ball-gun theory."

I smiled at the dig and said, "But why was it in the pond? I mean, if one of those guys brought the hammer with them to the golf course, say in their golf bag, why not take it out the same way? And then get rid of it where no one would ever find it."

"They feared they'd be searched," Vance said. "There's no way they could have known how law enforcement would react to their mystery golfer tale. Disposing of the hammer in the pond was the logical choice. Then later, one of the men returned to retrieve it, possibly with the aid of a metal detector, but was unable to locate it."

I chewed on that for a minute and decided Vance was probably right.

"So what do you think, Davis?" Lana said. "We've determined the crime was planned, so what was the motive?"

I looked for an answer in my bowl of yogurt. "I don't know. I guess there's basically two options. It either has to do with Wells's business and the escrow account stuff, or somehow it's connected to that accident back in '88. But I've got to get this hammer to Dale. Can I borrow a phone? I don't get service here."

"This way," Lana said to me. "We still have a land line. In case of emergencies."

I followed Lana across the kitchen and around a corner, to a doorway that opened into a large pantry, where tall shelves sat stacked with bottles of olive oil and vinegars, boxes of pasta, cans of beans and tomatoes. It was like a small gourmet grocery store. A small desk sat in one corner of the room, a slimline telephone atop it amid some index cards and a couple of open cookbooks. Lana picked up the receiver of the phone and held it up. "Do you remember how to work one of these?"

"It's been a while," I said, tapping on my phone to find Dale's number. I called. No answer. I left a message for him to call me back at this number ASAP. "That means 'as soon as possible,'" I added, just to be snarky.

Before the Roths left for Asheville, I asked them for their Wi-Fi information and told them I would like to go talk to Bill Rhinehart.

"Take the golf cart," Vance said. "The key is in it. There's a keypad by the garage door on the right. The code is five-one-five-zero-hashtag. And here." Vance reached into a kitchen drawer, then handed me a dark green keycard with the letter "R" written in white script. "Front door key. I believe the maintenance crew breaks for coffee at nine forty-five. That would be a good time to speak to Bill."

"Make yourself at home," Lana said as they walked to the door. A minute later I was alone in the giant house, sitting at the kitchen island, waiting for my laptop to come to life. When it finally did, I found their Wi-Fi account and typed in the password.

I checked my email—one unread message, from Elizabeth, asking me to contact her, along with a phone number.

I hurried into the pantry and dialed the number. She picked up on the first ring.

"It's Davis," I said. "I just got your email. I'm at the Roths' house. A lot's happened since I saw you yesterday."

"Can you come to the Asheville office?"

"No, I don't have a car. Like I said, a lot's happened."

"I'll be there in forty-five minutes. I've found something."

29

The Roths' golf cart was a shiny black beast with oversized tires, a built-in cooler, a built-in ball washer, and a long slender speaker attached above the windshield. It was a gas model, and the engine came to life as soon as I pressed on the accelerator. The cart sputtered for a few seconds, then took off at a speed a little brisk for my taste. I let up on the accelerator and slowly eased onto Country Club Drive.

The air was much cooler than it had been in recent days, and a dark gray cloud cover hung low, like a blanket draped over the mountains. I considered going back for my new trench coat, but couldn't work up the nerve to actually go get it and put it on.

When I arrived at the maintenance building, I pulled the cart to where Lana had parked the Range Rover a couple of days prior. An army of mowers and utility carts sat idle on the concrete pad. I limped over to a door positioned near a soda machine. I gave it a knock and when no one answered, I pushed it open, revealing a short hallway that smelled like motor oil, fresh-cut grass, and coffee. I could hear voices and laughter. I followed the noise to a room where ten or so maintenance workers sat around a long rectangular table, drinking coffee or sodas and munching on various snacks. When they noticed me, the talking abruptly stopped.

"Help you?" It was Bill, sitting at one end of the long table.

"Do you have a minute?" I said.

Without a word Bill stood, picked up a dark green coffee mug, and led me to his office, a small, dusty room with a particleboard desk and a bookcase stacked with trade magazines and hardcover books, many of which had the word *Turfgrass* written on the spine.

Bill sat behind the desk and pointed to a side chair. I took a seat and said, "Did you know Prentiss Wells was involved in an accident back in 1988?"

Bill's face turned to stone. "Yeah," he finally said.

I waited for Bill to add on to that, but he didn't. "Do you remember anything about it?" I asked.

"Hit a guy with his car. Killed him."

"That's right. You remember anything else?"

Bill shook his head, then took a sip from his mug, which I now noticed read: "Superintendents do it in the grass." I waited again, and after a few moments Bill said, "What's this about?"

"I'm looking into Prentiss Wells's death. I'm trying to get as much background information as I can."

"Looking into his death? You saying what happened to the man wasn't an accident?"

"That's what I'm trying to find out."

"What's it got to do with me?"

"I spoke with Roberta Ritter Allen yesterday."

Bill's nostrils flared.

"She told me she knows you from church," I said. "And that you knew her brother, Adam."

"I know who he is. But I didn't know him. I met him. Once. That's all."

"Tell me about it."

"What business is it of yours?"

"Look," I said. "I'm not here to stir anything up. I'm just trying to find out what really happened to Prentiss Wells. The Roths—Vance and Lana—they believe he was murdered. And they've hired me to investigate. So that's what I'm doing."

"And you're investigating me?"

The answer was yes, but instead I said, "No. Absolutely not. I'm just trying to get a better understanding of who Adam Ritter was and what happened the night he died."

Bill huffed, then shook his head. "The Roths hired you. They've got money to burn." He leaned back and crossed his arms. "All right. Whadd'ya wanna know?"

"Tell me about meeting Adam Ritter."

"I bought a guitar amp off him."

"How did you find out about the amp?"

"My cousin Travis knew I was looking for a cheap one. He told me a guy he worked with had mentioned having one he'd be willing to sell."

"Your cousin worked at the Pizza Hut in Canton?"

Bill raised his eyebrows. "That's right."

"So what happened?"

"Travis gave me the number. I called the guy and drove over to his house that weekend and bought it. I was there all of ten minutes. Only time I ever saw the guy."

"How old were you then?"

"Fifteen. I was in ninth grade."

"You were driving at fifteen?"

"I had my permit. You were supposed to have a licensed driver in the vehicle with you, but I didn't always follow that rule."

"And that's the only time you ever saw Adam?"

"That's what I said."

"How long was this before the accident?"

"Not long. Couple of weeks maybe."

Over Bill's shoulder I noticed a calendar hanging on the wall, with a photo of a golden lab sitting on the seat of a golf cart. It made me wonder about Brett Wells's dog, Peanut. I'd not asked if he was ever found.

"Is that all?" Bill asked.

"Your cousin, is he still around? Any way I could talk to him?"

Bill rolled his eyes, then took out his phone and started tapping the screen. He was putting the phone back into his pocket when the office door opened, and a guy in a maintenance uniform entered. He looked to be in his early fifties and heavy set, a barrel of a man. I glanced at the name tag sewn just over his shirt pocket: "Travis."

"This is Davis Reed," Bill said to Travis. Then to me: "This is my cousin. He's worked here longer than I have. Lucky for him he was already here when I came on. I'd of never hired him."

Travis gave Bill a middle finger, then shook my hand. "You want to know about Adam Ritter?" he said, taking a seat next to mine.

"That's right. How long did you work with him?"

"About three months, I guess."

"The night he was killed, did he mention any plans about going out with someone?"

"Not to me. He pretty much kept to himself. He washed dishes in a little room in the back of the restaurant. I was a cook—I hardly saw him."

"But you knew him well enough to know he had a guitar amp for sale."

"Yeah, we talked about music every now and then. He had a little cassette player back in the dish room, played the Cure, the Smiths, the kinda stuff you didn't hear much around here back then. That's how I found out about the amp, us talking about music."

"Did you ever talk about anything else? Like his friends? Or a girlfriend? People he hung around with?"

"Nah. He was pretty shy, didn't say much. He opened up a little when I told him I liked the music he was listening to. He told me he played guitar and bass, and had just started taking piano lessons from some woman in Waynesville. Said his daddy would whup him if he knew he was learning piano. Said his daddy thought piano was for sissies." Travis shook his head. "I'll never forget that. A daddy telling his son piano was sissy. Guess the man never heard of Jerry Lee Lewis."

"Back to the night he died. Did you happen to see anyone pick him up from work that night?"

"No. Dishwashers were usually last to leave. He was still there that night, when I left."

I heard an engine crank and looked out the window. The maintenance guys were climbing on their mowers and carts and heading out.

"But someone had to pick him up that night," I said. "His car was still at the Pizza Hut the next morning."

Travis shrugged.

"Did anyone from the sheriff's department talk to you about Adam?" I asked.

"Yeah, a deputy came by the next afternoon and talked to everyone who was working. He asked us the same stuff you're asking."

I pulled the printout of the newspaper article from my pocket and handed it to Travis. "Is that the deputy?"

Travis looked at the photo of Marvin and frowned. "No. The guy I talked to had a big mustache." Travis raised a hand and wiggled his fingers. "And wore a bunch of turquoise rings."

30

Back at the Roths' I parked the golf cart in the garage and walked over to
Bad Luck Betty. I examined the damage on the back of the vehicle and
wondered how much hassle the insurance company was going to give me
about my car. And how long it was going to take to get it settled.

I wandered over to the workbench. The bonsai tree was gone, and in its
place sat two antique guns. The kind you see pirates fire at one another in
movies. Next to the guns were a couple of gun remodeling books.

I looked around the garage and tried to imagine having the time, and the
means, to be able to pursue any hobby or interest that tickled your fancy.

I spent a minute staring at the pegboard wall of tools while wondering
if Jimmy or Freddy or Rex had a workshop full of equipment. Was that even
necessary to make a golf-ball hammer? What had Floppy said? *"All you need
is a good vise and drill with a big ol' bit."*

I stepped over to the wide door next to the wall of tools and twisted the
knob. It opened into darkness, and I felt around until I found a switch. I
flipped it up, and the room was suddenly bathed in fluorescent light. It was
about fifteen foot square and crammed full of stuff: a kayak; a mountain bike;
an artist's easel; a small table with what looked like a fly-tying set; a lathe; a
table saw; and a tall, skinny blue metal machine with the words "Dayton 20"
Drill Press" stamped on it. I stared at it for a long moment, then laughed.

"Davis?"

I spun around. Elizabeth was standing in the doorway, holding a brown
leather tote bag.

"What are you doing?" she asked.

"Snooping," I said, only half joking.

"I rang the bell, no one answered. Where are Lana and Vance?"

I stepped out and closed the door behind me. "Asheville. Now c'mon. Let's compare notes."

* * *

Sitting across from each other at the kitchen island, I told Elizabeth all that had transpired since our meeting at her office the day before, including me being attacked at Bearwaters and the discovery of the hammer.

"Are you injured?" Elizabeth asked.

"I'm sore. But I've been sore for a long time so I'm used to it. Now tell me what you've got—proof that Rex was stealing from the escrow account?"

"Not exactly. Matching the escrow transactions to the contracts and closing statements will take time. I thought a better strategy at the onset would be to quickly look at as many documents as possible to see if anything peculiar caught my eye. The first thing I found was this." Elizabeth reached into her tote bag and pulled out a file folder. She opened it to reveal a stack of papers, and slid the top paper in front of me.

I gave the page a cursory glance. It was full of boxes and lines, like an IRS form. "I don't know how to read this."

"That's a settlement statement. It's one of the documents an attorney prepares to finalize the sale of a property. Some people refer to it as a closing statement. It's a document that details the finances of the transaction—what's owed and what's due, and to whom: the seller, the buyer, a lienholder, the county tax collector, the attorney, etcetera. That particular one is for the sale of a home in Waynesville, dated January 22 of this year. The sales price is $598,000. The buyer and seller are listed in boxes D and E."

I drew a finger down the page. "Okay, says here the buyer is Willis Tilby and the seller is Richard Anderson." I looked up. "So what's odd about it? Do you know them?"

"No. That's not what caught my attention. Go to box G, property location."

"Um, 349 Old Hayes Cove Road, Waynesville."

Elizabeth leaned back and crossed her arms. "My friend Abigail has lived on Old Hayes Cove Road for over twenty years. I know that area well. There is no 349 Old Hayes Cove Road. It doesn't exist."

I glanced down at the names on the paper. "So how did Willis Tilby buy a home that doesn't exist? And how did Richard Anderson sell it?"

"I have a theory," Elizabeth said. "Once I found that settlement statement, which is obviously fraudulent, I went through all of the settlement statements and verified each property location, using a mapping app." Elizabeth placed her hand on the papers in front of her. "Here are three more settlement statements. All for homes in Haywood County sold in February of this year. One sold for $430,000 to a buyer named Ethel Campbell. Another for $525,000 to a buyer named Harriett Rachlin. And another for $379,000 to a buyer named Charles Dearmond."

"And now you're going to tell me none of those homes exist?"

"Now I don't need to." She paused. "Have you ever heard of something called an air loan?"

I shook my head.

"It's a form of mortgage fraud," Elizabeth said. "And for it to work, you generally need three people: a dishonest mortgage broker, a dishonest appraiser, and a dishonest real estate attorney."

"You've got to be kidding."

Elizabeth smiled.

"So how does this scam work?" I asked.

"The first step is to create a fake property and give it an address that doesn't exist. The appraiser then creates a fraudulent appraisal document that contains all of the necessary information about the property, square footage, year built, etcetera, as well as the appraiser's opinion of the property's value. Once the appraisal is complete, the mortgage broker creates fraudulent loan documents in the name of a straw buyer. These would include . . ."

"Hang on. Hang on. What's a straw buyer?"

"If my theory is correct, all the names I just listed are straw buyers: Tilby, Campbell, Rachlin, Dearmond. These people may not exist. They may be creations of the scammers, total false identities. Or they may be real people who have had their identities stolen and who are completely unaware they have a new mortgage in their name."

"So the homes don't exist. The buyers may or may not exist. What about the sellers?"

"They're not real. Just names on a contract." Elizabeth cocked her head. "Are you still with me?"

I wasn't sure but I nodded anyway.

"So now," Elizabeth continued, "the mortgage broker creates fraudulent loan documents in the name of the straw buyer. These documents would include the mortgage application as well as proof of the applicant's financial ability to repay the loan. This could be employment records, bank statements, credit history . . ."

"And the broker just makes up all of this stuff?"

Elizabeth raised an eyebrow. "That's why it's called fraudulent. Creating a false identity from scratch is difficult. It's easier to steal someone's identity and then create the fraudulent documents necessary to apply for a loan. That way you have a real name, a real Social Security number, a real credit history."

"So you think these straw buyers are real people?"

"I think it's likely, yes."

"Okay, so the mortgage broker creates all these bogus documents, and then what happens?"

"The broker signs off on all of the documentation, including the loan application and appraisal, and sends it to the lender, which is most likely a bank or financial institution located hundreds of miles from here, and the loan is approved. The only thing left now is the closing of the sale."

An image of Rex in his powder-blue suit and pink bow tie flashed through my head. "And that's where the dishonest real estate attorney turns a blind eye to a straw buyer purchasing a nonexistent home with a loan secured with fake documents."

"Exactly," Elizabeth said. "Rex Pinland is listed as the settlement agent on all four of these transactions."

"Is there anything that shows that Freddy did the appraisals? And that Jimmy was the mortgage broker?"

"No. The lender is listed on the settlement statements, since they're the lienholder, but there's nothing to identify the mortgage broker. And I haven't found any appraisals. But they must exist. You can't get a mortgage without an appraisal."

"So what happens to the money from the loan?" I asked.

"The three men split the money. Probably through a shell company they've created or an offshore account."

I thought about all of the pictures I'd seen of Jimmy surrounded by white sand and palm trees.

"All right," I said. "But what about the deeds and titles for these fake properties?"

"Just more fraudulent documents created by the scammers."

I leaned back and rubbed my temples, I was trying to crank start my brain. "I think I get it, but at the end of the day, it's still just a loan. It's supposed to be paid back, even if it's a loan on a home that doesn't exist. So what do the guys do?"

"It depends on the scope of the scam. In some cases the objective might be to purchase many properties quickly, then to let those properties fall into foreclosure. The lender is stuck because there is no asset on which to foreclose. But in that scenario the scammers need to disappear quickly because the lender will soon discover the fraud. Other times the scammers keep up with the mortgage payments."

"They actually pay back the loans?"

"Not completely, no. But consider this, the payment on a thirty-year mortgage for one million dollars at four percent interest is around five thousand dollars a month. You could make that payment for years and still have a lot of money to play around with. And then, when things get tight, simply refinance using an updated fraudulent appraisal that shows the property has appreciated."

I sat still for a minute, staring blankly at the Roths' gleaming commercial refrigerator. "Wells was going to retire," I finally muttered.

"Yes, I know," Elizabeth said. "I told you he mentioned that during our meeting."

"But Brett Wells told me his dad had changed his mind. He made a big announcement that he was going to retire, but then, when it came time to do it, he said he'd decided to work a couple of more years."

Elizabeth began nodding her head. "They got greedy."

I began nodding too.

"JoAnne Butler retired in January, remember?" Elizabeth said. "That was when Prentiss gave Rex control of the escrow account. Rex thought Prentiss would be out of the picture in a couple of months, and he went ahead and moved forward with the first fraudulent transaction in late January."

"But all of a sudden Wells has a change of heart," I said. "He tells Rex, '*Oh by the way, I'm not going to retire after all.*'"

"If Prentiss continued to work," Elizabeth said, "he would undoubtedly uncover the scam."

I suddenly realized my pulse was racing. "There's no way Rex acted alone. You said for this type of thing to work, you need an attorney, a broker, and an appraiser. If this mortgage scam is the reason Wells was murdered, all three of those guys are in on it. One of them hit Wells with that hammer, but they're all three guilty."

Elizabeth nodded.

"Would you write that stuff down for me, the names and property addresses?" I asked. "I'll do some digging myself."

The phone rang and I convulsed as if I'd just brushed up against an electric fence. "Are you okay?" Elizabeth asked.

"I'm a little skittish these days," I said as I slowly crossed the kitchen, toward the pantry. I was expecting to hear Dale's voice on the other end of the line, but it was Deputy Mike.

"You're not going to believe this," Mike said.

I wanted to tell Mike that the distance between what I could and couldn't believe had narrowed significantly since moving to Cruso. But instead I just said, "What?"

"Three members of the Steel Stooges are tied up 'round the hydraulic lift post inside Floppy's garage. Rusty Baker's one of 'em."

I didn't know what it said about my state of mind, but I believed it without question—or even much surprise. "Are you there now?" I asked.

"Yeah. Dale's here too. So's Earl and Boner and half the Lake Logan volunteer fire department. Dale got your message, asked me to call you. He's out back of the garage, tearin' Floppy a new one."

I knew why Dale was pissed. He'd wanted the glory, or at least the satisfaction, of nabbing Rusty Baker himself.

"Look, I've got something I need to give to Dale," I said. "It's important. I'm going to come up there."

I hung up and hobbled back to Elizabeth. "I need a ride."

31

When we arrived at Floppy's, the dirt lot out in front of his garage was packed with patrol cars, firetrucks, and ambulances. Elizabeth stopped in the middle of the road. "I'll go through more of the files tonight," she said as I stepped out of her car. "Maybe I'll find something that connects Jimmy and Freddy."

"We make a good team," I said. "Maybe when all this is over, you and I can—"

"I'm late for a meeting. Please close the door."

I did as instructed and watched Elizabeth drive away.

"What are you doing here?"

I turned to see Deputy Tommy approaching, the deputy who'd acted suspicious of me since the Graveyard Fields mess, and my least favorite law enforcement official, not counting half of the Charleston Police Department.

"I need to talk to Dale," I said.

"He's busy. Now get outta here and mind your own business."

"Were you always this helpful, or did you have to take special classes?"

Tommy stood like a statue. I wasn't sure he realized I'd just insulted him.

"Whatcha doin' here, Davis?" I heard Earl say. He stepped around Tommy and pointed to the dish towel I was holding. "Whatcha got there?"

"A murder weapon."

Earl snickered. "C'mon—you gotta see this."

"Hang on a second." I put my hand on Earl's arm and led him out of earshot of Tommy. "I talked to a guy today who worked with Adam Ritter back in 1988. He said you came to the Pizza Hut the day after Ritter died, to question the staff."

Earl looked me hard in the eye. "What are you after, Davis?"

169

"I think Wells might have paid Marvin off."

Earl didn't flinch. He didn't respond either.

"I talked to Byrd," I said. "He told me Marvin retired not long after the Wells accident. And that it was two years early."

Earl pointed a finger at my face. "I've been a deputy in this county for thirty years, and not once have I spoken bad 'bout anybody I've worked with. I ain't 'bout to start. Got it?"

Earl's tone suggested strongly that I get it, so I nodded, and he punched my arm. "C'mon—you ain't gonna believe this."

Earl led me past a sneering Deputy Tommy, through one of the open doors of Floppy's garage, where about twenty assorted deputies, EMTs, and local fire department volunteers milled about. My car was in one of the bays; I tried not to look at it. In the next bay a blue sedan was elevated six or so feet off the ground by a column of shiny metal that rose out of the concrete floor. Around the column, with their backs to it and their heads down, sat three men. Each wore ragged blue jeans, a dark-colored T-shirt, and one heavy boot. The other foot of each man was wrapped in bandages. A thick rope circled the three, holding them tightly against the column. One of the men raised his head and looked at me. Then he spat in my direction. I didn't recognize any of the men as the bikers I'd seen at Bearwaters.

"We're waitin' for Byrd to show up," Earl said. "Wanna take a picture?"

"I'll pass."

* * *

I left Earl in the garage and walked around the outside of the building, toward Floppy's trailer. Vicky and Sally were parked side by side behind the garage. I wondered how Sally had gotten home. Past the cars, Dale was sitting at the picnic table, the same one I'd been standing next to when Floppy attacked a rusty water heater with a golf-ball gun.

"That's quite a scene in there," I said, sitting down across from Dale. I put the towel-covered hammer on the table, but Dale didn't even give it a glance.

"Fuckin' Floppy," he barked.

"Where is he?"

Dale motioned toward the green trailer. "In there givin' his statement to Boner. Floppy won't let me in his trailer, I probably ain't been in there since Clinton was gettin' it on in the Oval Office."

"So, what happened here?"

Dale snorted. "Peckerhead said 'cause of all this Rusty Baker shit, he surrounded his trailer with bear traps. 'Bout fifty or so. Took us for fuckin' ever to disengage all of 'em."

I tried, and failed, to hold back a laugh.

"He heard some sort of racket outside at around five in the mornin'," Dale continued. "Then he heard screamin'. Came outside and found those three assholes, layin' on the ground, tryin' to get the traps off their ankles. Then he knocks each one of 'em out with a blackjack and hauls 'em into the garage and ties 'em up to that hydraulic post, like witches to a stake."

I put my face in my hands and cackled.

"It ain't funny!" Dale yelled.

I collected myself and said, "Did you find anything on them?"

"Damn straight we did. All three of 'em was carryin'. Baker had a thirty-eight S and W short on him."

"I assume that's a gun."

"It's a goddamn parole violation is what it is. He's goin' back inside. And one dude had a baggie of little white pills on him. We'll get 'em tested, but it looks like Oxy to me."

"Any of those guys injured in the face or neck?"

"What are you talkin' 'bout?"

"The screwdriver. I told you, I stabbed the person who attacked me. Probably in the face or neck."

"I don't think so. EMTs checked 'em over pretty good. They didn't say nothin' 'bout a face or neck wound."

We sat in silence for a minute, then I said, "So do you think this puts an end to it?"

Dale shrugged. "Yeah, at least for a while."

I glanced at the dented water heater. "In other news, I've got something to show you." I pointed at the towel. Dale looked down at it as though it has just magically materialized.

"The day I talked to the woman who lives next to hole sixteen at Springdale, I went down to the pond and looked around. I found a black knob or dial—actually I didn't find it; Lana Roth did—but anyway, it looked like a dial that may have come off a metal detector. Put that together with the flashlight the woman saw, and it seemed clear to me somebody was out there looking for something, either near the pond or in it. So last night Floppy went scuba diving in that pond."

"You idiot—that's trespassin'," Dale hissed.

"I know, but listen. He found this in the water, not twenty yards from where Wells fell dead." I unwrapped the towel to reveal the hammer. Dale looked at it as though a waiter had just placed the wrong dish in front of him.

"What the hell is it?" he said.

"Hit someone in the head with this, and voilà: death by golf ball."

"Did you just say *voilà*?"

"I'm serious—listen to me. I told you last night that I'd found out Wells suspected Rex of stealing from his firm's escrow account. Turns out it's worse than that. It's full-on mortgage fraud, and Rex's name is all over it."

"How do you know that?"

I explained to Dale who Elizabeth was and how she'd come to acquire the thumb drive, and most importantly, what was on it. I also explained that the type of fraud Elizabeth found generally requires two other people to pull it off: a mortgage broker and an appraiser. "Know any people who fit those descriptions?"

Dale stared into space for a bit, then put the towel back over the hammer and said, "Davis, I ain't got time for this shit right now. I've gotta clean up Floppy's mess first."

I pointed at the towel. "This is the murder weapon. And I just gave you the motive. Don't sit on this."

"What happened to Wells was an accident. This thing coulda been sittin' in that pond for a year, for all you know. And hell, it could be a joke thing. When I used to work at Springdale, one of the maintenance guys would nail golf balls to the bases of trees just to fuck with golfers. So I'm tellin' you, this hammer don't mean shit. And until your accountant lady hands over what she's got and our fraud division looks over it, your mortgage fraud thing don't mean shit either. And do I have to remind you there's someone out there who knows the person who accidently hit Wells and is tryin' to convince 'em to turn themselves in? You just need to stay out of it and go write that damn book."

I banged a fist on the table. "Listen, Wells was murdered and—"

"I'm the one with the fuckin' badge!" Dale shouted. "*I* make the decisions. You know, ever since Graveyard Fields, you think everythin's a damn mystery just waitin' to be solved. Man accidentally gets killed by a golf ball—well, here comes Davis Reed, hittin' the ground limpin'. I know you're pissed your big check ain't showed up yet and that you really need money. But it's time to knock this shit off."

"You knock it off and stop being so stubborn. I know you're angry about what Floppy did. And I know you don't want to think your ol' buddy Jimmy might be involved in a crime, but I'm telling you he is. I don't think he's the one who hit Wells with this hammer; I think that was Freddy. But Jimmy is in on this or else he wouldn't've been out there that day. Those three guys took Wells to that golf course to kill him and make it look like an accident. They wanted him out of the way so they could keep working their mortgage fraud scam. Now you need to find Freddy. The guy's turned into a ghost. Find him and confront him with this, and I bet you he'll give up the other two."

Dale stood and looked down at me. His beet-red face told me it was time to stop talking. I heard a rattle and turned around to see Boner and Floppy coming out of the trailer door. Floppy noticed me and waved. "Hey, there, Davis," he yelled.

I looked back at Dale, his face still red. He grabbed the towel off the table. "You go back to the cabin. And stay there."

32

Dale and Boner went around to the front of the garage, and Floppy took a seat across from me.

"Bear traps?" I said.

Floppy nodded furiously. "Those men aimed to hurt me. I stopped 'em."

Floppy was in the middle of giving me a very long and detailed account of what had happened when Boner came back around the corner of the garage. "Sheriff's Byrd's here, Floppy," he said. "He needs to talk to you."

Floppy stumbled away, and I sat at the table, feeling a mixture of relief and frustration. Relief that Rusty Baker was going back to jail and frustration that Dale was a stubborn ass.

I tried to forget about Dale's obstinance, my demolished vehicle, and my empty bank account, by imagining various scenarios of how Prentiss Wells's death played out. In each one Jimmy and Rex helped in some way, but it was always Freddy who hit Wells with the hammer.

About an hour had passed when I heard someone yell my name. It was Fern Matthews. She was walking quickly in my direction, her cameraman struggling to keep up.

"No comment," I yelled.

Fern turned to the cameraman and raised a hand. He stopped and leaned back on Vicky's fender. Fern took a seat across from me.

"I hope you didn't try to get a quote from Dale," I said. "It would be un-airable."

"Sheriff Byrd was happy to comment on the situation. And I let Floppy add a little local color."

I tried to stifle a laugh, but it snuck out.

Fern gave me her TV smile and pushed a few stray hairs behind her ear. "I hear you're investigating Prentiss Wells's death?"

"That's true. My theory is somebody hid behind a tree and shot him with a golf-ball gun. I can get Floppy to give you a demonstration if you'd like."

"I'm tempted to believe you. When it comes to you, Floppy, and Dale, things tend to play out like a *Three Stooges* episode."

"Please tell me I'm Moe," I said.

Fern smiled again. "Any leads so far?"

I didn't answer.

"I know," Fern said. "How about we do the reporter–detective quid pro quo thing?"

"It's a bit clichéd, don't you think?"

"My sources tell me that someone at Long Branch Brewery gave Rusty Baker your home address."

Something inside me sank. I wasn't sure if it was my heart or my stomach. "Who? Diana?"

"Your turn," Fern said.

"All I can tell you is this: my personal opinion is that Prentiss Wells was murdered. And I think an arrest will happen in the next forty-eight hours. Now who gave my address to Baker?"

Fern stood up. "Can't tell you that—sorry. So what's your next move with the Wells case?"

"My next move? I'm going home and drink beer for the rest of the day."

"Good idea," Fern said as she turned to walk away. She took a few steps, then twisted her head in my direction. "And stick to beer. I hear daiquiris can be dangerous."

A few minutes after Fern and her cameraman disappeared around the corner, Floppy reappeared. He told me everyone had gone but that before they left, Sheriff Byrd had shaken his hand and called him a hero in front of the crowd. "Earl took a video of it with his phone," Floppy said. "And then that TV woman talked to me."

I didn't even want to think how pissed off Dale probably was. Instead, I pointed at Sally. "Did she find her way home on her own?"

"Uh-uh. My buddy Cecil picked her up last night. He lives on Birch Street. He can walk to Bearwaters in five minutes."

"Can I borrow her again? I've got some errands to run."

Floppy rose up and stood rigid. "Kato at your service."

* * *

"Where we goin' first?" Floppy said. We were in Vicky, the engine revving, Floppy in his wraparound sunglasses.

"Ernie's Motors," I said.

Floppy shot me a curious look, nodded, then floored it. We fishtailed around the back of the garage, through the gravel lot, and onto the skinny two-lane highway. Less than twenty minutes later, we were rolling down the street near Ernie's. I pointed to Freddy Sizemore's office, and asked Floppy to pull into the drive. The black BMW was still there.

Floppy waited in the car while I once again gave the front and back doors a good rapping. No response, and both doors were locked. I tried Freddy's phone number again and got the same message that his voicemail was full.

"Ain't nobody home?" Floppy said when I crawled back into Vicky.

"No, the guy's vanished. Let's go to the Roths' house."

We did, but the Roths weren't back yet. "Strike two," I said. "Let's go over to that house by the pond. I want to look around some more."

We were there in a flash. I rang the bell a couple of times, anticipating a warm welcome, but there was no answer. "C'mon," I said to Floppy as I turned and headed around to the side of the house.

When we reached the pond, I told Floppy to look around carefully for anything unusual. Once again I wasn't sure what we were looking for. Maybe Freddy Sizemore's business card? Or better yet, a notebook with the initials "F. S." on the front along with a page titled "My Detailed Plan To Kill Prentiss Wells."

I stayed close to the pond while Floppy went deep into the trees in the direction of the pump station, where I'd heard rumbling the previous night. I was scanning the edge of the pond when the water suddenly splashed up not ten feet from where I was standing. *Another golf ball for Floppy to dive for,* I thought. *White gold.*

"Davis!" Floppy yelled.

I turned toward the trees but couldn't see him.

"Davis, hurry—it's that ol' lady."

I rushed in the direction of Floppy's voice, ducking under limbs and pulling briar-covered vines from my pants. When I spotted him, he was bent down, and Dot Davidson was lying at his feet, curled up with her arms around her knees.

*   *   *

My phone didn't have service. Floppy didn't have a phone. And Dot Davidson was alive but either asleep or unconscious.

"Drive to the pro shop," I shouted. "Tell them to call an ambulance. Quick!"

Floppy hopped through the trees like a rabbit being chased by a pack of dogs. I stared helplessly at Dot. She was wearing a down jacket, pajama pants, socks, and garden clogs. She had a purple bruise on her forehead. I put a hand on one shoulder and gave it a gentle shake.

"Dot? Dot, are you okay?"

I shook the shoulder again, harder. Dot's eyes fluttered for a few seconds, then shot open. Her whole body jerked at the sight of me.

"It's okay. It's me, Davis."

Dot twisted her head around, then straightened her legs. When she tried to push herself up, I put my hand back on her shoulder and gently held her still. "Don't try to move. An ambulance is coming."

Dot resisted for a couple of seconds, then relaxed and took a few deep breaths.

"What happened?" I asked.

Dot's cheeks flushed. She stared past my face, up to the gray sky. "I must have fallen," she said. "Last night."

"You've been out here all night?"

Dot looked me in the eyes. "I saw the flashlight again."

"And you came down here to check it out?"

Dot nodded.

"Oh, Dot, you shouldn't have done that."

A sly smile crept across her face.

"Did you see the person?" I asked.

Dot's smile widened.

"What did he look like? Short guy? Curly black hair?"

Dot shook her head. "It was a woman."

33

Less than fifteen minutes had passed when Floppy came back through the trees, followed by two first responders from the Cruso Volunteer Fire Department. Dot was now sitting up, and the first responders checked her over while she kept repeating, "I'm okay. I'm okay."

A couple of minutes later, one of the first responders helped Dot to her feet and said, "She seems all right."

Dot rolled her eyes and brushed herself off. "He can take it from here," she said, threading her arm through mine. "Let's have some tea."

Floppy led the way through the trees, to the edge of the pond, and on to the narrow path leading up to Dot's house. We were almost to the driveway when Dot suddenly spun around and looked back toward the pond. "Where's my shotgun?"

* * *

It was a fruitless search. Me, Dot, Floppy, and the two first responders scoured the area but only came up with a few beer cans, an empty tin of Skoal, and fourteen golf balls.

"Are you sure you had the gun with you?" I asked.

Dot shot me a look. "Hon, is that something I'd likely forget?"

One of the first responders appeared and said that someone from the sheriff's department was on their way. I wondered who it would be. Anybody but Deputy Tommy, I hoped.

* * *

It was Deputy Tommy. We were in Dot's living room. Me and Dot on the couch, Tommy and Floppy in armchairs across from us. Each of us held a

178

Disney coffee mug full of hot tea. My mug featured Donald Duck; Floppy's, Goofy; Tommy's, Piglet; and Dot's, Mickey Mouse. It seemed Dot had a wry sense of humor.

"I'm not sure what time it was," Dot said, "but it was very early in the morning, probably close to four. I couldn't sleep because of all the excitement about finding the hammer. I went to make some . . ."

"Hammer?" Tommy asked.

"It's not important," I said.

"I'm talking to Mrs. Davidson, not you."

Dot smiled at Tommy. "It's not important," she said. "Anyway, I went to make some tea and happened to look out the window to the pond. I saw a small light. It was moving around." Dot looked up at the ceiling for a second. "I don't know what came over me. I put on my coat and shoes and got a flashlight and went outside."

"With your shotgun?" Tommy said with a smug look I wanted to slap off his face.

Dot nodded. "That's right. I went down there and I saw the person. I snuck up on them. They were looking for something on the ground, and when they heard me, they turned around. I was close enough to them to see it was a woman."

"What did she look like?" Tommy asked.

"It's hard to say. She was bundled up in a big coat and had a ski mask pulled down over her head. But I shined the flashlight on her and saw she had long eyelashes and purple eyeshadow. It was a woman—I'm certain of it."

"Did you talk to her?" Tommy asked.

"No. She took off through the trees. I was going back to the house to call 911 when I tripped and fell."

Tommy took a sip of his tea and made a sour face. "Ma'am, I'll report the stolen gun, but I should let you know you were trespassing on private property. You know the land surrounding that pond's owned by the golf course."

"Then go find the other woman who was trespassing," Dot said.

Tommy asked a few more questions, and Dot gave a few more snippy answers. In the end he said he'd keep her informed. He left after giving Floppy a pat on the back and me a sneer, which I returned with great enthusiasm.

"Is it possible you didn't fall?" I asked Dot. "Maybe somebody else was there and they pushed you."

"I don't know, hon. I wish I could remember."

"Are you sure you're okay?"

"I'm sure. Now you go find them. And get my gun back."

* * *

The Roths were walking from the garage to the house when Floppy wheeled Vicky into their driveway.

"You ain't gonna believe what happened," Floppy yelled as he limped quickly toward them.

"How wonderful to see you again," Vance said. "Please come in."

The four of us huddled together around the kitchen island, and I let Floppy tell the Roths about his capture of Rusty Baker et al., and what had happened to Dot Davidson. Actually I didn't "let him"—I didn't have a choice. His mouth was moving so fast it would've taken a fully charged defibrillator to get his attention.

"Good heavens," Vance said when Floppy finally finished.

"And Dot's okay?" Lana asked.

"Yeah, she's fine," I said. "But listen, there's more to report. Elizabeth found something in the files."

"Who's Elizabeth?" Floppy asked. "What files?"

Vance cleared his throat. "Perhaps we should move into the living room."

"Good idea," Lana said, glancing at her watch. "Oh, look at the time. It's gin thirty."

I looked at my watch. It was 2:16.

* * *

Floppy declined a gin and tonic but happily accepted an Orangina. I downed my drink in three gulps while standing in the kitchen. Lana raised her eyebrows but quickly refilled my glass.

When we were all comfortable in the living room, I laid out what Elizabeth had found—the four fraudulent sale transactions, all closed by Rex Pinland.

"How do you sell somethin' that ain't there?" Floppy asked.

"Buddy, I don't fully understand it either," I said. "But it's all about money. It's basically lying to get a loan."

"I ain't got no loans," Floppy said. "I pay for everythin' in cash."

"You are a wise man," Vance said.

Floppy beamed at the compliment.

"So what now?" Lana asked.

"What now indeed," Vance said. "We have the murder weapon. And now, thanks to Elizabeth, we have a possible—I dare say, probable—motive for the crime. All that's left now is to identify the murderer."

"My money's on Freddy Sizemore," I said.

Vance smiled. "And if you are correct, you shall have your money."

"I was hoping the sheriff's department would prove me correct," I said. "I gave the hammer to Dale this morning and suggested he find Freddy and confront him with it, but he didn't seem all that interested."

"Did you tell him about the mortgage fraud?" Lana asked.

"Yep. He thinks that's a separate issue. He's not convinced it has anything to do with what happened to Wells."

"Phooey," Vance said. "What a nincompoop."

"Amen!" Floppy shouted.

"But there's also the Adam Ritter incident," I said. "I'm not ready to give up on that. It might have nothing to do with Wells's death, but there's something off about it. It's like a pebble in my shoe."

"Did you speak with Bill this morning?" Vance asked.

"Yeah. He confirmed what Adam's sister told me. He said he met Adam once, to buy a guitar amp from him. Claims that's the only time he saw him."

Vance cocked his head. "Why do you say *claims*?"

"I don't know. I just get a weird vibe from Bill. He got hot when I started asking questions about him and Adam knowing each other. But he did introduce me to his cousin Travis who works on the grounds crew, and he worked with Adam at the Pizza Hut. He says he has no idea who picked up Adam that night."

"Interesting," Vance said.

"But maybe Bill and Adam hit it off when Bill went to buy that amp, and they became friends. Maybe he was the other person out there that night. I'm going to keep digging until I find out."

"That's the spirit," Vance said.

I downed the last of my drink and said, "Listen, thanks for putting me up for the night, but since Rusty Baker's no longer a threat, I'd like to get back to the cabin. I've got a mountain I need to stare at."

I grabbed my duffel bag and laptop and left the Roths, with a promise to stop by at ten the following morning to discuss next steps. Floppy drove me to the cabin, and despite me thanking him and saying goodbye, he followed me inside.

"You're welcome to hang out," I said, "but I need to think. And I can't think if you're talking."

Floppy did his zip-the-lip routine, and I grabbed an Old Crab and a Coors Light out of the fridge. I put on a coat and a knit cap, and we went out onto the deck. The top of Cold Mountain was hidden by the blanket of low gray clouds. The odd snow flurry drifted by, like ash from a distant fire.

I was shocked he could manage it, but for the next hour Floppy sipped his beer and didn't say a word. I sipped my much better beer and stared at Cold Mountain, trying to will it to tell me what to do. It was characteristically silent, so I listened for the angel. When that didn't work, I listened for the devils. But it seemed everybody was taking the afternoon off.

"I ain't ate nothin' all day," Floppy announced at a little past four.

"I might have a burrito in the freezer," I said.

"Uh-uh. Today's when El Bacaratos puts chimichangas on sale. They got cheese ones and beef ones and chicken ones and bean ones. They's all real good." Floppy hopped up. "You want anythin'?"

I wanted chips and guacamole but couldn't afford it. "I'm fine, thanks."

"Can I come back and eat here?"

I nodded.

Floppy grinned. "I'll be back 'fore you can say *chimichanga*."

* * *

Floppy is fast but I probably could've said *chimichanga* a thousand times before he returned. When he did, he was carrying a white plastic bag, out of which he pulled two large tinfoil cylinders. He then removed a plastic tub and a grease-soaked paper bag.

"I got ya some of that guacamole ya like, and some chips too. My treat. I don't eat guacamole on account it feels real weird in your mouth. It's mushy and slimy and chunky all at the same time. And it's green. I don't eat a lot of stuff that's green. 'Cept pickles."

I patted Floppy's shoulder. "You're a good man."

We took our food and a couple of fresh beers to the deck. During Floppy's absence the angel had finally begun whispering in my ear. I now knew what I needed to do.

When we finished eating, I turned to Floppy. "Tell me something, Kato. Do you have a set of lockpicks?"

34

It was full-on night when we turned onto the street near Freddy's office. The cloud cover blocked the stars and the moon, the only light coming from Vicky's headlights and the street lamps along the sidewalk.

"Pull over here," I said when we were about a hundred yards from Freddy's.

"You can't park here on the street," Floppy said.

"Yeah, I know. I just don't want to park in the driveway like we did earlier. We need to park Vicky somewhere she won't be noticed."

Floppy pointed to Ernie's, where about fifteen used cars sat out in front of a small trailer. There was no fence and no gate, and the only security seemed to be four giant floodlights that blanketed the lot in bright yellow light. "Park in there and nobody'd notice," Floppy said.

We pulled in between a big Chevy SUV and a tiny Mazda Miata. Floppy popped Vicky's trunk and rummaged around for a minute before finally pulling out a small black case.

"Do you have any gloves?" I asked.

Floppy rooted around again and produced two pairs of blue surgical gloves. We put them on and headed across the empty street. I led Floppy up the drive, where the BMW was still parked, and around to the back door. I gave it a knock, waited a minute, then pointed at the lock. Floppy nodded and got busy. With a tiny flashlight secured between his teeth, he took two picks from the small black case. As he worked, I paced back and forth across the backyard, glancing at the surrounding homes, hoping not to see anyone staring through a window back at me.

"Got it," Floppy said. He opened the door, and we both stepped inside and then froze, listening for any sound. The place was eerily silent.

Using Floppy's mini flashlight and the light on my phone, we searched the lower level of the building, which looked to have been recently renovated. Along with the kitchen there were a living room, two decent-sized bedrooms, and one bathroom. All with bare walls and not a stick of furniture. Upstairs was a different story, no joke intended. There were four rooms and a small bathroom. The first room I checked was a bedroom, with an unmade bed and clothes all over the floor. I moved through the room, shining my phone light on every surface, and saw a wallet, wristwatch, and phone on a bedside table. The sight of them gave me a bad feeling. I glanced quickly into the bathroom, then Floppy and I moved on, and I opened a door that revealed Freddy's office.

In the middle of the room sat a wooden desk topped with file folders, a laptop, a legal pad and pen, and an almost empty bottle of Crown Royal. I circled around the desk, and my foot hit something—a rocks glass, on the floor but unbroken.

I touched the spacebar on the laptop with a gloved finger, and the screen illuminated, showing an image of the fountains in front of the Bellagio Hotel in Las Vegas. In the center of the screen, a small white text box invited me to enter a password. I didn't bother trying to guess it. Instead, I sifted through the file folders, which were full of appraisals. I checked the piece of notebook paper where Elizabeth had written down the names of the straw buyers and the property addresses of the fraudulent transactions—none of the names matched. But the dates on the documents were recent, so I knew that Freddy worked with hard copies. Which meant there were more somewhere.

I checked a bookcase that sat along a back wall and ran my phone light along the shelves. They were crammed full of books and trinkets, but no folders.

I checked the third room, another bedroom, probably a guest room. It was neat, bed made and the closet empty except for a few plastic hangers.

When I looked into the fourth room, I thought I'd hit the jackpot. It was full of file boxes stored on metal shelves that ran along one wall, with year and contents listed on the front of each box. On the other side of the room were a rectangular worktable and a large trash bin, the kind you use to roll your garbage to the curb for pickup. But the bin had a thin slit cut into the lid, which was secured with a padlock.

Floppy stepped over to it and gave it a shake. "They got one of these at the bank," he said. "I asked 'em 'bout it. They said it's where they put stuff they want to get rid of that needs shreddin'. Stuff with, like, your social security number on it and such. It's got a lock so nobody can open it and go through it. When it gets full, a company comes and picks it up and shreds all of the stuff inside. Imagine that bein' how you made a livin'. Rippin' up paper."

I went to the shelving unit and found a box dated 2019 that was labeled "Appraisals and Comps." I handed Floppy my phone so I could work with both hands, pulled down the box and sat it on the worktable, and had Floppy hold his flashlight over it. It was full of tan file folders, all labeled with names. I went straight to the "T's". I sifted through the folders quickly and slowed when I got to a file marked "Thomas." Next came "Thompson," then "Thorton," then "Underhill." No Tilby. I searched through the "R's," the "D's," and the "C's," but did not find appraisals for Rachlin, Dearmond, or Campbell. "Dammit." I shoved the lid onto the box and kicked the shredding bin.

"Whatsa matter?" Floppy asked.

"This was a stupid idea. C'mon, we need to get out of here."

I put the box back on the shelf. We were walking out of the room when I asked Floppy to give me back my phone.

"I put it on top of that shreddin' thing," he said.

I turned toward the bin and Floppy shone his flashlight on it. There was nothing on the lid. I pulled the bin away from the wall and Floppy scanned the floor with his flashlight. "I betcha it fell through that little slit when you kicked it," he said.

I grabbed the lock and tugged on it. "Tell me you've got a pair of bolt cutters in your trunk."

"I loaned Cecil my bolt cutters."

"Can you pick the lock?"

Floppy grabbed it and turned it upward, revealing a set of numbers. "Nope. This is a combination lock. But I can cut through it with my acetylene setup. We just need to get it back to the garage." Floppy bent down and reached under the bin. "I'll get this end. You get the top. Ready? One, two, *heave*."

The bin was heavy, and I could feel the tightness in my back. Plus I couldn't see. Floppy had his flashlight in his mouth, shining directly at my face.

Somehow we made it to the bottom of the stairs, through the kitchen, and down the back door steps, where we set the bin in the driveway behind the BMW. I was trying to catch my breath when lights from a vehicle shone against the side of the building.

"Somebody's coming," I said.

Floppy and I grabbed the bin and pulled it across the backyard. It was tough going; the ground was soft, and the bin's plastic wheels sank into the grass. When we reached the far end of the back of the house, we turned the corner and ducked down under a window. I leaned over and peeked around toward the back door. The driveway was now illuminated in blue light. I heard a vehicle door open, then close. The sound of a police radio echoed across the yard.

"It's the cops," I whispered to Floppy. "A neighbor must have seen the flashlight inside the house and called it in."

Floppy nodded but didn't offer any suggestions. I looked over his shoulder toward the street. I could see Vicky sitting in Ernie's lot.

I heard a knock. "Did you lock the door when we came out?" I whispered. Floppy shook his head.

I heard another knock, followed by the sound of the door creaking open. I slowly rose and peeked through the window into one of the empty bedrooms. Through the room's open door I saw lights flicker on in the kitchen.

"Let's go," I said.

Floppy and I dragged the bin along the side of the house and up to just a few feet from the street. I looked back. More lights were now on inside Freddy's.

"Hurry," I said.

We moved forward fast—at least fast for us—and for a second I thought we might make it. Then the bin hit the curb at the edge of the street and twisted, its weight pressing against my bad leg. I lost my balance and fell onto the pavement. Floppy swung the bin around and righted it, then reached down to help me up. Suddenly we were bathed in bright light. I twisted my neck and saw a vehicle approaching. A horn blared and Floppy waved his arm for the driver to go around. The car sped by in a blur of noise and lights, and I pushed myself up. Floppy and I grabbed the bin's handle and resumed our mission, this time much slower.

Then a voice boomed from the direction of Freddy's: "What are you two assholes doin'?" I turned around and saw Dale standing on Freddy's front porch.

35

Floppy and I ignored Dale's gaze as we pulled the bin up behind the patrol car, which was parked directly behind the black BMW.

"I told you to stay at the cabin," Dale said. He was walking up the driveway, pointing a giant finger in my direction. "And you"—Dale moved the finger toward Floppy—"I don't even wanna see you."

"You should be thankin' me!" Floppy shouted. "I saved your butt from them bikers."

"I would've taken care of 'em myself if you hadn't a gotten in the way, you skinny idiot."

"I ain't skinny, I'm *toned*."

"Bullshit! You're so skinny I'm surprised you ain't disappeared down the shower drain."

"Least I don't look like I've spent the last two years locked inside a Hardees."

"Stop it!" I yelled.

Floppy and Dale shut their mouths and glared at each other.

"What are you doing here?" I asked. "Did a neighbor call it in?"

Dale didn't answer, and suddenly it dawned on me. "You're here looking for Freddy, aren't you? You finally decided to get off your ass—"

"Shut up," Dale barked. "Tell me what you and Peckerhead are up to. And why're you wearin' gloves?"

I explained to Dale, in more detail, about the mortgage fraud Rex was involved with, the air loans, the straw buyers, and the fact that there had to be fraudulent appraisals somewhere.

"You trespassin' motherfuckers," Dale said when I'd finished. "First the pond at Springdale and now this man's residence. I oughta drag both of you'ns in right now."

"Speaking of that pond, did you hear—"

"Yeah, yeah, I talked to Tommy this afternoon. He told me 'bout the ol' lady and the missin' shotgun."

"He seemed about as interested in that as you were about the hammer," I said. "So Floppy and I came here 'cause somebody needs to find out what's going on."

Dale huffed for a few seconds, then pulled out a tin of Copenhagen and filled his jaw with tobacco. When he put the tin back in his pocket, he said, "Well, did ya find anythin'?"

"Not any appraisals with the names or addresses I was looking for," I said. "But I've got a bad feeling. There's no sign of Freddy, and his voicemail's full. And there's a wallet and a phone on a nightstand upstairs. Who leaves their house without those things?"

Dale glanced at the bin. "What's that?"

"They've got one at the bank," Floppy said. "They told me it's where they put stuff—"

"It's where you put documents that need shredding," I said. "My phone fell into it. And it's locked. We were going to take it to Floppy's garage so he could cut it open."

Dale's face twisted, and for a moment I thought we were in for an explosion. But then he chuckled, and it built and built some more, and then Dale was bent over with both hands on his knees, laughing so hard I was afraid he might choke on his tobacco. When he finally straightened up, his face was bright red. He pulled a blue bandana out of his back pocket and wiped his eyes. "If it weren't for bad luck, you wouldn't have no luck at all."

I nodded. "I'll file that under 'No Shit.'"

"All right," Dale said. "You two wait here."

Dale went inside Freddy's, and Floppy began rambling about all the things he disliked about his cousin. I listened for a couple of minutes, then told Floppy to hang tight.

I went into the house and could hear Dale walking around upstairs. I found him in Freddy's office. "Find anything?" I asked.

"His license is in his wallet, along with some credit cards and a couple of twenties. The phone's dead."

I stepped around him to the bookcase, where now, with the lights on, I could better examine the shelves. Most of the books were motivational and get-rich-quick schemes: *The Seven Laws of Passive Income, Retire Young*

Through Real Estate, Cryptocurrency Investing for Dummies. On one shelf a golf ball sat on a small wooden base with a plaque that read: "Hole in One, Waynesville C.C. #8, 06/15/2004." There was an Atlanta Braves bobblehead, a small silver bowl holding a few foreign coins, and a short stack of casino chips from Caesars Palace.

"C'mon," Dale said. "Ain't nothin' here. Let's go."

I didn't move. I was transfixed by what was next to the casino chips. A small white ceramic horse.

"I said let's go," Dale shouted, from what sounded like the first floor.

I grabbed the horse and hurried down the stairs. "I knew it, I knew it, I knew it," I said, rushing into the kitchen and grabbing Dale's shoulder.

"What the hell's wrong with you?"

"That accident, when Wells hit and killed a guy who had just robbed a house? That guy wasn't alone. Someone drove him out there to that house and then saw the accident. They witnessed what happened. That person was Freddy. That's why he killed Wells. Revenge."

"You've lost your damn mind."

I told Dale about my visit to Susan Wallace's house and how she said that the only thing not recovered from the robbery was a small, white, ceramic horse. Then I told him about what Marvin Singleton had said when Prentiss Wells's photo came on the television during my visit. "He had to be talking about Freddy," I said. "*'That poor boy. He was so scared. I let him go.'* Freddy saw what happened and was freaking out. Marvin let him go so he wouldn't get in trouble. But Freddy's held a grudge against Wells for all these years. Or maybe Marvin let Wells go when he shouldn't have. I found out Marvin retired not long after the accident, and that it was two years before he was supposed to. Maybe Wells paid Marvin off. And that's why he said, *'I let him go.'* Who knows? But Freddy having this horse has got to mean he was there that night."

"And the man waits thirty somethin' years 'fore gettin' revenge? No way. That's crazy."

I stopped and thought. "What if Wells paid Freddy off as well? And kept paying him all these years. I spoke to the sister of the guy Wells hit and killed. Prentiss Wells has been sending her family a check for five hundred dollars each month ever since a few years after the accident. So what if he was paying Freddy too, but suddenly decided to stop. That would be motive, even beyond the revenge angle."

Dale sighed and looked around the kitchen. "The only thing for certain is the man ain't here."

I put the horse in my pocket, and Dale and I went back outside. Floppy was sitting on the trunk of the BMW. "Get offa there!" Dale yelled.

I jerked a thumb toward the garage. "We didn't look in there," I said.

Dale grabbed the handle on the garage door and gave it a tug. The door raised an inch and then stopped. There was a keyhole under the handle. I pointed to it. "Floppy?"

It took him less than thirty seconds while Dale looked the other way. When the lock clicked, Dale gave the handle another tug. The interior of the garage was pitch-black until Dale grabbed a flashlight from his duty belt and shined it inside.

Freddy Sizemore was wearing a blue golf shirt, tan shorts, and white sneakers that hovered two feet above the cement floor.

36

Within the next twenty minutes, two firetrucks arrived, as well as two ambulances, five sheriff's department patrol cars, and three Waynesville police cars. Then Phil, the medical examiner, appeared in a beige sedan.

Four deputies began working to cut Freddy down, but I couldn't stand to watch. I walked to the front of the building and sat down on the steps leading up to the porch. Not long after, Dale appeared and handed me my phone. "You can thank the fire department for that. They love their bolt cutters."

"So what's the story?"

"I don't know yet," Dale said, then disappeared toward the garage.

I used my phone to check my email. There was nothing from Elizabeth or Allison, just a message from a representative from my auto insurance company who said he'd meet me at Floppy's garage at eleven the following morning to assess the damage to my vehicle.

About a half hour later, Dale reappeared and sat down next to me.

"So?" I said.

"He left a note. Said he'd been wantin' to kill Prentiss Wells since 1988, but when he finally did it, he couldn't live with the guilt."

"How long does Phil think he's been there?"

"Not long, maybe five, six hours."

"Definitely suicide?"

"That's what Phil thinks. But he'll check him over good."

"Did you see the drill press in the garage?" I asked. "He used that to make the hammer."

"Yeah. They's a bunch a tools and shit in there too, but guess what? No hammer." Dale paused and lowered his head. "I shoulda known somethin' was off 'bout this whole thing."

I bit my tongue.

"Byrd put me in charge of it, and I didn't pay it 'nuff attention," Dale said.

"Why is that?" I asked.

"Truth is, I just didn't wanna deal with it."

"Why? Because of Brett Wells? And Carla?"

"That was part of it. But hell, I believed what they told me out on the golf course. It was too stupid of a story to make up. Then when Phil's report came out sayin' Wells was definitely hit with a golf ball, I figured that settled it. That's when I checked out and told Earl to take over." Dale kicked one of the steps with the back of his boot. "I shoulda found that fuckin' hammer. Shoulda had that whole area searched that very day. But as soon as Brett Wells showed up on that golf hole, all I could think 'bout was wringin' his neck for what he did to me."

"What you thought he did to you."

We were silent for a long stretch. Then Dale said, "Well, go ahead and say it."

"What? That I was right about Freddy?"

"No, that you somehow stumbled your way into five thousand dollars."

"Yeah, and not a moment too soon. I heard from my attorney yesterday. That big check I was expecting isn't coming after all."

I waited for Dale to say *"I told you so."* Instead, he said, "Sorry."

We were silent for a while, then I said, "Pretty ballsy of Freddy, don't you think? Killing Wells when Jimmy and Rex were close by."

"Only takes a second to hit somebody with a hammer," Dale said.

"I don't know. It's hard to believe Freddy could do it undetected. What if Jimmy and Rex saw what happened and made up the mystery golfer story to protect Freddy?"

"If that's how it went down it means Double F lied right to my face." Dale bit his bottom lip. I could tell his gears were starting to turn. "C'mon—let's go put an end to this bullshit."

* * *

Dale's patrol car had been moved out on the street just down from Ernie's Motors, and I saw that Vicky was still in the lot. I wondered where Floppy had gotten to. Probably in Freddy's garage, talking Phil's ear off.

When we got into the patrol car, Dale used the radio to get Jimmy's address. We'd barely started moving when I heard a noise coming from behind me. When I turned around, I saw Floppy sitting up from the back seat. "Where we goin'?" he asked.

"What the hell are you doin' in here?" Dale yelled.

"I got sleepy," Floppy said. "I had a long day. First I trapped them bikers and tied 'em up to the—"

Dale slammed a fist on the dash. "Shut up!"

Jimmy lived on the south side of town, not far from the Waynesville golf course. The house was a decent-sized ranch-style home with an attached one-car garage. There were a few lights burning inside the house, and a white Mini Cooper sat in the driveway.

Dale banged on the front door, waited a couple of seconds, then banged on it again. The light in the peephole darkened for moment. Then, a few seconds later Jimmy opened the door. He was barefoot and dressed in blue boxer shorts, a plain white T-shirt, and an Atlanta Braves cap with matching scarf. It was quite a look. "What's up, buddy?" Jimmy said to Dale. He glanced at me and Floppy. "What's going on, guys?"

"We need to talk," Dale said, taking a step forward.

Jimmy backed away and let us inside, as if he had a choice. He closed the door and turned to Dale. "Is everything okay?"

Dale looked around. "Is there a place we can sit down?"

"Who is it?" a woman's voice yelled from somewhere in the back of the house.

"Who else is here?" Dale asked.

A young woman with short black hair appeared and walked toward us. She was wearing boxer shorts as well, and a skin-tight tank top. She looked familiar. Then I realized it was the woman I'd seen in some of Jimmy's Facebook photos.

The woman stared hard at Dale, the only one of us wearing a uniform.

"This is my girlfriend, Calista," Jimmy said.

"Do you live here?" Dale asked. Calista shook her head. "Is that your Mini outside?" She nodded. "Get in it and go home."

The woman turned to Jimmy. "It's okay," he said. "These are buddies of mine." He put his hand on Dale's shoulder. "This is Dale Johnson. We went to school together. We just need to talk. That's all." When the woman didn't move, Jimmy stepped over to her and whispered something in her ear, and she turned and went back toward the rear of the house. A minute later she returned, wearing black yoga pants, a baggy white sweatshirt, and suede boots with what looked like yak fur sticking out of the tops of them. She kissed Jimmy on the cheek, then went out the front door.

"So yeah, c'mon—back here," Jimmy said. We followed him down a hallway and into a living room where a giant TV hung on a wall, a Braves game filling the screen. I saw a couch and a couple of side chairs and a coffee table topped with an iPhone, beer bottles, a baseball glove with a ball in it, and an open pizza box with two slices remaining. Jimmy grabbed a remote and turned off the TV. "Have a seat," he said. "Can I get you anything? Beer?"

Dale, Floppy, and I sat down on the couch. "Nah, we're good," Dale said. "Now, listen, Freddy Sizemore's dead."

Jimmy collapsed into a chair. "Dead? Are you serious? When? What happened?"

Dale stayed silent.

"C'mon, man, talk to me," Jimmy said. "Tell me what happened."

"It was suicide," Dale said. "Hung himself in the garage out back of his house. We just came from there."

Jimmy bent over and put his head in his hands. "Oh my god," he said. "I just talked to him yesterday. I've been trying to keep tabs on him. He's been such a mess since, you know, what happened to Prentiss." Jimmy looked up at Dale, who stared back but said nothing.

"What?" Jimmy asked.

"Freddy left a note sayin' he killed Wells, and killed hisself outta guilt."

Jimmy's eyes almost popped out of their sockets. "Killed Prentiss? What the fuck? That's crazy." He looked at me for a second, then back to Dale. "C'mon, buddy—stop messing around. It's not funny."

"Tell me again what happened on the sixteenth hole," Dale said.

Jimmy threw his head back in his chair. "You serious? It's crazy. How could he do it? Rex and I were right there."

Dale said it slower this time. "Tell me again what happened on the sixteenth hole."

Jimmy went through the story. As far as I could tell, it was identical to the one he'd told Dale on the golf course while Prentiss Wells lay dead in a bunker.

"So while Wells was gettin' ready to hit, you're on the phone with your girlfriend," Dale said. "And Pinland's on the other side of the fairway, checkin' his voicemail. And Freddy said he was goin' down by the pond to take a piss. Did you see Freddy go down to the pond?"

Jimmy shook his head. "No. Like I said, I was on my phone. I wasn't paying attention to Freddy."

"I talked to Rex," I said. "He didn't see Freddy go down to the pond either."

Jimmy nodded slightly, as if the realization of what had happened was starting to sink in.

"Then you finish your call and turn 'round and see Freddy runnin' toward the sand trap," Dale said. "And Wells is layin' face down in it. Ain't that right?"

"Yeah. That's when I yelled for Rex, and we both ran over to check on Prentiss."

"Rex told me he'd spent a minute to ninety seconds checking his voicemail before he heard you yell to him," I said. "Does that sound about right? How long was your phone call with your girlfriend?"

Jimmy grabbed the iPhone off the coffee table. He slid his finger around the screen, then turned it toward us. Dale took the phone and read from it. "Calista. March eighteenth. 3:42 PM. Incomin' call. One minute." Dale tossed the phone back to Jimmy. "One minute's a long time. Freddy had plenty of opportunity to hit Prentiss in the head without bein' noticed."

Jimmy leaned forward, waiting for Dale to continue.

"We found a hammer with a golf ball attached to the head, in the pond next to the sixteenth hole," Dale said. "That's what Wells was hit with."

Jimmy's face turned pale. It reminded me of Freddy's face at the course.

"Now look at me," Dale said. "Look me right in the eye and swear to me everythin' you've told me is the truth."

"Dale, I swear," Jimmy said, sweat starting to bead on his forehead. "I am not lying."

"So there really was someone playing behind your group that day?" I said.

"Yeah, that's what I've been saying the whole time," Jimmy said. "Wait a minute. Do you think—"

"Did Freddy have a girlfriend?" Dale asked.

I was wondering the same thing. If Freddy had a girlfriend, had she played the role of the mystery golfer to help pull the wool over the eyes of Jimmy and Rex? And had she been the one Dot Davidson had caught searching near the pond?

"Not that I know of," Jimmy said. "Freddy was pretty private about that kind of stuff." Jimmy turned to me. "You weren't joking about that golf-ball gun were you? You knew Prentiss had been murdered."

"What reason would Freddy have to kill Wells?" Dale asked.

Jimmy stared at his bare feet for a while, then said, "Just a minute." He left the room and returned a moment later, holding four bottles of Michelob Ultra. He put three bottles down on the coffee table and kept one for himself. Floppy grabbed a bottle and popped it open.

"The only reason I can think of is this," Jimmy said as he twisted the top off his beer and sat back down. "Back in the eighties, Prentiss was involved in an accident. He hit a guy with his car, and the guy died." Jimmy pointed at me. "You asked me about it. On the driving range."

"I know," I said. "But you didn't tell me everything. Did you?"

Jimmy shook his head with shame. "No. I didn't."

"Then let's hear it," Dale said. "All of it."

"The guy Prentiss hit and killed had just broken into a house close by," Jimmy said. "Freddy was friends with that guy. He was with him that night. He was there."

"And Freddy saw the accident?" Dale asked.

"Yeah. Freddy said Prentiss was drunk."

"Did Wells see Freddy that night?" I asked.

"Yeah. A deputy showed up right after it happened. He told Freddy to get lost and keep his mouth shut or else he'd arrest him. Freddy said he was scared shitless. He'd just helped rob a house. He was only sixteen. He knew he'd be in big trouble. Said his parents would kill him."

"All right," Dale said. "So Freddy kept his mouth shut."

"No," Jimmy said. "That's the problem: he didn't. When Freddy got older, he used that accident as leverage against Prentiss."

"Like blackmail?" Dale said.

"Can I have a piece of that pizza?" Floppy asked.

"Yes, and no," Jimmy said. "I mean yes, have the pizza. But no, I don't think Freddy was blackmailing Prentiss—I mean not in the traditional sense. Freddy had a gambling problem. Spent almost every weekend over in Cherokee, and he'd fly out to Vegas two or three times a year. He ran hot and cold. Sometimes he'd be way up, sometimes way down. But apparently whenever he needed money he'd go to Prentiss, 'We have an understanding' is how Freddy put it."

"Sounds like blackmail to me," Dale said. "And Freddy just willingly told you all this?"

"He was three sheets when he told me. We were pretty deep into a bottle of WhistlePig that night."

"So why'd he do it?" Dale asked. "If Wells was Freddy's ATM, why'd he kill 'im?"

"I think it came to the point where Prentiss felt he'd paid Freddy enough. The timing was bad because Freddy had gotten himself in a pretty good-sized hole. Evidently, he owed some people that you don't want to be in debt to. That night we were drinking together, when he told me about seeing that accident, I loaned him nearly five grand, but he said he needed a lot more than that. Exactly how much he wouldn't tell me. But he did tell me Prentiss had refused to help."

"When was this?" Dale asked.

"About three weeks ago."

Dale grabbed the last piece of pizza, then leaned back. "Well, I guess that's that," he said. "But you need to come down and make a statement tomorrow. First thing in the mornin'."

"Yeah, buddy, of course," Jimmy said.

"Does Pinland know any of this?" Dale asked. "The stuff 'bout the old accident and Wells givin' Freddy money?"

"I don't think so. Freddy and Rex weren't really tight. Rex can be a little stuffy. I certainly never told Rex about it. Hell, I didn't tell anybody about it. Not even Calista."

"How well do you know Rex?" I asked, offhand like.

"Not all that well. We've golfed together a few times, but always with Prentiss. We're both members at Waynesville Country Club. Freddy was a member there too. So was Prentiss."

"Was Prentiss ever suspicious—"

"Was Freddy remodelin'?" Dale asked, throwing a chunk of crust into the pizza box.

Jimmy paused at the interruption. "Uh, yeah. Slowly. He was wanting to sell his place, but it needed work. He moved a bunch of his furniture to a storage unit somewhere. I think he was almost finished with the downstairs but then ran out of money. Like I said, as far as finances went, Freddy ran hot and cold."

As Jimmy spoke, Floppy slowly leaned forward. I thought he was going to grab Dale's discarded pizza crust, but instead he picked up the baseball glove and slipped it over his hand. Suddenly the angel began babbling in my ear. I was trying to decipher it when Dale slapped my leg and stood up.

"First thing in the mornin'," he said to Jimmy. "Ask for me when you come in. I'll be waitin'."

"I'll be there," Jimmy said. "Hey, do you mind if I call Rex and tell him about this? He's not going to believe it."

"Yeah, I guess that's fine," Dale said.

"Oh god," Jimmy blurted. "Brett. Someone has to tell Brett. He and Freddy were friends, not real close, but—"

"We'll contact Brett," Dale said. "Sheriff Byrd'll want to do it personally."

We all walked to the front door, where Dale and Jimmy gave each other a man hug, that bizarre ritual that's half handshake, half awkward embrace.

* * *

When we got back to the patrol car, Floppy asked Dale if he could drive.

"Shut up and get in the back," Dale barked.

We headed back toward Freddy's, and I asked Dale why he'd interrupted me when I was asking Jimmy about Rex.

"'Cause I didn't want you to start blabbin' 'bout all that mortgage shit," Dale said. "Until the fraud guy can go through those files your lady friend's got, they ain't nothin' to talk 'bout."

"Fraud guy? Earlier you said it was a whole division."

"It is. It's a division with one dude in it. Stan. Now get him them files in the mornin'."

37

When we arrived back at Freddy's, six vehicles were parked out front, three from the Sheriff's Department, two from the Waynesville Police Department, and one van from the local ABC affiliate.

"Shit," Dale mumbled.

"Ooh, I can talk to 'em," Floppy said from the back seat.

Dale pulled to a stop next to Ernie's Motors. "You ain't talkin' to nobody. You're goin' home."

"I'll wait here," I said.

Dale walked across the street to Freddy's, where Fern Matthews suddenly appeared in the driveway. Dale rushed by her like a celebrity dodging paparazzi, and like paparazzi she trailed after him.

"You need a ride to the cabin?" Floppy said.

"No, I'll get Dale to take me back. But are you free in the morning? I need a ride to the Roths'. I'm supposed to be there at ten."

"Kato won't let you down."

Floppy opened the back door of the patrol car and began to slide out. "We had us a big day, didn't we?"

"We did indeed."

Floppy stepped out, then put his head back inside. "Turns out it wasn't that rich couple who killed Wells after all. Good thing I'm a mechanic and not a detective."

Floppy slammed the door, and I watched as he limped over to Vicky and drove away. Fifteen minutes later Dale reappeared in the driveway. He was half jogging and hiking his pants back up under his belly every few steps. Fern was right behind him. I slid down below the window. In a few seconds the driver's side door opened, and Dale climbed in and wedged himself behind the steering wheel. In one fluid motion he cranked the engine, put the car in gear, and buried the accelerator.

"That woman's like herpes," Dale said as we flew down the dark street on our way back to Cruso.

I laughed. "Why? Because you can't get rid of her?"

Dale turned and gave me a frantic look. "Yes."

We barreled down Main Street, then turned onto 276. After a couple of miles of silence, I said, "In a roundabout way Fern let me know it was Daiquiri who told somebody from the Steel Stooges where I lived."

"Don't surprise me," Dale said. "I told ya Daiquiri's a psycho."

"Yeah, but you never told me why."

"You know me and her went on one date, right? 'Bout a week after I shot Sindal Baker."

"Yeah. And?"

"We had dinner and a few beers, and the whole time she kept askin' me all kinda details 'bout that drug bust. What I knew. When I knew it. If they was gonna be more arrests. I didn't think much of it 'til I took her home and was standin' by her front door, hopin' she's gonna ask me in. But instead she tells me she can't wait 'til Rusty Baker gets outta jail and comes after my fat ass. Then she walks inside and slams the door in my face."

I wondered how Diana fit into the Rusty Baker saga, if it all. Then realized I didn't really care. I had more pressing thoughts swirling through my head.

"So did they find anything at Freddy's?" I asked.

"Nothin' so far," Dale said. "We'll start callin' 'round in the mornin', see where his storage unit's at."

I didn't speak for a while, and Dale glanced at me. "What's wrong?"

"It's going to sound like a cliché."

Dale sighed. "Go ahead."

"Some things don't add up."

"Like what?"

"Like who was out at the pond last night? If it was Freddy and a woman, why would he be searching for evidence that connects him to a murder, only to kill himself a few hours later?"

"'Cause he didn't find that evidence. Knew he was probably close to gettin' caught."

"Okay. What about this: If Freddy didn't go down to the pond to piss that day at the golf course, why were his shoes muddy?"

Dale thought for a moment. "Maybe he went to piss later. Maybe when Jimmy and Pinland were ridin' 'round lookin' for that golfer."

"Yeah, maybe." I paused. "And another thing. Who was calling the sheriff's department, claiming they knew the identity of the person who hit the golf ball?"

"That's easy. Somebody just lookin' for a reward. That's why they was so curious 'bout what the charges would be if the person turned themselves in. If it was just gonna be a slap on the wrist, one person turns themselves in, the other collects the reward, then they split it."

I blinked. "Does that really happen?"

"Damn right it happens. People are crazy."

"Speaking of crazy," I said. "There was a tiny part of me that was beginning to suspect the Roths might be involved in Wells's murder."

Dale laughed. "The swingers? Why?"

"Floppy put the idea in my head, which, I know, should have been a red flag to begin with. But there are some weird coincidences."

"Like what?"

"Like the Roths have a drill press."

"Big deal," Dale said. "So does my buddy Burrell and a shitload of other people."

"I know, it's stupid. But then there was that plastic knob down by the pond. I didn't find it—Lana Roth did. I must have stepped right over it. And the Roths knew Freddy. He did an appraisal for them a few years ago. And they were at the golf course at the time Wells was killed. They were in the restaurant, remember? That's when I met them. Lana had on a neck brace, and I started to wonder if that was just a prop. Then Floppy made that golf-ball gun, and I started to imagine—"

Dale cackled. "And I thought you'd gone crazy back when you were searchin' for that gold."

38

The low gray clouds finally made good on their promise. When I woke up the next morning, the trees outside the cabin were dusted with freshly fallen snow. It wasn't a blizzard, just a mild flurry, but it made everything outside look clean and fresh.

On the laptop I checked the local news. So far nothing about the death of Freddy Sizemore.

I sent an email to Elizabeth, asking if she could get the thumb drive to the Sheriff's Department ASAP. I added that there was a lot I needed to talk to her about and that I'd call her when I had service.

Floppy showed up in Vicky at nine forty-five, to collect me. The drive down to the main road was covered in white, but 276 was clear. "Light snow all day," Floppy said. "Then it's s'posed to warm up a little and turn to rain. That'll make a mess."

We pulled up to the Roths' house at a couple of minutes before ten. "You coming in?" I asked.

"Nope," Floppy said, twisting a knob on the radio. "I'm gonna listen to the *Swap Shop*."

* * *

Vance opened the door and led me inside. He was wearing a different ascot, a blue one with white polka dots. "How many of those do you have?" I asked.

"I've never counted," he said as we walked into the kitchen, where Lana gave me a kiss on the cheek and then made me a cup of coffee. "Black and weak," she said. "Just the way you like it."

We moved to the living room, and I was reminded of my first visit here. Sitting in the same room, drinking gin and tonics, wondering if Prentiss Wells really had been murdered. We'd come full circle.

"Well," Lana said. "Anything new to report?"

"It's over," I said. "Freddy Sizemore was found dead last night. Suicide. He left a note confessing to Wells's murder."

Lana's jaw dropped.

"Good heavens," Vance said.

I gave the Roths a full report of the previous evening's activities, including the motive that had led Freddy to kill Wells.

When I finished, Vance and Lana stared at each other for a long moment. Then Vance turned to me. "Extraordinary," he said.

"So, anyway. Elizabeth will get the files to the sheriff's department, and they'll handle that through their fraud division. Dale's right: it's a separate issue."

"You no longer feel Jimmy and Freddy were involved in the mortgage fraud?" Vance asked.

"I searched Freddy's files and didn't find any appraisals with the names or addresses Elizabeth gave me. I know she said you generally need three people to make that kind of scam work, but if Rex was creating fake closing statements and fake deeds and titles, why not just create the rest of the fake documents as well? Why cut in two other guys when you can keep the money all for yourself?"

"Perhaps," Vance said.

"Anyway, I hope we can still hang out. When it warms up again, I'd like to have you guys over to the cabin. I've got a big deck."

"I bet you do," Lana said with a wink.

I waited for Vance to leave the room and return with a luxurious leather checkbook and an antique fountain pen. But he didn't move.

"So, listen, I need to get over to Floppy's to see the insurance guy about my car. I hate to ask, but could I get my check now? My rent's due soon, and I'm going to need to rent a car until they figure out what they're going to do with mine."

Vance frowned. "I'm sorry, Davis, but no, not yet. The story is not finished."

"What are you talking about? It's over. Freddy confessed. Case closed."

Lana leaned back and crossed her legs. A gold anklet sparkled above the strap of her black heel. "There's one more thing you need to do," she said with a confident smile.

"We'll have to act quickly," Vance said. He turned to Lana. "Do you think we can put it together on such short notice?"

Lana waved a hand in the air. "Puh-lease."

"I don't follow," I said.

"The final chapter," Vance said. "The summing up."

I looked back and forth between the Roths. I was lost, and I guess it showed.

"We'll get everyone together," Lana said. "Everyone involved in the case. And then you pace around the room and explain how you solved it."

I waited for the Roths to start laughing. They didn't.

"No offense," I said, "but that's absurd."

"Phooey," Vance said, rising to his feet. "It's not absurd. It's essential. Now, if you don't mind, Lana and I have work to do."

I slowly stood and Vance put an arm around my shoulder and ushered me toward the front door. When we reached it, he said, "We'll see you this evening at seven for the summing up. Wear the coat."

* * *

"Did ya get your money?" Floppy said when I opened Vicky's passenger door and climbed inside. "It'd be funny if it was one of them big ol' checks like they give ya on TV when ya win a sweepstakes or such."

I didn't speak. I just stared through the windshield at the gently falling snow.

"You okay?" Floppy asked.

"I used to think the Roths were eccentric. Now I'm thinking they're bat shit crazy."

"Eccentric is just crazy with more money," Floppy said. "Hey, I wonder if I'll turn eccentric after I find Grandaddy's gold?"

* * *

The insurance guy turned out to be fairly nice, as far as insurance people go. He took some photos and filled out some forms that I signed and said that his recommendation would be to total the car. That was after Floppy told him that he'd inspected the vehicle thoroughly and had discovered severe damage to the engine and electronics. I didn't know whether that was true or not, but I didn't argue. I asked the guy about a rental car, and he told me my policy didn't cover that expense. He gave me his card and said I'd hear from him in the next couple of days.

When he left, I called Elizabeth. I got her voicemail, left a message, and she called back five minutes later.

"Did you get my email about the files?" I asked.

"Yes, I took the thumb drive to the sheriff's office this morning. I asked for Dale, but he wasn't there. I gave the drive to someone named Stan, and explained to him what I'd already found."

"Good—thanks. Where are you now?"

"In the Asheville office."

I told Elizabeth about Freddy's suicide and confession, but just said that Freddy had killed Wells over money. I didn't want to get into a discussion about Marvin's possible complicity in the whole thing, at least not over the phone.

"Now you can go back to writing your book," Elizabeth said.

"Not quite yet. Vance and Lana are planning some sort of get-together, and they want me to act like Poirot at the end of a mystery. You know, go over the investigation, the clues, how I solved it."

She paused a moment. "But the murderer is dead. And he confessed."

"Yeah, I know. That will make it a bit anticlimactic."

Elizabeth giggled and the butterflies took flight. "I'm sure I can bring a plus one," I said. "So what do you say? It's tonight at seven."

"All I can say is, maybe."

Elizabeth hung up and I called Dale.

"What's up, numbnuts?" he said.

"Any luck with Freddy's storage unit?"

"Yeah, we found it. Place over near Dellwood. Mike and Earl's headed out there now. Did your lady friend get them files to Stan?"

"I just talked to her. She gave him the drive personally this morning and told him what she'd already found."

"Good. Once Stan goes through all that shit, I can get a warrant to get the rest of the files from Wells and Butler."

"How long will that take?"

"Beats me. A few days at least. Hey, did that couple give you your money? Your rent's comin' due."

I described how the Roths expected me to give a performance before getting paid.

"They ain't swingers," Dale said. "They're lunatics."

* * *

I borrowed Sally and went back to the cabin. I nuked a burrito, grabbed an Old Crab, and checked the internet for news about Freddy Sizemore. There was one short report on the website of the local ABC news affiliate, Fern's station. It mentioned that the body of a Waynesville appraiser named Freddy Sizemore had been found at his home and that the cause of death was an apparent suicide. The report ended by saying the story was developing.

I spent some time searching Google and Facebook for the names I had gotten from Elizabeth: Willis Tilby, Ethel Campbell, Harriett Rachlin, and Charles Dearmond. Straw buyers. Folks who'd had their identities stolen or folks who might not exist at all. I found plenty of people with those names, but nothing to suggest any of them were connected in any way.

I'd put the white ceramic horse I'd taken from Freddy's on the table next to my laptop, in hopes it would serve as a good luck charm as I searched the web. It didn't seem to get the message.

After an hour I wondered why I was even bothering. My part was over. All I needed to do was don my expensive trench coat, give a short speech, and collect my reward. Not exactly a performance I was looking forward to, but when your bank account's empty, your car's totaled, and your rent's due, integrity becomes negotiable.

39

There were three cars in the Roths' driveway when I parked Sally by the garage: Elizabeth's SUV, Dale's patrol car, and a gray Ford F-150.

I waited for a minute before getting out. The snow had turned to rain, and I was hoping it would lighten up before I made a dash to the front door. I was also hoping to quiet the whispering I'd been hearing since putting on my trench coat and leaving the cabin. I didn't know if it was the angel or the devils, but the muttering was constant, and messing with my concentration.

I stepped out of Sally, but instead of heading to the house, I ducked over to the garage and entered the code into the keypad. Once inside, I made a beeline for the door next to the wall of tools. I opened it, stepped through, and turned on the lights. I examined the drill press. There was a bit in it, a big one. I went out and got a hammer from the pegboard and then matched the hammer's face against the bit. It was close to the same size. Then I pushed through all of the recreational equipment toward the back of the room. I found what I was looking for sitting against the wall, as pretty as you please: *a gray metal detector with one black knob missing.*

At the front door I rang the bell, and a guy I'd never seen before answered. He was thirtyish, with short dark hair and dressed all in black. "Good evening sir," he said.

"I'm looking for the Roths."

The man took a step back. "This way, sir. May I take your coat?"

"No, thanks. I think I'm supposed to keep it on."

"And your name, sir?"

I told the guy and he asked me to follow him. When we reached the wide doorway of the living room, he stopped and loudly announced, "Mr. Davis Reed."

I scanned the room and saw Vance. He was standing near the couch in a black tuxedo with a bright white scarf draped around his neck. Lana sat nearby, holding a champagne flute and wearing a slinky, red sleeveless dress and silver heels. A red feather boa hung loosely around her shoulders. She was talking to Chris and Roberta Allen. In the back of the room, a fire roared in the fireplace.

"The man of the hour," Vance said, walking toward me. He turned to the guy who had led me in. "Benjamin, get Mr. Reed a glass of the Glenmorangie eighteen." Then to me, "This type of night calls for scotch."

Benjamin nodded and disappeared.

"Exciting, isn't it?" Vance said. "And the weather is perfect." He gently pushed my shoulder. "Now, go mingle. I'll announce when we're ready for you to begin."

I stepped over to Lana. "You look perfect," she said.

"May I have a word?" I asked.

Lana flashed a mischievous smile. "In a few minutes, dear. I'm in the middle of something. Go talk to your friends. I'll come find you."

Dale was standing next to the bookcase full of mysteries, talking to Elizabeth. He was wearing his uniform, but not his duty belt, and he held an empty beer glass. Elizabeth sipped a glass of white wine. I wandered over and said, "So I guess you two have met."

Elizabeth smirked. "Is that the kind of stellar detective work we're in for this evening?"

I smirked back. "This is absurd," I said, motioning toward Vance and Lana. "It's like they're cosplaying at a mystery convention."

"You're the one in the trench coat," Elizabeth said.

"They bought it for me. And actually it's worse than just dressing up. I think they've been manipulating me."

Elizabeth gave me a look, and she and Dale leaned in close.

"I just went inside their garage a few minutes ago," I whispered. "Not only do they have a drill press, which is what Floppy said you'd probably need to drill a hole in a golf ball big enough to fit a hammer face into, but they have a metal detector with one knob missing."

"Seriously?" Dale said.

Elizabeth was silent, but her face showed an expression I'd not seen on her before: uncertainty.

"The drill press might mean nothing," I said. "Vance has all kinds of tools and gadgets in there. But a metal detector with a missing knob can't be a coincidence."

"Whatcha thinkin?" Dale said.

"I think the Roths are rich and bored. And that's a hazardous combination."

Benjamin appeared, carrying a silver tray with my drink on it. Dale handed him his empty glass. "Keep those comin', buddy," he said.

The doorbell rang and Benjamin hustled out of the room. A moment later he appeared in the doorway and called out, "Mr. Floppy Johnson."

Floppy stepped in, grinning from ear to ear. He had on camouflage cargo pants and a black T-shirt printed to look like a tuxedo.

"Jesus Christ," Dale mumbled.

Floppy noticed us and limped over. "Hey, y'all," he said. Then he looked me up and down and chuckled. "They oughta call you Inspector Cruso. Get it? Like that Inspector Clouseau in them Pink Panther movies."

I was introducing Floppy to Elizabeth when a familiar-looking woman approached, dressed all in black and, like Benjamin, carrying a silver tray. I suddenly realized she was the waitress from the golf course restaurant who had served us the day I first met the Roths.

"Crab Rangoon?" she said.

Elizabeth and I declined. Dale and Floppy both grabbed four each.

The doorbell rang again, and soon Benjamin shouted, "Mrs. Dot Davidson."

Over the next fifteen minutes, the other guests arrived: first Bill Rhinehart, then Susan Wallace, and finally Jimmy and Rex. Aside from Floppy and the Roths, everyone was dressed casually. Even Rex had forgone a suit for khakis and a dark blue sweater. Jimmy was wearing black jeans and a baggy gray turtleneck.

"How did they get all of these people to come?" I said to Elizabeth.

She reached in her handbag and removed a small pale blue envelope. Her name was written on the front in elaborate script. "Didn't you get one?"

I shook my head. Elizabeth handed me the envelope, which was already open. I removed the card and read it.

Mr. and Mrs. Vance Roth
request the pleasure of the company of
Ms. Elizabeth Harper
at a small soirée
this evening at seven o'clock
545 Country Club Drive, Cruso
Evening attire suggested

"You've got to be kidding," I said.

"The two of them showed up at my office this afternoon to deliver this," Elizabeth said. "They said they were hand-delivering all of the invitations."

I looked at Dale. "Mine was waitin' for me at the sheriff's office," he said. "It said my name plus guest, so I told cowboy he could come."

"Hey, did he and Mike find anything in Freddy's storage unit?" I asked.

"Nope. Just furniture and rugs and shit," Dale grimaced and looked at Elizabeth. "Sorry, ma'am. I meant *stuff*."

"No drill press?" I asked. "No shotgun? No boxes full of fake appraisals?"

Dale shook his head. "No, but Boner called a little while ago and asked if he could go back to Freddy's house. Said he had an itch he needed to scratch."

"What's that about?"

Dale shrugged.

"All right, what about Freddy's computer?" I asked.

"The tech guys got into it," Dale said. "Ain't no work files on it, just emails and stuff like that. Looks like all his appraisals were done by hand. We took all them file boxes from that upstairs room to Stan. It's gonna take him a month to dig through all that. I told him to concentrate on that thumb drive from Wells—that's the priority."

I glanced over at Rex, who was speaking with Vance. He looked as calm and collected as he had that day on the sixteenth hole. He had no idea the hammer, figuratively in this case, was about to drop. "Did Jimmy show up this morning?" I asked.

"Yep," Dale said. "He brought Pinland with him. I took their statements."

"And you didn't mention anything about the mortgage fraud?"

"No. I told ya, until Stan can compile the evidence, there ain't nothin' to mention."

"And Freddy's death was definitely suicide?"

"That's what Phil thinks. No signs of a fight or struggle. Nothin' on his neck to suggest he was scratchin' to get the rope off. Dude's alcohol level was point two. Guess he needed some liquid courage to wrap that noose 'round his neck."

Elizabeth frowned.

"Sorry, ma'am," Dale said.

"I checked the news right before I came," I said to Dale. "There's nothing about Freddy's connection with Wells. It's weird. I thought Fern would be all over this."

"Well, Sherlock, I guess everybody's gonna know 'bout it soon 'nuff, when you give your big presentation."

Presentation. I had no idea what I was going to say. At the cabin I'd come up with a short speech summarizing the investigation, but the discovery of the metal detector in the Roths' garage had me wondering if I'd gotten it all wrong. If this was really just a game to the Roths, was I the one getting played?

I surveyed the room. Susan Wallace was standing alone next to the fireplace, in what appeared to be the same track suit she'd had on when Floppy and I had visited her house.

"What is all this about?" she asked when I stepped over and said hello.

"The indulgences of a bored rich couple," I said gesturing toward the Roths. "Tell me, did they deliver your invitation personally?"

"Yes. At first I thought they were trying to sell me something, but they said it was going to be one of those murder mystery nights where the guests try to solve the crime. They said they were friends of yours and that you had mentioned me to them. They said you were coming to the party, but I told them I wasn't interested."

"What changed your mind?"

Susan leaned in close. "They said if I would attend, they would donate one thousand dollars to Barney's Fight."

"What's that?"

"It's an online fundraiser my daughter set up. Her dog Barney has liver disease and the treatments are very expensive. It's on my Facebook page. A thousand dollars will be a huge help."

I surveyed the room again, this time wondering what various bait the Roths had used to reel in a bunch of strangers.

I turned back to Susan. "This is going to sound odd, and I'll talk more about it to everyone in a bit, but I was with the sheriff's department last night when they searched the house of a man who'd committed suicide. It turns out that man was with Adam Ritter the night he robbed your sister's house."

Susan's face stiffened.

"Anyway, during the search I noticed this." I reached in my coat pocket and removed the ceramic horse. "I thought you might want it."

"What for?"

"This is your sister's horse. The one that was stolen."

"No, it's not," Susan said. "Greta's horse was bigger and had a bright gold mane."

Before I could process this, someone tapped on my shoulder—Roberta Allen, Adam Ritter's sister. "Can I talk to you for a minute?" she said.

"Yeah, of course," I said. Then to Susan, "Are you sure? It's been over thirty years. Maybe—"

"That is not Greta's horse," Susan said firmly.

I followed Roberta over to the wall of glass. The rain was coming down harder.

"So what made you guys decide to come to this affair?" I asked.

"That couple, the Roths. They said they were friends of yours and that you'd be here tonight, and I wanted to talk to you." Roberta turned and looked out at the rain. "They told me and Chris about someone being with Adam the night of the accident. And that Mr. Wells was drunk that night."

"Who knows what really happened," I said.

"Whatever happened, it was enough for Mr. Wells to keep paying that someone off. No wonder Mr. Wells felt guilty. 'Cause he was guilty." Roberta looked at me. "And the sheriff's department turned a blind eye. Nobody's talking 'bout that. It's just swept under the rug."

Roberta's expression was a mix of anger and sadness. She reached into her pocket and removed a slip of paper. "This came today. Right on time. Just like every other month."

Someone began clinking the side of a glass, and Roberta and I both turned to the center of the room. "May I have everyone's attention," Vance said as the chatter fell to a hush. "Thank you for joining Lana and me on this gloomy evening and on such short notice. It is our pleasure to have you here in our home. Please enjoy the hors d'oeuvres, and have Benjamin or Patty freshen your drinks. Our program will begin shortly."

Roberta handed the paper to me. It was identical to the check she'd shown me on her iPad. It was for five hundred dollars, made out to Roberta Ritter

Allen from the account of Philos Adelphos Dikaios LLC. The only thing different was the date. "Huh," I said. "I guess he had it set up so someone would take it over at the time of his death."

"I don't want it anymore," Roberta said. "It's blood money." She turned and walked away.

I put the check in my pocket and rejoined Dale, Floppy, and Elizabeth by the wall of mysteries. I showed Dale the ceramic horse. "This isn't it," I said.

"What are you talkin' 'bout?"

"This isn't the horse stolen from the house Adam Ritter robbed."

"So? That don't mean nothin'. Maybe Freddy never even had the horse from that robbery."

"Floppy, you look impeccable," Lana said. I turned to see her standing just behind me. She put a hand on my elbow. "Do you still want a word?"

"Give me two minutes," I said.

Lana winked. "I'll meet you in the foyer."

I limped over toward Dot Davidson, who along with Bill Rhinehart, was studying the shelves of photos and collectibles.

"Look at this," Bill said, holding up a small plastic box that contained an autographed golf ball. "Tom Watson." He pointed to some other boxes. "Jack Nicklaus. Arnold Palmer. Gary Player."

"Impressive collection," I said.

"I can't read this one," Bill said, holding up a white golf glove with an illegible signature scribbled in black next to the Velcro strap.

I'd not noticed the glove before but figured since it wasn't encased in plastic, it probably wasn't that valuable. I took a closer look at the signature, then shrugged.

"Lefty, whoever it is," Bill said. "Maybe Phil? Or Bubba?"

I turned to Dot. "Hello, hon," she said.

"How are you feeling?"

"I'm tip-top. You know I don't think I ever thanked you for rescuing me. Maybe I could throw together a good home-cooked meal for you and Floppy one evening."

"That would be much appreciated."

"He's a mechanic, isn't he? I think I need a new battery for my Camry. It wouldn't start tonight. I had to drive my cart over here in this weather."

"Listen, Dot, I need to ask you something. This is important. Are you one hundred percent sure you saw someone by the pond last night?"

"Of course I'm sure."

"And you're certain it was a woman?"

"Yes."

I leaned close to Dot's ear and whispered, "Could it have been Lana?"

"Lana," Dot blurted out loudly, causing Bill to give us a side glance. "Why on earth would it be Lana?" Dot asked, lowering her voice.

"You said the woman had on a big coat and a ski mask. And you only saw her for a split second. Now think back. Is there any chance it was Lana?"

"Absolutely not. What's gotten into you?"

I left Dot and hurried to the foyer. Lana was waiting for me by the front door, sipping her champagne. As I approached, she began to speak, but I cut her off. "What are you and Vance up to?"

Lana giggled. "It's just a silly party. Sometimes we like to get dressed up and pretend we're in a cozy mystery."

"This is far from cozy. And it's certainly not pretend. Be honest with me. Were you the person Dot saw by the pond last night?"

Lana looked stunned. "Are you joking? No. Why would I be out there?"

"Was it you or Vance out there the first time she noticed the flashlight?"

"No. Absolutely not."

I reached into my coat and removed the black plastic knob. I held it up close to Lana's face. "This belongs to you. I found the metal detector in the garage."

Lana stared at the knob for a few seconds, then seemed to make a decision. "Okay, fine. I faked finding it. I didn't know Dot had seen a flashlight by the pond until we talked to her that day. But I already had that thing with me. Vance and I wanted to make sure you would be interested in searching the pond."

"Why? How did you know something was in there?"

"We didn't. Vance and I just wanted to draw out the investigation as long as possible. It was so much fun playing detective."

"I already said it isn't pretend."

"To us it was. At least at the time." Lana gave me a pitiful look. "Don't be mad, but we really thought Prentiss was accidentally hit and killed by a golf ball."

I took a couple of much-needed deep breaths. "So to you guys I didn't stand a chance of earning that five grand. I was just a toy to play with."

"Even if Prentiss's death had been an accident, Vance would have paid you for your time. But it wasn't, and you uncovered the truth. Think about it.

If Vance and I hadn't prodded you, Prentiss's death would have gone down as an accident."

"No, it wouldn't. Freddy confessed. I didn't catch him."

"Maybe he killed himself because he knew you were investigating and getting close to the truth."

"Is that supposed to make me feel better?"

Lana put her hand on my cheek. I could feel heat coming from my neck, and I was tempted to open the front door, hop in Sally, and go back to the cabin and get drunk. *Five grand be damned.*

"Tell me again it wasn't you out there by that pond last night," I said.

Lana gave me a disappointed look. "Dot said the woman she saw was wearing purple eyeshadow. Darling, would I wear that?"

The doorbell rang, and Lana and I stepped aside so Benjamin could answer it. It was Earl, wearing his carpenter jeans and Western shirt. He looked around curiously as Benjamin ushered him off to be announced.

"I'm sorry," Lana said. "I really am. But everything turned out swimmingly. Now please, indulge us. Just for a little while longer. All you have to do is go in there and describe the investigation and how you discovered Prentiss Wells was the victim of a violent murder. Afterward we'll all raise a glass and toast your achievement. Then Vance will write you a check."

"I don't how Jimmy and Rex are going to feel when I announce that they were too oblivious to realize a murder occurred right in front of them."

Lana responded with a smile.

"How did you convince them to come?" I asked. "Does one of them have a beagle with distemper?"

"Ha ha," Lana said. "These people are here because Vance and I can be very persuasive." She took a step back and eyed me smugly. "You're proof of that."

I heard the clinking glass again.

"C'mon," Lana said, putting her arm around my waist. I wiggled free, then followed her to the doorway of the living room. Vance was standing in the center of the room, holding court. Rex and the Allens were sitting on the couch. Jimmy was on the modern art chair. Bill Rhinehart was standing by the fireplace, next to Susan Wallace and Dot Davidson. Floppy and Elizabeth stood by the shelves of collectibles, and Dale and Earl both leaned against the bookcase of mysteries.

Everyone was present, except . . . "Where's Brett Wells?" I whispered to Lana.

"He's the one holdout," she whispered back.

"And now, ladies and gentleman," Vance announced, "it is time for what I like to refer to as the summing-up." Vance turned and raised his arm in my direction, as if commanding me to dance.

All eyes turned toward me. The only sound came from the crackling logs in the fireplace. Lana stepped away and joined Vance. The butterflies in my stomach were having seizures. I tried to think of how to begin. Then a loud clanging broke the silence. The opening guitar riff of "Highway to Hell."

40

Dale put his phone up to his ear. "'Sup, Boner?" he said loudly. As Dale listened, his brows began to furrow. He glanced at me, and I could see his neck turning a dark shade of red. With the phone plastered to his ear, he marched across the room, grabbed my arm, and pulled me toward the foyer.

When we were by the front door, Dale moved the phone away and said to me, "Do you remember those names you were lookin' for? On those appraisals?"

I pulled the notepaper out of my wallet and handed it to him. "Okay, you ready?" Dale said into the phone. "Willis Tilby, Ethel Campbell, Harriett Rachlin, Charles Dearmond."

Dale listened for a moment, then glanced at me, his nostrils flaring. "Pack it all up and put it in the lockup. We'll get it to Stan in the mornin'."

Dale ended the call and sneered. "Guess what? That was Boner. That itch he needed to scratch at Freddy's? Apparently Boner remembered seein' a remodelin' video on YouTube sometime back, and the dude that was remodelin' was one of these conspiracy theorists—ya know, didn't trust banks and shit like that. Anyway, when he remodeled, he put a false wall in one of his closets that opened up into a hidden room that had a big ol' safe in it, bolted to a cement floor. Had lotsa guns and canned food in there too. Point is, Boner wondered if Freddy did somethin' like that when he remodeled."

"I get the feeling he did," I said.

"Yeah, not to that extent, but Boner found that the carpet in one of them little downstairs closets was just Velcroed down. He pulled it up and found a panel built into the floor. Pried that up and found a lockbox. Had twenty grand in cash in it. Hundreds, bundled up like at the bank. And there was a big envelope in there. Guess what was in it?"

I felt a jolt of electricity. "The fake appraisals."

"Nope. Four mortgage applications for them fake buyers, prepared by Jimmy Fuckin' Fletcher."

I thought for a moment. "Freddy kept that for insurance. He had to have prepared the fake appraisals. And if he got busted, he was gonna make sure Jimmy went down with him."

"I'm gonna rip his nuts off."

"Is there a problem?" Vance said.

I turned to see him walking in our direction. I threw up a hand and he stopped. "All's good. I just need a couple of minutes."

Vance nodded solemnly and headed back toward the living room.

"Whatcha gonna say in there?" Dale asked.

"I have no idea."

"Don't mention any of this shit we just found out. Just stick to what happened to Wells. I'll get Stan to verify what Boner found in the mornin'. Then I'll go pick up Jimmy and Pinland myself."

I didn't speak, and Dale slapped my chest and chuckled. "All right, Columbo. Go in there and tell everybody how you solved a murder right after a dude confessed to it. And make sure you say you couldn't a done it without me. 'Cause that's the truth."

Dale started to walk away, but I grabbed his arm. "Hang on." I reached in my coat pocket and pulled out the ceramic horse. "Why did Freddy have this on a shelf if it wasn't from the robbery? There was nothing else like this at his place."

"I don't know," Dale said. "People collect all kinds of things. Look at all the weird shit these swingers have." Dale slapped my chest again. "Now c'mon. Get in there and do your thing 'fore Lord Fartbottom comes back out here and gives us the stink eye again."

"What if Wells's murder had nothing to do with that old accident? What if it's all about the mortgage fraud? What if Jimmy, Freddy, and Rex were all in on the murder just like they're all in on the fraud?"

"And Freddy just happens to confess to the thing and kill himself?"

"Pretty convenient if you're Jimmy and Rex."

Dale blew out a long breath. "Davis, don't go in there and embarrass yerself." He pointed a finger at my face. "And don't say nothin' 'bout this mortgage shit. That's mine. I'll handle it after Stan verifies it. If Jimmy and Pinland were involved with Wells murder, I'll get to the bottom of it. Got it?"

I didn't speak. "Got it?" Dale snapped.

I nodded.

"Now go in there and get your money so you can pay your damn rent."

* * *

"Finally," Vance said when Dale and I walked into the living room. "I was about to ask Deputy Pless to form a search party."

I stopped next to Vance, and Dale took his position by the bookcase.

"Are you ready?" Vance whispered to me.

I wasn't, but nodded anyway.

"Wonderful," Vance whispered. He gestured toward Floppy and Elizabeth. "Wait over there for a moment. I've prepared a few opening remarks."

As usual with the Roths, I did as I was told.

"Ladies and gentlemen," Vance said, "it's no secret that Lana and I are great lovers of mysteries and detective fiction. So it should come as no surprise that when we first learned of the death of Prentiss Wells, we pondered how a murder on a golf course could be made to look like an accident. Of course we had no reason to think Mr. Wells had been murdered, but—and at the risk of sounding macabre—we delighted in imagining various scenarios of how such a feat could be accomplished. And as fate would have it, we soon connected with Davis Reed, the private detective who solved the Graveyard Fields mystery last fall."

I glanced at Dale. He looked at me, made a fist, then moved it back and forth in front of his crotch.

"We offered Mr. Reed a challenge," Vance continued. "Prove Mr. Wells had been murdered and identify his killer. We had no idea Mr. Reed would actually succeed. He gathered facts and collected evidence. It is to his credit that . . ."

Floppy jabbed my side with an elbow. I turned to him. He was holding up his right hand. The golf glove with the illegible signature was on it.

"Look," he whispered. "This thing fits like a glove. Get it? Like a glove. 'Cause it is one."

It was like someone pushed a mute button on a remote. All the sound in the room died. Even the logs in the fire stopped crackling. I looked at Vance. He was speaking, but I couldn't hear a word. He was staring straight at me with one eyebrow raised. Everyone else in the room looked directly at him. Except Lana. She was staring at me too, an expectant look on her face.

I rushed over to Dale and told him to follow me.

"Please hurry back," Vance said as Dale and I left the room.

Back in the foyer I said, "The glove. Don't you see? *The glove.*"

"What's wrong with you?" Dale said.

"When you talked to Jimmy the day Wells died, he shook your hand, remember? And you told him to take off that sticky golf glove."

"Yeah. So?"

"Jimmy's right handed. Right-handed golfers wear their glove on their left hand. Just like right-handed baseball players. Dammit, I should've figured this out last night when Floppy put on Jimmy's baseball glove."

"What the hell are you talkin' 'bout?"

"Every picture I've seen of Jimmy on a golf course, his glove is on his left hand. When I talked to him at the driving range, his glove was on his left hand. Here, look." I pulled out my phone and found Jimmy's Facebook page. I scrolled to a photo of Jimmy on a golf course and showed it to Dale. "Look: his glove is on his left hand. So why would he have a glove on his right hand the day Wells died?"

Dale's neck began to turn red again.

"Wells's death had nothing to do with Adam Ritter," I said. "It's all about the mortgage fraud. Wells was going to retire, but he changed his mind. Those guys needed him out of the way. Jimmy's the one that swung that hammer. He wore the glove so there wouldn't be any fingerprints, or to get a better grip—I don't know. But there's no other explanation for the glove."

"And he and Pinland just made up all this shit 'bout Freddy seein' that accident back in the eighties?"

The angel was chattering at hyper speed. "That's why Rex searched the old newspapers. He and Jimmy were looking for any information about the accident. Marvin's name is in that article. I bet they tracked him down to Sunset Seasons, and he told them the same thing he told me. *'That poor boy. He was so scared. I let him go. We never found that little white horse.'* If the mystery golfer story didn't work, they were going to frame Freddy. They were going to get him drunk, fake his suicide, and put that horse on his shelf. Framing him was their plan B."

Dale looked stunned. "Well, plan B was elaborate as shit."

"Oh god," I said. "The scarf. Why was Jimmy wearing a scarf last night? He was barefoot and in his underwear. And tonight he's wearing a turtleneck." I shoved Dale's chest. "He's the one who attacked me at Bearwaters.

It wasn't a biker from the Stooges. Jimmy moved his car somewhere, then waited. He saw you leave and he waited for me to come out."

Dale stomped his feet, then did a one-eighty. "Now I know why they played at Springdale," he said.

"What do you mean?"

"They was all members at the Waynesville golf course, but they took Wells to Springdale 'cause it's outside city limits."

I suddenly understood. "Meaning the sheriff's department would be in charge of it instead of city police," I said. "Jimmy figured, as head deputy you'd be the one to investigate."

"Gentlemen?" It was Vance.

"We're busy," Dale barked.

"I imagine so," Vance said, "but everyone's waiting. And we've finally reached the climax of the story. It's time, Davis. Come tell us who killed Prentiss Wells."

41

It did not go smoothly. Dale rushed past Vance toward the living room, and by the time we caught up with him, he had Jimmy by the arm and was tugging at the top of his sweater. "What's wrong with you, man?" Jimmy shouted.

As Dale tugged, I caught a glimpse of a white bandage on Jimmy's neck.

Earl ran over to help, but Dale shouted, "Go get my handcuffs!" That prompted everyone who was sitting to stand and move away. I got Floppy's attention and pointed to Rex. Floppy nodded, then sidled up next to him.

I heard a loud grunt and turned to see Dale bent double. Jimmy was running for the doorway, and I took off after him.

When I reached the front door, it was standing wide open, and Fern Matthews was stepping in. I pushed around her and the guy behind her holding a camera. In the driveway Earl was running past Dale's patrol car toward the backyard.

"Where is he?" I heard Dale yell. A second later he was standing beside me, one hand curved around his groin. A light snapped on, and I turned to see the cameraman approaching. Fern was at his side, holding an umbrella in one hand and a microphone in the other.

"Where is he?" Dale yelled again.

I pointed in the direction Earl had run. "That way—toward the golf course. Earl's after him."

Dale stared at the driveway full of cars and yelled, "Shit!" His patrol car was blocked in by the Allens' truck and Elizabeth's SUV. He cursed again, then opened up the passenger door of his car and yanked out his duty belt. He struggled to get it around his waist as he jogged across the drive.

With my limp there was no way I was going to catch up, much less keep up. So I hopped behind the wheel of the closest vehicle. A moment later I was bouncing down the Roths' backyard in Dot Davidson's old electric golf cart, chasing after Dale, Earl, and Jimmy Fuckin' Fletcher.

* * *

It didn't take me long to find Dale. He was talking to Earl at the bottom edge of the yard, where a narrow, shallow ditch separated it from the eighth hole. Dale and Earl were both soaking wet.

"Slide over," he said to me. Then to Earl, "Get goin'."

I moved over to the passenger side, and Earl trudged back up toward the house. Dale gently eased the golf cart over the ditch, then sunk the accelerator, which had little effect.

"Where's Jimmy headed?" I asked.

"Probably toward the highway. Earl's gonna call it in."

It was practically pitch-black, and I could barely see three feet in front of me. Dale felt around on the cart's dash, then pulled back a knob, and the cart's headlights turned on. Now I could see four feet in front of me.

"Goddammit!" Dale yelled. "I could walk faster than this. Shit, *you* could walk faster than this."

I had no idea where we were or where we were going. After a minute or so, I saw the headlights of a car half a mile or so in the distance, on Highway 276. Dale swung the cart to the right, and we bounced over a rough stretch of terrain and through a small stand of trees. Suddenly a berm appeared before us. Dale hit the brakes, but we continued forward and slid over the edge of it. When we came to a stop we were parked in a bunker.

"I thought you knew this place like the back of your hand," I said.

"When the hell did they put this here?" Dale yelled.

We pulled forward over the lip of the bunker and continued toward the highway. I heard an engine rev. I turned around and saw headlights approaching. They were moving fast and soon caught up with us, illuminating the cart.

Dale twisted around just as a small pickup pulled beside us. Bill Rhinehart was driving, Floppy in the passenger seat. We all came to a stop, and Floppy rolled down his window.

"I told you to watch Pinland!" I yelled.

"Earl's got him," Floppy said.

"Any sign of Fletcher?" Bill asked.

"No, but go down to 276," Dale said. "He's gotta be headed for the road."

When Bill and Floppy took off, Dale buried the accelerator under his boot, and we proceeded onward at the speed of a floor buffer. We'd gone about a hundred yards when Dale slammed on the brakes and spun the wheel, causing us to do a one-eighty on the wet grass. We came to a stop, and Dale growled.

"What wrong?" I asked.

"I'm cold. And I'm wet. And I'm pissed off."

I was fairly warm, and aside from my feet, completely dry. I was beginning to love my new trench coat. "C'mon," I said. "We're not going to catch Jimmy in this old thing. Let's go back up to the Roths'."

Dale didn't speak. I knew he was hoping anyone other than Floppy would catch Jimmy. While I was waiting for Dale to stop pouting, I noticed a tiny flash of light fifty or so yards in the distance. I waited a few seconds, but it didn't reappear. I pointed to where I'd seen it and said, "What's over there?"

Dale looked around, trying to get his bearings. "Bathrooms. Little buildin' by the sixth hole."

I told Dale what I'd seen, and we headed in that direction. Soon the building came into view. It was about the size of a garden shed. Dale put his finger to his lips, and we both slowly stepped out of the cart and into the rain. Dale pulled a flashlight off his belt and aimed it at the building, which had two identical doors, one standing wide open, one closed. Dale gently put his ear against the closed door, listened for a moment, then gestured for me to come over. I put my ear to the door and heard Jimmy's voice. He was talking to someone on his phone.

Dale pulled me back and unholstered his service weapon. With the gun and light aimed at the door, he gently pushed on it. It didn't budge. "Come outta there, dumbass!" Dale yelled.

There was no answer.

"Jimmy, open this fuckin' door 'fore I kick it down."

"I have a gun!" Jimmy shouted.

Dale took a step back, then kicked the door. It still didn't move. He lowered his gun and took out his phone. A moment later, "We got him. He's in the bathroom on six. You gotta key?" Dale hung up and kicked the door again. "Open up!" he yelled.

"Dale, please," Jimmy said. "You gotta help me out."

"I ain't gotta do shit," Dale said. "Now get out here!"

A few seconds passed, then Jimmy called out, "I got a Glock under my chin, Dale. Help me out or I'll use it."

Dale slung his head back. "You've lost your damn mind."

I turned and saw Bill's truck approaching.

"C'mon, man," Jimmy said. "We were buddies back in the day. Remember all the trouble we used to get into? Remember we'd fill up a flask with my daddy's bourbon and sneak through the back door of the movie theater in Waynesville?"

"Jimmy, shut the fuck up and open the door," Dale demanded.

Bill's truck pulled to a stop next to the golf cart, and he and Floppy walked up to me. "He claims to have a gun under his chin," I said.

Bill unsnapped a large keyring dangling from his belt, and cycled through the keys. He removed one and held it up. Dale nodded, then put up a finger, signaling for Bill to wait.

"And that girl, Denise, you dated in eleventh grade?" Jimmy said. "Acne so bad she looked like—"

"Jimmy!" Dale yelled. "You don't want me to come in there and get you! Now open this door, and step out slowly."

There was a long stretch of silence. Me, Dale, Bill, and Floppy all exchanged looks. Finally Jimmy spoke. "Remember the graveyard? Up in north Canton? Me and you'd park up there and sit and drink beer on the tailgate of my truck. You had that old IROC."

Dale motioned for Bill to give him the key.

"We'd race back to Cruso, remember?" Jimmy continued. "My piece-of-shit truck. You'd always give me a one-minute head start."

Dale took the key from Bill and moved it to the lock on the door.

"Please, Dale," Jimmy said, his voice pleading. "That's all I'm asking for—one minute. I've got thirty-five thousand in cash in a safe at the house. It's yours. All you gotta do is hang back for one minute."

In one motion Dale twisted the key and pushed the door open. Jimmy rushed out, knocking Dale off-balance, then ramming into me. I fell face-first onto the wet grass. I glanced up and saw Jimmy running past Bill's truck. Floppy stepped in front of me and pulled out something from one of the side pockets of his camouflage cargo pants, and a second later his arm thrust forward. I heard a yelp and saw Jimmy grab at his back, then stumble and collapse.

42

"**G**imme back my throwin' star," Floppy yelled from the passenger seat of Bill's truck, where he'd been ordered by Dale to sit.

"Shut up," Dale yelled back. He was standing over Jimmy, who was face down in the grass and in obvious pain.

"Get it out," Jimmy shouted through clenched teeth.

Dale had his flashlight aimed at Jimmy's lower back, where a shiny piece of metal was sticking out through Jimmy's sweater.

"I ain't touchin' it," Dale said.

Dale called for an ambulance, and Bill drove down to the highway to meet it and escort it out to our location. While we waited, Jimmy continued to beg Dale to remove the throwing star from his back, and Dale continued to refuse.

A few minutes later Bill and Floppy returned, trailed by an ambulance and two patrol cars, one driven by Deputy Tommy, the other by Deputy Mike. Despite Jimmy's apparent agony, his throwing star injury turned out to be mild, and after being bandaged, the EMTs and Deputy Tommy loaded him into the back of Tommy's patrol car and took off. Dale asked Bill to lead Deputy Mike to the Roths' and to take Floppy with him.

"Earl's up there with a man named Rex Pinland," Dale said to Mike. "Take him in and wait for me."

When they'd gone, I sat down in the golf cart and waited for Dale to join me. He didn't. "Come on," I said. "Let's go."

"I ain't goin' back just yet," Dale said.

"Why? There's a fire and good scotch up there, and I could use both right now."

Dale slammed himself down on the golf cart seat and crossed his arms over his belly. He was pouting again.

226

"You caught him," I said. "Floppy just assisted, that's all. It wouldn't have happened without you. So let's get back to the Roths' before Floppy can get in front of Fern's camera and take all the credit."

Dale growled, then stomped on the accelerator.

* * *

"It was a throwing star," I said to Elizabeth. "Like in kung fu movies."

We were sitting on the couch in the Roths' living room, where I was enjoying the warmth of the fire and a glass of Vance's expensive scotch.

The rain had finally stopped, and everyone else had gone outside to watch Dale and Floppy talk to Fern. I didn't need to see it to know it wasn't going to be pretty.

I was telling Elizabeth more of the details of Jimmy's capture when Roberta Allen appeared in the doorway. She glared at me for a moment, and I got the message and walked over to her.

"Find out what really happened to Adam," she said.

"I'll do my best. But listen, I talked to a guy who worked with Adam at the Pizza Hut. He said Adam was pretty shy and mostly kept to himself."

"That doesn't surprise me."

"He also said Adam told him that he'd recently started taking piano lessons from a woman in Waynesville and that he didn't want his dad to find out. Do you know anything about that? It's a long shot, but if I can track down this woman maybe she can tell me if Adam might have become friends with someone there while he was taking lessons."

Roberta thought for a moment. "I don't remember him ever talking about piano lessons, but him not wanting Daddy to find out makes sense. Daddy was always telling Adam he needed to man up."

I walked with Roberta to the front door, where my trench coat was drying out on a peg. I reached into one of the inside pockets and removed the check she'd handed to me earlier. "This is to balance the scales," I said. "As long as these keep coming, keep cashing them."

Roberta hesitated, then took the check and walked out the door.

"What was that about?" Elizabeth asked when I sat back down beside her on the couch.

"A pro bono investigation." I took a healthy sip of scotch, then turned to Elizabeth and said, "Hey, do you think we could go to Sunset Seasons tomorrow?"

Elizabeth considered it, then said, "Sure. But it would need to be at around ten."

I nodded and was once again trying to remember how to initiate a kiss when Vance and Lana strolled in, both carrying champagne flutes. "Everyone has gone," Vance said as he sat down on the modern art chair.

Lana squeezed beside him. "What a fun party."

"I have to get home," Elizabeth said as she stood up. "As always, thanks for a fascinating evening."

I was pushing myself up when she said, "Stay put. I'll see you in the morning. Ten o'clock." She extended her hand and I shook it. She turned to the Roths. "I'll show myself out. Goodnight."

When Elizabeth had gone, Vance said to me, "I owe you some money."

"I'll take it," I said. "Along with an explanation."

"There's nothing to explain. You solved the mystery. Well done."

"Did you tell Floppy to put on that glove? And to make sure I saw it?"

Vance looked confused. He was a better actor than I'd previously thought.

"When did you guys know it was Jimmy who'd killed Wells?"

The Roths said nothing.

"And how did Fern Matthews know to show up here tonight? Were you guys able to convince her to keep a lid on the story about Freddy's connection to Wells? And then get her here tonight for an exclusive, when you knew the truth would finally come out?"

Silence.

I pointed at Lana. "You said you two can be very persuasive. Now tell me, how much of this whole thing has been a charade?"

More silence.

"What's next?" I said. "Will the entire cast run in here and join hands and take a bow? Including Freddy? And Prentiss Wells, for that matter?"

Vance chuckled. "An ending even beyond our capabilities."

"Why don't you two enlighten me on your capabilities."

Vance studied his champagne, then said, "Have you ever read Raymond Chandler's *The Big Sleep*? Or seen the film with Humphrey Bogart?"

I shook my head.

"It's a classic of hard-boiled detective fiction and included in many lists of best crime novels." Vance paused. "Early in the story a chauffeur to a wealthy family dies. He's found inside a sedan in the water, near a pier. The death is never resolved. When making the film, the director sent a telegram to

Chandler, asking whether the chauffeur was murdered or died by suicide. Chandler responded that he didn't know."

I waited for Vance to continue. He didn't.

"So, what?" I asked. "Are you telling me not every mystery has a solution?"

Vance leaned forward and gave me a consoling look. "No, Davis. I'm telling you not every mystery needs one."

43

At nine thirty I rolled Sally into the parking lot of Sunset Seasons. I pulled out my phone and opened my banking app. I tapped the icon for "Mobile Deposit," then took a photo of the front and back of Vance's check. When the deposit was accepted, a screen appeared saying the funds would be available in five to seven business days. If I was planning a celebration party, it was going to have to wait.

Then I called Dale.

"Whatcha want? I'm tired," he said by way of answering.

"Up all night?"

Dale grunted.

"So what's the story?" I asked.

"Whose? Pinland or Fuckin' Fletcher?"

"Start with Jimmy."

"He ain't got one. Clammed up tighter than a gnat's ass. Says he ain't got nothin' to say 'til his attorney shows up. Some big shot from Charlotte. S'posed to be here this afternoon. I can't wait to watch Byrd pick him apart."

"What about Rex?"

"Pinland? He's the other side of the coin. Won't shut up. Fully admits to the loan fraud shit. Probably 'cause we showed him proof of it this mornin'. But he says everythin' was Jimmy's idea, the loan fraud, takin' out Wells, takin' out Freddy."

"Hang on. Hang on. So Jimmy definitely killed Freddy? Faked his suicide?"

Dale snorted. "Ya know, I've always thought it was weird that Ernie's Motors ain't got no fence 'round it. Only used car lot I know that ain't surrounded by chain link. You know why there's no fence? 'Cause Ernie's got

230

ten security cameras mounted 'round that place. Boner got him outta bed at four this mornin' to get the footage. One of the cameras is pointed across the lot, right at Freddy's. We got Jimmy's car goin' to Freddy's every day since the Wells killin'. And two days ago Jimmy shows up and goes into Freddy's house, and a couple of hours later the two of 'em walk out and go into the garage. An hour after that Jimmy comes out of the garage and closes the door and leaves. We got him dead to rights. His Charlotte big shot ain't gonna mean shit."

I kind of wanted to see the footage of me and Floppy pulling a shredding bin across the road but didn't think it was the time to mention that.

"It's just Jimmy on the camera footage?" I asked. "Not Rex?"

"That's right, just Jimmy. Pinland says Freddy was freakin' out pretty good. Convinced the whole thing was gonna come down any second. Jimmy was goin' over there every day to keep Freddy soused and quiet. But it got to the point Jimmy made the decision to keep Freddy quiet for good. Pinland swears he tried to talk him out of it, but I don't know if I believe that. And get this: Pinland also swears up and down he didn't have nothin' to do with killin' Wells other than helpin' to cover it up. Claims he thought Jimmy was just gonna threaten Wells out on the course, but when it went further than that, he followed Jimmy's orders to go along with the golfer story out of fear Jimmy would rat him out on the fraud."

"So Jimmy hit Wells with the hammer, but how did it end up in the pond?"

"Accordin' to Pinland, right after Jimmy whacked Wells in the head, Wells grabbed the hammer and lunged for him. Jimmy took off like a scared cat, and Wells threw the hammer at him. Flew over his head down toward the pond. Jimmy ordered Freddy to go search for it."

That explained why Freddy's shoes were muddy at the golf course, but not why he looked like a motion-sick ghost. I asked Dale for the answer.

"'Cause like Pinland said, Jimmy had just let on that he was gonna threaten Wells."

"Why?" I asked. "To try to force him to retire?"

"That's the story. But then Jimmy pulls out that hammer and whacks Wells in the head, and Wells fights back for all of five seconds, then he croaks and falls down in the sand. Pinland said Freddy 'bout lost his shit when that happened. But Jimmy threatened Freddy and Pinland. Told 'em the story they needed to stick to or else they were all goin' to jail."

"Jimmy wasn't out there to threaten Wells. He had that hammer and wore that glove for the sole purpose of killing the guy."

"That's what I think too. Accordin' to Pinland, when Wells fell down in the sand, he ran over and checked for a pulse. When he told Jimmy he couldn't find one, Jimmy said, 'Problem solved.'"

"All right, last thing," I said.

Dale huffed. "I doubt that."

"What about Jimmy's story of Freddy being with Adam Ritter that night in '88. Is there any truth to it? Did Jimmy make it up and plant that horse at Freddy's to try to frame him?"

"Pinland claims he don't know shit 'bout that."

"But then why was he looking at newspapers from back then at the library?"

"He says a few months ago Jimmy told him there was somethin' off 'bout that old accident Wells was involved with. That somethin' wasn't right. And if they could figure out what that was, it might be worth somethin'. Pinland's wife's got cancer and he needed money for the medical bills, so he dug in to it but claims he didn't find nothin'."

"But they had to have talked to Marvin. At Sunset Seasons."

"Pinland didn't. If he's tellin' the truth."

"Somebody did. Because I can't believe that ceramic horse on Freddy's shelf was a coincidence."

"You know somethin'? Coincidences have been known to happen."

"And I still don't trust Bill Rhinehart despite his help last night. He met Adam Ritter not long before that accident. Maybe they became friends. Maybe he was with Adam when—"

"Knock it off, will ya. It's over. You got your money. Now go write that damn book."

I stayed silent.

"And hey," Dale said, "Brett Wells is here. He's pretty shocked. I told him how everythin' went down. He asked for your number. I gave it to him. I didn't think you'd mind."

"He seems like a decent guy."

There was a short pause. "Yeah. I guess he might be."

"Get some sleep," I said. "I'll buy you a beer soon."

"Pay your rent first, dickhead."

* * *

At five minutes to ten Elizabeth's SUV pulled into the Sunset Seasons parking lot. I hustled over and met her at her car. As we walked inside, I updated her on what I'd learned from Dale.

"Any information on the mortgage fraud?" Elizabeth asked.

"Rex has admitted to it," I said. "But I didn't ask how deep it goes. Earlier, Dale told me it would take a while to go through all of the files. The fraud division is very small. As in Stan small."

"It occurred to me the straw buyers listed on the documents I found might be individuals who applied for loans at Eagle's Fork Financial and were turned down. Their applications would give Jimmy all of the information necessary to steal and use their identity."

"I bet you're right. We'll just have to wait and see what Stan uncovers."

As we passed the nurses station, Elizabeth smiled and said a pleasant "Good morning" to Sheila, who nodded and smiled back. Then Sheila turned to me and sneered. I blew her a kiss.

Elizabeth knocked on Marvin's door, pushed it open, and we both stepped inside. Marvin was in his wheelchair by the window. He was wearing a white T-shirt and baggy gray sweatpants.

"You're looking casual today," Elizabeth said.

Marvin frowned at Elizabeth. "It's been a long time since I've seen you," he said.

"Well, here I am," Elizabeth said with a big smile. "And I'm very happy to see you." She bent down and kissed Marvin's forehead.

Marvin smiled and my heart swelled a bit.

"This is my friend Davis," Elizabeth said. "He's writing a book about the bomber that crashed into Cold Mountain in the forties. You helped search for that crash. Do you remember?"

Marvin glanced at me and squinted. I sat down in the recliner across from him. "Hi, Marvin. Before we talk about the search for the plane crash, I'd like to ask you about this. I pulled out the newspaper article I'd printed at the library and handed it to him. Elizabeth leaned over his shoulder, and I pointed to the photo. "That's you, Marvin," I said. "Do you remember that night? That accident with Prentiss Wells? He was a real estate attorney."

Marvin stared at the photo for a long moment, then looked up at me and said, "That poor boy. He was so scared." Elizabeth came around and sat on the arm of my chair. Marvin looked at her. There was concern in his eyes, or maybe it was regret. "I let him go. I'm sorry." Then back to me. "We never found that little horse. I searched that field myself. Never found it." Marvin looked back at Elizabeth. "I let him go. I'm sorry."

"What else do you remember about that night?" I asked. "Was there someone else there besides the boy who died?"

Marvin looked down at the photo again. "He was so scared," he said.

"Who was scared?" I asked. "Who did you let go? Who else was there?"

"I let him go," Marvin said. Then louder, "I let him go."

"Does the name Bill Rhinehart mean anything to you? Was he there that night?"

Elizabeth jumped up and put her hand on my shoulder. When she stepped to the door, I joined her.

"Wait outside for a few minutes," she said. "He's getting agitated. It's common in people with Alzheimer's. Now what exactly are you trying to find?"

"There's something about that accident. I think somebody else was out there that night with Adam Ritter, the guy who died. Jimmy claims it was Freddy, but we now know Jimmy's a liar, so I don't know how much credence to put into what he says. But my gut's telling me somebody else was out there, and it's bothered Marvin for decades. And it's bothering me too."

"Okay. I'll talk to him and see if he remembers anything else."

* * *

I'd been leaning against a cinder block wall outside Marvin's door for about ten minutes when a woman who looked old enough to have voted for Coolidge slid her walker up to me and asked if I knew the name of this hotel.

"Sunset Seasons," I said.

She repeated the name, then asked where she could go to collect her luggage and check out. I pointed in the direction of the nurses station. "Ask for Megan," I said.

The woman was slowly shuffling down the hall when Marvin's door opened, and Elizabeth stepped out. "I'm sorry," she said. "He keeps repeating the same phrases. The only thing different he's said is 'His daddy begged me to change it.' Does that mean anything to you?"

I thought for a moment. "He might be talking about Adam Ritter's dad. Apparently, he was furious that his son's last act was robbing a house. The kid had never been in trouble before. So maybe Adam's father asked Marvin to modify the report, or at least to keep that detail out of the newspaper."

Elizabeth handed the printout to me. "It didn't work," she said.

I shook my head. "No. It didn't. Marvin did his job. By the way, I talked to the sheriff a couple of days ago, and he said Marvin retired two years early. Do you know why?"

"I'm not sure exactly. He didn't like to talk about it. I think he'd just had enough. You were a police officer—you know the toll the job takes."

"I was a traffic cop for all of two months. Not exactly the most trying experience."

Elizabeth smiled and the butterflies in my stomach started their calisthenics. "Anyway," I said, "what do you say me and you go have dinner soon? Sometime after five to seven business days from now."

Elizabeth's eyes narrowed. "A date?"

"Yeah, a date. You know, the romantic kind. Wine, candles, maybe even a bit of hand-holding."

Elizabeth smiled sweetly, and I wondered if I was finally about to get the kiss I'd been unable to initiate. Instead, she said, "I'm too old for you."

I took a step back. "No you're not. That's ridiculous."

"Couples with a ten-plus-year age gap are almost forty percent more likely to divorce than couples who are the same age."

I started to argue, but Elizabeth put up a hand. "And you're not my type."

I know she didn't mean for it to sting, but it did.

"Davis, I am your friend," Elizabeth said. "And as your friend I would love to have dinner with you. But only as friends. Okay?"

I nodded because it was easier than speaking, and Elizabeth said, "Good. Now do you want to ask my grandfather about searching for the plane crash?"

I was deflated and just wanted to go home. "Nah. I'll save that for another time."

"Okay. Come on. I'll walk you out."

We worked our way through a maze of wheelchairs, walkers, and unsteady senior citizens. When we reached the door leading to the waiting area, Elizabeth extended her hand. I shook it, and she smiled and pulled me in for a tight hug. "You're a good man, Davis," she whispered in my ear.

As we hugged, I stared at the staff photos hanging on the wall, and just as Elizabeth and I were both pulling away, the angel whispered in my ear.

"That looks like . . ."

Elizabeth turned around. "Who?"

I stepped forward and pointed to the face of a young girl with short black hair. I read the caption under the photo: "*Calista Maldano, Administrative*

Assistant. She looks like Jimmy's girlfriend. I've seen photos of her on his Facebook page. And she was at his house when I was there. I can't be certain, but it sure looks like—"

"Oh my god," Elizabeth said. Her eyes were bulging.

In a flash Elizabeth took off down the hall. I had to stagger after her at full speed to keep up. At the double doors she shoved the key card hanging from the lanyard around her neck onto the card reader. The doors clicked and Elizabeth pushed through them in a rush. I followed a few feet behind as Elizabeth darted from room to room, back and forth across the hallway, looking at every door. I had no clue what she was doing.

"Here!" Elizabeth yelled, pointing at a door. As I approached it, she continued on. I stared at the door for a good fifteen seconds before I realized what I was looking at. Just under the room's number hung the nameplate of the occupant: Willis Tilby.

"Dearmond," Elizabeth called from somewhere around the corner. I was heading in her direction when I heard her say, "Rachlin." Followed quickly by "Campbell." Elizabeth had found the straw buyers.

Four real people. Residents of the memory care facility at Sunset Seasons.

44

Back in the parking lot, I called Dale.

"You're not going to believe this," I said when he answered. I gave him the rundown of what Elizabeth had just discovered.

"She didn't show up for work today," I said. "Not all that surprising since her boyfriend has been arrested for murder. But still, I bet if you search her house, you'll find purple eyeshadow and probably a bunch of Costco products. Maybe even a sleeve of smiley-face golf balls. Maybe even Dot Davidson's shotgun."

"Fuckin' Fletcher," Dale said.

"She's the administrative assistant. That would give her access to all of the residents' files. Everything Jimmy would need to prepare a loan application in their name. It's awful to say, but I guess if you're going to steal identities, it's smart to steal them from people who can't remember theirs."

Dale growled.

"That's probably how he got to Marvin too," I said. "And got that information about the old Wells accident."

"All right, I'll find out where she lives and send a couple of boys over to check it out. But, hey, listen, there's 'nother plate spinnin' down here. One of Rusty Baker's boys that was tied up 'round Peckerhead's hydraulic lift wants to make a deal."

"A deal about what?"

"Says he knows things 'bout Long Branch. Says there's pills flyin' out the back door of that place. Says he can finger a couple of women responsible."

"I can't believe you said that without laughing."

"I'm too tired to laugh."

"I've always wondered if Diana and Daiquiri were somehow involved with the Stooges' business."

"Well, Byrd's puttin' together a team to investigate. I'll let you know what pans out. But don't you go down there snoopin' 'round. Even if somebody offers ya five grand."

* * *

I was headed through Clyde, on my way back to the cabin, when my phone buzzed. It was an 828 number I didn't recognize. I answered it anyway, hoping it might be Elizabeth, calling to say she'd changed her mind and that she was open to a romantic date.

"Davis, this is Brett Wells."

"Oh yeah, Brett, hi. Look, I'm really sorry about how everything turned out. I know you and Jimmy were friends."

"Why didn't you tell me you were suspicious of the circumstances surrounding my dad's death?" Brett sounded pissed, so I asked him to hold for a minute and then pulled into the meat-and-three restaurant and turned off Sally's engine.

"I didn't mention it because I didn't want to put any ideas in your head I couldn't prove."

"If you had told me you were actively investigating my dad's murder—"

"Brett, when I came to your office, I didn't know for sure your dad had been murdered. I was just concerned that no one was looking into other possibilities, that's all."

"And you should have shared that concern with me," Brett snapped.

There was a long silence before Brett said, "This is hard to comprehend. That someone you know—a friend—is capable of such violence and deception. I've known Jimmy for over fifteen years. He was someone I trusted. And Rex. His involvement in this is . . ."

Brett needed to rant, and I let him go on for a while. Finally I interrupted. "Brett, listen—I understand. Someone I considered a dear friend betrayed me. Actually, he tried to kill me and came very close to succeeding—that's why I limp. It made me angry at the world and not want to trust anyone. But I finally realized that's no way to live."

I could hear Brett breathing. I gave him a few seconds to speak, and when he didn't, I said, "I recently learned this phrase: Philos Adelphos Dikaios. It means—"

"Love of humanity and justice for all," Brett said in a rush. "It's the motto of my law school fraternity."

For a moment I sat silent and watched the cars pass on the four-lane that runs through Clyde.

His daddy begged me to change it.

I closed my eyes and pictured myself in Brett's office, staring at him across his giant desk. Brett wiping his eyes with a tissue and saying things like *"I was a wild child. My parents made a lot of sacrifices for me. Dad told me I wasn't destined to be a failure."*

"Brett, this is going to sound like an odd question," I said, "but what did your mom do?"

"What?"

"For a living. Your mom, what did she do?"

"She taught piano. She had a studio in our home."

My eyes began to well up. "Somehow I knew you were going to say that."

"What are you talking about?"

"The checks aren't enough, Brett. You need to tell Roberta Allen the truth."

After a moment of silence, the call disconnected.

* * *

I thought about how it might have happened. The best I could come up with was that Brett and Adam had met when Adam began taking piano lessons from Brett's mom. Roberta had said Adam didn't have a girlfriend and was interested in art and music. I was stereotyping, but sometimes those shoes fit. The two couldn't exactly parade their relationship around, especially not in a tiny Southern town in the eighties, so they kept it secret.

Brett picked Adam up after work and drove him to the house that sat across the field from the Wells's. Wild child Brett decides to break in and rob it, and Adam follows his lead. When they almost get caught, Adam takes off across the field toward Brett's house, and Brett heads that way on the road, in the station wagon. Adam either falls down the bank or jumps out into the road, and Brett accidently runs into him. Adam is killed instantly.

Marvin, responding to the break-in, soon appears on the scene, as does Brett's dad after hearing the siren from Marvin's patrol car. Some kind of agreement is made, money is promised—enough to let Marvin retire a couple of years early. And suddenly Prentiss Wells was behind the wheel that night. A sacrifice to his son's future success.

When Brett graduates law school several years later and has his own money, he begins sending checks to the Ritters. A way to balance the scales.

By the time I pulled into the parking lot of El Bacaratos, I was fifty percent sure I had it right. But I was a hundred percent sure that there were only two people alive who knew what really happened that night: Brett Wells and a ninety-nine-year-old man with Alzheimer's.

45

I only had about twenty dollars to get me through until Vance's check cleared, but that wasn't going to stop me from spending half of it on chips and guacamole. I figured I deserved it.

After acquiring said delicacy, I put the to-go bag in Sally's passenger seat/cooler and called my attorney. By some miracle the receptionist put me through.

"Davis, I'm so sorry," Allison said. "This has been a roller coaster, I know."

"Just tell me what the odds are right now. I mean, is there still a chance they're going to settle this thing?"

The longer Allison hesitated, the more my stomach sank. Finally she said, "It's doubtful. Actually, I think at this point it's over. I'm sorry. But I did say at the very beginning this was a long shot. The CPD's position has always been the two men in question were not acting in their capacity as law enforcement officers when you were injured."

"I was injured because one of them shot me in the leg."

"I know. I'm sorry Davis. Really." There was a long pause. "But on the bright side, with a settlement off the table, you're no longer bound by the NDA. You can shout your story from every mountaintop if you want to."

"I'd rather have the money," I said.

"It would make a great book. I know you're working on the plane crash thing now, but once that's finished, why don't you write a gritty true crime story? Your story. Or you could do a podcast. Those are really popular right..."

I hung up.

* * *

When I pulled up to the cabin, Vicky was parked in the clearing, and Floppy was sitting on her trunk.

"Where ya been?" he said.

"Getting my heart broken. My overactive imagination stimulated. And my dreams dashed." I held up the to-go bag. "And I got some chips and guacamole."

Floppy followed me up and around the side of the cabin. When we reached the front door, I froze. Another unexpected gift was sitting on the welcome mat. Not a shotgun shell, but a fancy metal detector with all of its knobs intact. An envelope sat on top of it. I handed Floppy the to-go bag and picked up the envelope, which featured an engraved pineapple on the back flap.

Floppy pointed to it and said, "Did you know pineapples are the universal symbol of hospitality?"

I shook my head and ripped open the envelope.

"And swingers too," Floppy said. "They use it to signal other swingers. Like on cruise ships and stuff. If you see a picture of a pineapple hangin' on somebody's door, it means they're hopin' to get it on."

"Stop!" I yelled, and removed the card.

Dear Davis,

Thanks to you, Lana and I have had the most exciting week in recent memory. And while you may be frustrated at not knowing all of the answers, believe me when I say, Lana and I don't know all of them either. (Lana just said that was her cue to wink.)

You performed admirably, my friend. Now please accept this gift, and let it serve as a reminder of our thrilling search for a killer. We hope it will now lead you to lost treasure.

Vance and Lana Roth

I turned to Floppy. I started to ask him if the Roths had instructed him to put on the golf glove and show it to me, but I stopped myself. I suddenly didn't care. Vance was right—not every mystery needs to be solved.

Inside the cabin Floppy examined the metal detector like it had fallen off a spaceship. "This is a PI detector," he said. "That stands for 'pulse induction.'"

These are real expensive. And they're real good at findin' gold that's underground." He looked at me, his eyes wide with excitement. "C'mon. It's a pretty day. Let's go up on Cold Mountain and start searchin'. With this thing we's bound to find somethin'."

"Be my guest," I said as I unpacked the chips and guacamole. "Knock yourself out. Take that thing and go find that gold."

Floppy's face dropped.

"You ain't comin'?"

"I've got work to do here."

"On your book?"

I nodded.

"You'll get it finished one of these days," Floppy said. "I have faith in ya."

"And I in you."

Floppy grinned and headed for the door. When he opened it, I said, "Hang on a second." Floppy turned and gave me an inquisitive look. "If you do find that gold," I said, "don't go turning eccentric on me."

Floppy nodded solemnly. "I'll try real hard not to."

After Floppy left, I loaded up a tray with the chips and guacamole, an Old Crab, and a pen and legal pad, and carried it out to the deck. When I sat down, a warm breeze drifted through the budding tree limbs. I tried to remember Floppy's word for that but couldn't.

A few low clouds drifted over Cold Mountain, and for some reason the shadows they cast on the gray trees made me think of troubled ghosts looking for a home. I grabbed the legal pad, where what amounted to almost six months' worth of notes about the bomber crash barely filled three quarters of a page. As I read the notes, I realized I couldn't tell the story because it wasn't my story to tell. I tore off the page and at the top of a blank one wrote *Book Title: Graveyard Fields*. Then I stared at Cold Mountain and waited for it to tell me what to do next.

Author's Note

Cruso, North Carolina, is a real place. I should know—I was born and raised there and lived in the small community for over forty years. And Springdale is a real golf course in Cruso. My dad built the course in the late 1960s and opened it the year before I was born. That course was like my sibling. I was constantly fighting against it for the attention of my parents, who worked liked the dickens to keep the place going. I worked there too—from the time I was a kid washing golf carts and mowing greens; to when I was an adult, as the golf course superintendent; and later when I was the general manager, a position I held until I was thirty-nine. That age may seem a little young to have a mid-life crisis, but I figured, *Why not go ahead and get it over with?* I left the golf world behind and started writing, which, similar to golf, is a hard way to make an easy living.

This book is a love letter of sorts to the golf course my family operated for fifty years. My father passed away in 2005, and my mom sold the course in 2018 to a family who are showering it with attention and affection. This book is also my thank-you to Cruso, a community full of some of the most warmhearted and generous people I've ever come across. It's also home to a few bizarre folks who I've slightly fictionalized in these pages. I'm proud to say Cruso will always be my home, no matter where I hang my hat.

Acknowledgments

Many thanks to the following:

The fine folks at the Haywood County Sheriff's Office.

My agent, Miriam Kriss.

The folks at Crooked Lane Books.

Nathan Galbreath for helping me try to understand real estate law.

Editor Sara J. Henry for her talent, patience, and ball-busting honesty.

Blair Knobel, Jack Bacot, and Seth Jones, magazine editors who were willing to give me a chance to write after I ditched the golf business and couldn't decide what to do with my life.

Peter and Brenda Hennessey; my wife, Jess; and my kids, Emily and Julian for their love and support.